Praise

Velve ...*ysm*

'HF

"I was enthralled. I'd recommend this read to anyone and everyone."

~ *Two Lips Reviews*

"Beth Kery   bestselling

~ *Larissa*

author

"Velvet Cataclysm is a fast paced, action packed, and emotional erotic paranormal romance that had my adrenalin flowing and heart twisting."

~ *Closetreader Blog*

Look for these titles by *Beth Kery*

Now Available:

Take a Stranger No More
Holiday Bound

Velvet Cataclysm

Beth Kery

SAMHAIN
PUBLISHING

Samhain Publishing, Ltd.
577 Mulberry Street, Suite 1520
Macon, GA 31201
www.samhainpublishing.com

Velvet Cataclysm

Cover by Kanaxa

First Samhain Publishing, Ltd. electronic publication: May 2010
First Samhain Publishing, Ltd. print publication: March 2011

Dedication

To all the ladies who encouraged me when I doubtfully entered the realm of vampires, unsure if I could make a unique contribution to the genre: Fi, Lea, Sabra, Robin—thank you for the encouragement and support.

Chapter One

Christina peered through the dense shadows cast by towering oaks, sprawling maples and trembling locusts. This was Saint's world—the silence, the darkness, the odor of fresh earth and dewy grass filling her nose. The excitement and mystery clinging in the warm, balmy air made the blood race in her veins.

A distant howl pierced the night. More than likely it was Scepter, the half-domesticated wolf to which her son, Aidan, had become so attached. Saint's property attracted a surprising number of wild animals. Christina supposed it was due to Whitby being one of the few wooded urban areas. Animals made their way down the lakeshore from Wisconsin or suburban forest preserves, foraging for food and finding a haven on the wooded acreage.

Saint's property occupied six full city blocks, but at night it seemed to transform into an otherworldly landscape that stretched without end. Christina wondered if Saint knew she was aware of this night characteristic of his house and grounds.

That she knew so much of *his* singular character, for that matter.

Knowing Saint, he thought she rested as deeply and sweetly as Aidan had at age two, when she and her son had first moved to the coach house on Whitby's grounds. Saint always denied it, but Christina knew he'd taken pity on them back then, offering the coach house for a ridiculously low rent after learning from her boss that she could no longer afford her rent in the Lakeview neighborhood.

He'd been a friend and subtle protector over the years, but tonight, Christina Astor planned to force Saint to acknowledge she was a woman who desired him. She'd lived on his property for nearly a decade now and it was past time for him to acknowledge her as more than a renter and friend.

She'd been hyperaware of him at the charity function tonight. Since Saint sat on the board for the non-profit organization that operated several therapeutic group homes in the city for runaways, emotionally disturbed teenagers, and young adults, he'd volunteered to have the party on his grounds. It wasn't uncommon for Christina to be hyperaware of Saint—that was the norm, in fact—but tonight she sensed he was just as aware of her.

How many times had she looked up while standing amidst the crowd to see him watching her with those exotically tilted blue eyes? Too many to count. Christina had never been able to fathom how Saint could possess such a singularly cold stare and yet make her feel so hot. Raging flame trapped in ice—that was the essence of his gaze.

She longed to set that fire on a rampage.

She stopped dead in her tracks when she heard a woman sigh in the distance. Her bare feet wiggled in the cool grass as she hesitated. Something fluttered sickeningly in her gut, only to settle like hot, burning lead.

Saint wasn't alone.

What had she expected? Just because tonight seemed so perfect for what Christina had come to consider their fated union didn't mean Saint shared her opinion. He obviously didn't. The painful ambivalence she'd sensed in him earlier tonight must have gotten the best of him, given the fact that he was entertaining someone from his ever-changing harem of avid female worshippers.

She heard an ecstatic cry and a low moan.

Correction, Christina thought bitterly. Several someones.

Eyes narrowed in disbelief, she didn't do an about-face like her mind screamed for her to do.

After all of it—after all the buildup, all the heart-throbbing anticipation tonight, *this* was what awaited her? He'd come out to the gazebo in the silent early morning hours, just like she'd seen it happening as they'd locked gazes earlier.

He'd come all right. But he'd brought his own lovers.

She'd been so sure he knew precisely what she'd wanted tonight. And her intuitions were never wrong when they were this strong.

She anxiously sifted through her memories of the night. How could she have been wrong in what she'd sensed? One of their charged exchanges came to her in graphic detail.

She'd been networking and offering information on Altgeld House to various contributors, board members, and other sympathetic community leaders. She instinctively found Saint in the crowd—not difficult to do since his head towered over everyone who surrounded him. His tousled light brown hair, streaked with strands of incandescent gold, looked glossy in the flickering lanterns and the glow cast by the tiny white lights hanging in the canopy of trees. He'd continued to meet her stare as he conversed with a bald-headed man and a woman wearing a large hat.

A shiver of excitement had danced down Christina's spine.

"Is it true what they say?" Melinda Marquette, another

psychiatric social worker who managed a sister home to Altgeld House, asked as she leaned closer to her. Christina flushed, knowing the older woman had noticed where she'd been staring. "Did he really get the nickname Saint from all of his charitable acts and altruism? Or is it just an affectation to fascinate the ladies?"

"Come on, Melinda. Look at him. Do you really think he needs to use Hollywood devices to lure women into bed?"

Melinda chuckled softly. "No, I see your point. The man looks like a combination of a rock star and Jesus on steroids."

Christina pulled her gaze away from Saint's steady stare. "If it weren't for Saint Sevliss, you and I would be out of a job and all of our kids would be on the street. He's LifeLine's biggest contributor."

Melinda nodded wryly at the affluent crowd surrounding them. "The hype about this sicko who's been murdering young people, especially the lost ones like our kids, is certainly doing its fair share of bringing in donations to LifeLine, in addition to Sevliss."

Christina nodded, her mouth pressed into a hard line. It was a grim fact of life that the sociopath the media had dubbed the Youngblood Thief was bringing in tons of money to LifeLine from concerned philanthropists. The media had sensationalized the grisly murders to nauseating levels, but in doing so, had inadvertently highlighted the plight of a subpopulation of mentally ill and homeless young adults in Chicago.

Christina hated the fact that the sad end to four homeless, lonely kids by the horrific method of exsanguination—complete drainage of the blood from the body—was the cause of LifeLine's swelling coffers.

"They say Sevliss is the true leader of the city, you know, the shadow behind every union leader, neighborhood alderman, and councilman. They also say he doesn't need to avoid press because the media is in his pocket as well. But you must have juicy goods on him, living right here on his property?" Melinda prodded.

Christina just smiled and changed the topic. As much as she liked Melinda, she didn't gossip about Saint. She didn't because she knew instinctively how uncomfortable that would make him.

A few minutes later she'd spun around to snag a glass of champagne and an appetizer from a passing waiter. When she glanced up, Saint was standing directly beside her. He'd come without observable movement, without sound, and in typical Saint-fashion, without a shred of respect for the time it should have taken everyone else on the planet to cross the distance between them.

She quirked up one eyebrow as she looked at him.

"What?" he asked.

Christina laughed softly. She'd known him for eight years now and he still managed to pull off a poker face every time he exhibited yet another bizarre behavior. Did he really think she didn't notice?

She smiled up at him before she took a sip of champagne, never letting her gaze falter. "It's going very well, don't you think? We couldn't have had a better night for it."

He'd merely nodded as he stared down at her from his height of six-foot five-inches. He looked thin. Beautiful as an angel fallen from heaven, but too thin. She held up the pastry appetizer to his lips. It was a common thing for her to push food on him. He glanced down at her hand. His nostrils flared as he inhaled slowly but he shook his head in refusal.

Funny...he *looked* hungry.

"Go on, eat it. You're throwing this party, and I haven't

13

seen you touch a morsel of all this fantastic food."

"I can't eat anyone's food but yours, Stina."

She smiled. Saint was the only person she knew who shortened her name to Stina. Given his typical laconism, she'd always prized the sound of the pet name uttered in his deep, husky voice. Maybe it was wishful thinking on her part, but it always sounded like an endearment on Saint's tongue.

"*Right.* If that were the case, you'd be capable of surviving on what—three meals a week, tops? Why don't you just say you're not hungry?" She chewed and swallowed while he watched her.

"Aren't you at least going to cut the silent act to tell me I look beautiful tonight?" she asked him brashly, not concerned in the slightest by his refusal to chitchat with her. Saint wasn't one for small talk. Never had been. How many times had he walked across the grounds and sat on the front porch with her, or with her and Aidan, said a total of a dozen words the entire time, before uncoiling his long frame from an Adirondack chair and sauntering silently back to the big house?

She couldn't imagine how he thrived in a social gathering such as this. He always managed to get exponentially more money donated to LifeLine's shelters and group homes than any board member, so he must not be entirely backward. But if he possessed an ounce of social acumen, Christina had yet to see it.

Saint was just...*Saint.*

He'd shrugged and blessed her with a rare smile. "Do you really need to hear that you're beautiful? Why state the obvious? Might as well say the sun is bright."

She paused abruptly in the act of lifting her champagne glass to her lips, her eyes flashing up to meet his. Had he really just said that? Saint never complimented her. At least not with words. With her special ability to read people's minds, however, Christina had always known he admired her...wanted her.

Not enough to ever *do* anything about it, she'd thought irritably. Not even after eight years of knowing her. But still, she'd known. She'd seen the expression of longing in his eyes, noticed how even the slightest snarl on his shapely mouth resulted in her boyfriends preferring to stay clear of Whitby altogether. Certainly Aidan's deadbeat dad, Rick, had avoided Whitby like the plague, but Christina suspected that had just as much to do with Rick being a loser as it did Saint's intimidating frowns.

Saint was always her silent sentinel...her distant lover.

She'd recently made it her mission to narrow that distance to nothing.

She'd swallowed heavily as she stared into his mesmerizing eyes. She'd thought she'd understood the depth of his longing before, but she'd been wrong. It was as though he'd been blocking her from his desire and he suddenly released the barrier. Arousal flooded her awareness. A pleasurable tingling sensation buzzed just beneath her skin. Heat sunk from her belly to her sex. A mandatory need to touch him, to press her body against his long, hard length overcame her.

She'd stepped forward as if to do precisely that—yes, even in the midst of a party related to her work. His head lowered, as though to meet her in a kiss. For an electric second that stretched impossibly long, she was lost...gone...flying around in the depths of Saint's eyes.

A harsh moan scraped her throat.

For just a moment she'd existed in a different world—a place of rich, voluptuous pleasure. She could still feel the slight rasp of Saint's teeth brushing her inner thigh, his firm tongue sliding between the swollen folds of her pussy, the sensation of his big hand opened across her ribs and his fingertips lightly skimming the soft curve of her lower breast. She stared up at the roof of the gazebo, ecstasy nearly blinding her.

"No. Never again."

She'd blinked at Saint's roughly spoken words, the trance broken. The lights around her seemed to throb against the velvety black background of the night sky. In the distance, she heard the waves of Lake Michigan striking the beach rhythmically, or was that the sound of the blood surging in her veins? She'd felt hot. She touched her fingertips to her cheek. Her face wasn't the only thing that had grown warm and damp.

Warm moisture pooled between her thighs.

Had it really happened?

Her gaze locked on Saint's rigid features. She took a step closer to him, stunned by the magnitude of desire she saw etched on his features...hurt by the fact that he appeared to be struggling like crazy against that desire.

"Saint?" she asked in a hushed tone.

Her boss, Al Anderson, had stepped up to her and asked her a question about the renovations at Altgeld House, and Saint was gone.

That hadn't been just *her* fantasy that she'd seen graphically as she stared into Saint's amazing eyes, Christina thought bitterly as she stood alone on the shadowed Whitby grounds. *He'd* experienced it as well.

He'd wanted it, too.

So why did he make love to others beneath the gazebo on this sultry, sweet-smelling night that should have been theirs to share, Christina wondered, still shocked by the unexpected blow he'd dealt her.

Resentment swept through her when she gleaned the truth.

She'd never considered herself a masochist, so she couldn't imagine why she took one step, then two, and then was racing through the cloak of darkness.

She briefly glimpsed the gazebo set in a thirty-by-thirty-foot clearing before she ducked behind the trunk of an oak tree. Candlelight reflected off the white, high-roofed gallery, making the structure seem unnaturally bright, like a giant, glowing lantern set amongst the black canopy of trees.

Christina's lungs burned as she tried to catch her breath. A strange, nearly unbearable combination of excitement and dread mixed in her breast, making her limbs tremble. She took a shaky inhale and peered around the trunk of the tree.

For several moments, she stared, her muscles frozen. Nausea rose in her even as sexual arousal unlike anything she'd ever known before spread like wildfire to every nerve in her body.

Her position put her directly in front of one of the six-foot-wide entrances to the gazebo. Two females lay naked next to one another, their thighs spread. One of them still wore a pair of strappy high-heeled sandals while the other was barefoot. Christina saw the soles of her light brown feet flex as Saint leaned over her, his head between her thighs.

The other female had a long mane of blonde hair. She writhed against the pressure of Saint's hand moving between her thighs. Neither woman had been at the party, Christina was sure.

Neither was the type who would go unnoticed.

The candlelight caught the gleaming highlights in Saint's burnished hair as he moved his head more rapidly and the woman's rapturous cries cut through the still, humid air. He was clothed only in the dark pants that went with the suit he'd worn earlier at the party. Lean, powerful muscle rippled beneath golden brown skin.

The woman cried out sharply, her muscles stiffening, her bare feet flexing hard. He continued to eat her pussy hungrily while she climaxed.

He lowered his head to a smooth thigh; his jaw opened and shut. The woman raised her head and keened louder, her eyes going wide in stunned ecstasy, her pleasure so tangible it seemed to flow through Christina like palpable waves.

The thing that struck Christina most in that soul-wrenching moment was how natural he looked. It was as though she'd come upon a lion feeding on a fallen gazelle. There was no violence here, no sacrilege. His consumption was raw and primitive and as right as a summer downpour upon the thirsty earth.

She was so disoriented by witnessing the intensely carnal moment that she hadn't at first registered that both women's backs were arched, their hands above their head, wrists together as though they'd been bound. He didn't restrain either of them, however, and Christina could see no bindings. It must be their choice to hold the position.

Or Saint's preference?

Anxiety and the first inklings of fear entered Christina's awareness when his jaws remained fixed to the woman's thigh, his mouth moving ever so slightly. The woman's head fell back to the floor of the gazebo, her body sagging limply as she gasped for air.

Saint lifted his head. A whimper of anxiety escaped Christina's throat when she saw the long, sharp incisors that protruded onto his lips. With her sixth sense, she'd gleaned so much about him, so many secrets.

But she hadn't guessed *this*.

His head whipped around. Christina took cover behind the

tree, praying he couldn't hear her rough pants for air. The howl of a dog in the distance mingled with the hammer of her heart in her ears.

Why didn't she run?

Was she in too much shock to experience fear? He'd *bitten* that woman with teeth that looked like an animal's lethal fangs. The fact that the woman appeared to love every moment of it confused Christina even more. She felt anxiety over Saint's strange behavior, yes, but also an unbearable sexual excitement.

Not to mention fury that he'd chosen to bring two other females to what should have been a special meeting between them. Her anger frothed at the thought.

He was doing this on purpose, the bastard. He was doing this to push her away.

She gritted her teeth and poked her head out from behind the tree. He must have decided whatever he'd heard had been an animal or a sound from the distant city streets, because he was back to making love. He stretched across the woman he'd been pleasuring, his head now between the blonde's thighs. After a moment, he raised his head to inspect his handiwork.

The blonde's pussy had been shaved clean. It glistened in the soft candlelight. Christina's womb flexed inward in painful arousal as she watched Saint's head lower once again. The woman made a choking sound, as though pleasure had literally stolen her breath.

Christina watched, enthralled, as his limber, wet tongue drew sigh after moan after begging chant from the woman's throat. Her body had gone rigid, her back arched off the floor. The brown-skinned woman moved her hips restlessly against Saint's body. He responded by pressing a hand between her legs. The woman mewled appreciatively. Saint's head whipped around.

Suddenly his eyes were on Christina. She trembled in dismay and shock and arousal and she didn't know what else, but she couldn't bring herself to move. Tears soaked her heated cheeks.

He pushed his upper body up with his arms, pinning her with his stare.

Chapter Two

Misery finally overcame her.

She turned and ran through the night. She came up short not two seconds later when a wolf stepped into her path. At first she thought it was Scepter. But then she saw that while this animal was as tall as Scepter, it was bulkier. Its fur looked dark gray in the moonlight versus Scepter's mixture of dove gray and white around the neck and muzzle.

"Go away," she hissed. Tears continued to pour down her face. A dam of emotion felt as if it were about to break and explode out of her chest. All she wanted to do was to get home and stifle her groans of pain and agony into her pillow. She didn't have time for strays—wild or domesticated.

"Get," she repeated between clenched teeth. She started to charge toward the animal, made fearless by her volatile emotional state. Movement caught her attention out of the side of her eye, however, and she paused. Her mouth fell open in amazement when she saw that close to a dozen wolves surrounded her in a half-circle. Each of them stood utterly still, their moonlit eyes fixed on her.

A hand spread along the side of her neck, long fingers stretching into her unbound hair. He jerked her against his long, hard body, her belly thumping against his groin. Heat and the odor of aroused male filled her nose, the impact of the scent sending her body into a strange combination of fight or flight and lust so powerful it struck her awareness like a slap to the face.

"Get your *filthy* hands off me," she growled at Saint, outraged that he had the nerve to touch her with the women's essence still on him.

"Why do you run? You know perfectly well I'd never harm you."

She laughed mirthlessly. "I obviously don't know the first thing about you."

She saw his light blue eyes gleam in the moonlight, reminding her of the wolves that surrounded them. His nostrils flared when he inhaled. "You're right. You know nothing about me, lovely, or you wouldn't be having infantile fantasies about us sharing a romantic interlude in the darkness."

His eyes flashed; his head moved slightly as he inhaled again, clearly catching her scent. For some reason, the primitiveness of his actions made her want to respond in kind, made her itch to press her body against his hard length, to claw at his back until he came down over her in the fragrant grass...to force him to take what was his.

The thought made her flinch away from him.

"You're an animal," she hissed.

"Yes."

She started. He sounded so sure...so sad. Tears scalded her eyes.

"I've always known you weren't like other people, just like I'm not. I didn't mean you were an animal because you're different. I meant it because you called here tonight knowing perfectly well how much you were going to hurt me. You wanted to make *sure* of it, you bastard." She jerked violently out of his hold. "*That's* why you're an animal, Saint."

"Better I hurt you this way than to turn your foolish fantasies into reality."

She went up on her tiptoes, shoving her face as close to his as she could get. "It was your fantasy as well, you fucking hypocrite."

For several seconds they just stared at each other, Christina trying to catch both her breath and her splintering control; Saint holding himself preternaturally still.

"You won't harm those women," she stated fiercely.

"I never harm. I take, but only what's freely given." His gaze dropped down over her. "And not always that."

The image of him swam in a world filled with tears.

"Just stay away from Aidan and me, you son of a bitch."

As she ran blindly through the darkness.

Saint watched Christina run away. Her vitessence—her vibrant lifeforce—popped and snapped around her, shining brilliantly in his vision. That he could actually see her hurt and disillusionment like a human would see something as tangible as the sunrise made his pain exponentially more vicious.

His frozen stance belied a nearly overwhelming need to race after her. This was his life—always the mandate to restrain, ever the requirement to battle his hunger, to vanquish his need.

He sensed Fardusk standing near his right shoulder and spoke. "Have the others escort the women off Whitby's grounds."

"Have you become as mercenary in your feeding as your clone, then?" Fardusk asked.

Saint turned slowly. Fardusk's face looked as though it'd been carved from rock in the blue-tinged light of the moon. He

23

experienced the admonishment from the revered chief of the Iniskium like acid splashing on a raw wound.

"I have given them pleasure. I haven't shortchanged them," Saint said bitterly. "Why don't you just say what you're really angry about?"

"It was beneath you to trick Christina in that way. She deserves better."

His muscles convulsed with repressed emotion. He'd known Fardusk now for over five and a half centuries, and never *once* had his companion chastised him. This despite the fact that Saint was more deserving of Fardusk's condemnation than any other. Saint had been the one to rob Fardusk and so many members of the Iniskium tribe of their mortal lives, after all.

"She deserves *much* better," Saint hissed. "What would you have me do? She is life; I am the walking dead. Christina is the fullness. I am the void. Would you have me drain her of every ounce of her vitessence, only to make her like me?"

"I would have you face your fate instead of run from it."

Fury lashed through him. Saint lunged.

"I do not *run*," he snarled close to Fardusk's impassive face.

He didn't see the Iniskium chief's face, however. Instead, all he could envision was the image of Christina's hurt when she saw him pleasuring the women, Christina suffering from a wound he'd purposely inflicted.

Remorse flooded him, but what other choice had been left to him? He forced himself to take a step back from Fardusk.

"I do not run," he repeated. "I restrain. I endure. I will even put up with your condemnation tonight because I have no other choice."

Fardusk remained silent as Saint turned and headed toward the main house, alone.

Chapter Three

The silence stretched. Christina didn't move as she stared at the waifish young woman who sat in front of her desk. The girl's forearms rested in her lap, the bandages around her wrists looking starkly white against tanned skin.

"Do you think you're going to make me talk by staring at me like that, Christina? I ain't a member of your fan club, and I don't intimidate easy." Alison's thin, pretty face twisted in defiance.

Christina looked mildly surprised. "You, easily intimidated? I'd just as soon call life fair. Come on, Alison, you know I'm not trying to intimidate you. I'm waiting patiently because I think you want to tell me why you cut yourself this afternoon."

Christina waited. She hadn't been bluffing. She'd had the ability to read other people's minds for as long as she could remember. Occasionally she caught entire thoughts, but usually just overall emotional states. The reasons behind those emotional states were less defined—the difference between catching the scent of lilacs on the wind and holding the flower in your hand.

Alison Myers wanted to reach out to Christina. She longed for a sense of security and comfort. Whatever was haunting her, tempting her, was countermanding that desire. And whatever had its hold on her was far more troubling than Alison's typical demons.

Christina had long ago become familiar with the bitter ambivalence of teenagers and young adults. They longed to be independent, to be in full control of their lives, and yet...the longing to be taken care of and nurtured remained, causing a bitter emotional struggle. Hell, it wasn't just teenagers who fought the internal battle. All humans vacillated between wanting to be in total control of their destinies and being taken care of by someone they trusted.

For the majority of young adults at Altgeld House, the raw wounds and scars from childhood traumas made the battle a hundred times more potent and painful.

Alison flipped her jet-black dyed hair out of her eyes, her gaze on Christina hungry and suspicious at once. She licked at her lower lip, the silver stud piercing her tongue dragging slowly along damp flesh.

Christina understood the girl was purposefully being provocative. Not surprising. When Alison felt backed into a corner, she automatically reverted to the familiar security of the seductress role. It was how she found her power when she was feeling powerless, a pattern Christina had witnessed in abused children too many times to count.

"I know you want to trust me, Alison, but you're scared. You've only been at Altgeld House for four weeks now. Surely some of the others—Mirella, Eric, Andre—have told you that I can be trusted." Christina stood and came around her desk, sitting in the chair next to Alison. "I can't help you if you don't tell me what was going through your mind when you picked up that razor and cut yourself."

Another tense silence ensued. Christina noticed the tears welling in Alison's extraordinary midnight blue eyes. She reached out with her mind to read the twenty-year-old woman's primary emotion. Usually kids who cut themselves were either boiling with anger or so miserable they'd gone numb. But those weren't the primary emotions she sensed emanating from Alison.

"You're scared shitless," Christina said softly.

A sob racked the girl's slender torso. Tears that had been restrained until that moment gushed down her cheeks in a torrent.

"It was a sacrifice. A blood sacrifice. It was a test. I had to show that I give myself willingly—without doubt."

Christina crinkled her brow in concern. She hadn't observed any indication of delusional thinking from the girl in her original assessment, nor observed any psychotic thought processes since then. She must have missed something...unless Alison had gotten herself mixed up with some sick jerk who got off on forcing his girlfriends to cut themselves as a sign of loyalty?

Altgeld House wasn't a lock-down facility. The residents were expected to either be in school, working, or trying to find a job. There was an eleven-thirty p.m. curfew monitored by Marianna Jones, the night supervisor, but Lord knew residents had been known to get into plenty of trouble before the midnight hour struck.

"Who demands a blood sacrifice?"

Alison opened her lips to respond, but a knock sounded on Christina's office door. She mentally cursed whoever had interrupted at such a crucial moment. She apologized to the fragile young woman and flung open the door.

"Can't you read?" she demanded, referring to the *do not disturb* sign she put up when she was in session with a resident. She came up short when she saw Saint standing there, wearing jeans and a black T-shirt that highlighted the long taper from his broad shoulders to his narrow waist. He wore sunglasses and his hair had the wind-tousled, sexy look she associated with him just getting off his sleek Augusta F4 motorcycle. Fury swelled in her breast.

It'd been two weeks since the charity function. The fact that she'd been able to read Saint's monumental conflict and pain when he'd halted her amongst the trees only escalated her volatility and confusion. She'd never resented her ability to read others more acutely, but things would have been easier if she could just think of him as a freak and a jerk.

She'd been making plans to move off Whitby's grounds since the night of the gazebo. But when night came, she grieved for the loss of him...grieved for the loss of what might have been.

What should have been.

The incendiary thought kept occurring to her that perhaps Saint'd been right to show her what he was, justified in pushing her away when she'd become so insistent upon seducing him.

She'd kept her defensive barrier intact, however. Been proud of herself for shutting him out.

The realization that all she'd done was avoid the issue for two weeks slammed home as she stared at the vivid reality of Saint standing right in front of her.

What right did he have showing up here in her private domain, looking like a beautiful, suffering angel, when she was doing her best to squeeze the life out of her too-frequent thoughts of him?

"What do you want?" she asked ungraciously.

"I brought Aidan. He wants to talk to you. He's waiting in the day room."

"Is he all right?" Her anger at the fact that Saint had been hanging around Aidan when she'd specifically told him to stay away was forgotten in her concern for her son.

"He's fine. He just said he had something important he wanted to discuss with you and asked if I'd bring him over."

Christina glanced around at Alison, who was staring at Saint, slack-jawed. Christina mentally rolled her eyes. Was there a female on the planet whose brain wouldn't short-circuit at the sight of him?

"Alison, can you hold on just a moment? I need to speak with my son."

Alison swallowed heavily and nodded.

Christina sighed and stepped into the hallway, worried she'd lost crucial therapeutic ground with the girl by the interruption. She'd done a suicide assessment and spoken at length with Alison's psychiatrist. They'd agreed the girl wasn't actively suicidal. But Alison was in some kind of danger. Christina just knew it. And this business of a blood sacrifice alarmed her.

She glanced up when she noticed that Saint hadn't moved to make way for her and her nose was just inches away from a broad, cotton-covered chest.

As usual, he didn't speak, even when she stared into his eyes.

"If you want to say something, *say* it," she spat.

"Aidan's not the only one who wants to speak with you. I do, as well."

She rolled her eyes. "Miracle of miracles. Whatever it is will have to wait. You're at the very bottom of my list, Sevliss."

She felt his gaze boring into her back as she walked away.

He watched her as she strutted down the corridor.

Christina's fury burned in his nose and tasted like bitter spice on his tongue. Her never-absent arousal added a rich, intoxicating flavor to the complex array of emotions that always flavored the energy field that surrounded her. He forced himself to look away.

It shamed him beyond belief that he could have stared at her unceasingly for an eternity, drawing on her vast energy...feeding from her like the parasite he was until he'd drained every ounce of her vitessence, leaving nothing but a hollow shell.

Christina lit up his monochrome world like a blazing comet. Whenever he was near her, a lifeless, gray landscape flooded with vibrant, throbbing color.

He glanced into Christina's comfortable, messy office, his attention fixing on the pale, undernourished-looking young woman who stood facing him. She trembled. His gaze flickered down to her wrists. Vitessence glowed around her wounds—the color a watered-out gold against the gray outlines of the rest of her.

For one such as he, releasing blood to the air was like breaking a safety seal. He caught the scent of her blood, her fear and excitement.

He stepped into the room.

"You recognize me," he said. It wasn't a question, but a statement of fact.

"Of course."

"Where have you seen me before? Here?"

Confusion flickered across the young woman's expression. "I don't understand...what do you mean?"

"Tell me where you've seen me before." He removed his glasses and used his ascendancy, not to enslave, but to calm.

"At the Grand Avenue subway stop, of course. You listened to me play and sing for over an hour, and then you took me to the Black Velvet Lounge. And then afterwards, you took me to that place far, far down below the city." Her voice faded to a husky whisper as she stepped closer to him. The aura of her vitessence throbbed with the escalating beat of her heart. She rolled a thick silver barbell along her lower lip and laughed seductively. "You loved the feel of that on your cock, didn't you? Remember? How I took you so deep and hummed you a sweet tune, and you called me your little songbird...your sweet little pet? You've come for me early? Is it time?"

"No."

She started out of her entrancement.

"There's been a change of plans."

"But, you said if I showed myself worthy... You *saw*, didn't you? I didn't lie to you, did I?" She held up her forearms. Pale gold tears flowed down her gray face. "You said that if I showed myself willing, we could possibly live together for a glorious eternity."

Saint's muscles clenched in rising fury.

It'd been five and a half centuries since Saint's one and only night of unregulated bloodlust. His first memories of life were clear and hauntingly graphic, as much as he prayed to the gods to make them fade. Consciousness hadn't come in fits and starts, but in an abrupt slam. He and his clone, Teslar, had just suddenly been there, inhaling the verdant earth and the brackish water in the distance. One sensation had preceded all others. It had awakened him to the gray, shadowed world.

Hunger.

They had come upon a village not far from the banks of a river. Teslar and he had fed like ravenous wolves turned loose in a field filled with helpless cattle.

Saint lived daily with the knowledge of what he'd done to the Native American tribe, the Iniskium. It hadn't taken him long to learn the horror of his actions, to know the fires of remorse, but Teslar continued in his never-ending mission to drain his victims completely of their vitessence. Teslar craved the spice of fear in his food and enjoyed coming up with new ways to evoke it in his victims.

Teslar was a fear-eater.

Saint definitely sensed fear in the young woman who stood in Christina's office, but the most overwhelming misplaced emotions he read at that moment were excitement, infatuation, and idolatry. It worried him. He was responsible for his clone, after all.

Teslar's crimes were his own.

Ages ago, Saint had separated himself from Teslar, denied his bloodlust free access to rule his existence. Only then had the Magian named Kavya given him the primary mandate that ruled his existence.

Now Saint lived to keep Teslar in check, to control from the outside what could not be regulated from within.

Still, Saint knew the truth. He and Teslar were one and the same—parasites, creatures worthy of the look of disgust and fear Christina had given him the other night after she'd seen him feed off the women's vitessence—the vital essence exuded by the soul, the energy that surrounded humans in varying amounts. Vitessence was found in concentrated forms in the blood, sweat, tears, and sexual secretions—fluids associated with strong emotion.

Saint and Teslar were both energy vampires, but vampires in the classical sense as well.

Teslar was harvesting his energies for some purpose, carefully cultivating his power. Saint had suspected he was the

Youngblood Thief before, although the means of blood extraction had thrown him off the scent of his clone at first.

Why would a vicious and expert blood-drinker like Teslar bother to paralyze and then medically exsanguinate his victims? Teslar had the ability to exsanguinate utilizing his fangs and suction alone.

Why this change in method?

Saint thought he knew the answer. Teslar wanted to heighten his victim's fear. The captive bolt that had been found inserted in the young people's brain caused paralysis. Unfortunately, the victims were fully aware of what was happening to them while their blood was drained.

Despite Saint's suspicions, leaders of the Iniskium—Fardusk, Isi and Strix—had been unable to come up with any solid proof that Teslar was the Youngblood Thief. Even the opportunity to obtain proof had been negligible, as Teslar had found a new hidey-hole in the underground of the city—a den, which, as of yet, had remained a secret to Saint and the Iniskium.

Until now.

He stepped closer to the girl, automatically setting up an energy barrier between them, protecting her from his poisonous, parasitic nature, leaving only a narrow channel open. He turned his ascendancy up to its fullest strength.

"Listen to me. If you give yourself to Teslar or any one of the Scourge revenants for the Final Embrace, there is a ninety percent chance you will die."

"I know," the girl replied fervently, her eyes glassy with manic excitement. "I'm prepared to make the sacrifice."

Saint paused. She *knew*? Teslar had told her the truth?

Not all of it, Saint was willing to bet. He continued

ruthlessly.

"Your blood, and most likely your flesh, will be consumed with all the mindlessness and disregard of a fast-food meal. If they don't eat your flesh, there is a ten percent chance you will turn Scourge revenant, possessing no soul. You will be a monster, and the form of that monster will not even be something of your own choosing. There will be no point to your existence but to feed, to figure out how to feed next...to scheme how to feed well. And hear this. You will be one of many. Teslar has said you would be his special companion, his mate, but he lies. Teslar breeds and breathes lies."

For the first time, her worshipful expression fractured. "But *you* are—"

"I am *not* Teslar."

He tried to keep the passion out of his voice, but it was difficult. It was stupid to bemoan the fact that Teslar and he were identical in appearance.

We share more in common than just a face. I am him and he is me and we are all together.

"When were you planning on seeing Teslar next?" he asked the girl sharply, pushing aside the taunting voice in his head.

Alison bit her lower lip doubtfully. Saint pressed with his ascendancy.

"If...if you come with me later tonight, you'll see Teslar," she said.

"I'll follow you then."

Chapter Four

Christina stomped into her office and threw Saint a vitriolic glance. He sat in the leather chair behind her desk, unmoving.

His eerie stillness had been one of Christina's first indications that Saint wasn't normal. Human beings weren't capable of that sharp degree of focus while remaining immobile for so long. Unless they were a Buddhist monk or something.

"Where's Alison?"

"She went to her room," he replied evenly.

"You've got a lot of nerve, you know that?" She slammed the door shut and swept across the room like a wildfire on the rampage. "It's you who put this fixed idea in Aidan's head that we shouldn't move away from Whitby. Didn't I tell you to stay away from him?"

"You're wrong. No intervention was required on my part. Aidan is very upset about the idea of leaving Whitby. It's his home."

"Wrong. Whitby Manor is your home," she corrected, pointing accusingly.

She stepped back when he stood abruptly, quick as a

snake at the strike.

"It's my home because you're there," he growled.

Christina was set off-balance by his unexpected revelation accompanied by a focused explosion of feeling. The vivid memory of the gazebo made her recover. "Maybe you should have thought of that before you brought your girlfriends to what should have been our first date."

She'd never seen Saint show an emotion as mundane as incredulity until now.

"First date? You *saw* what I am! Saw it with your own eyes, and yet the only thing you consider is that I was unfaithful to your infantile fantasies?"

She snarled and picked up a heavy marble paperweight from her desk, fully prepared to hurl it at Saint's stunned expression of disbelief. A frustrated cry left her lips when he was suddenly beside her, restraining her wrists. He wrapped his arms around her and pushed her back into his chest.

"Calm down."

For a few seconds, she was dazed by his resonant, deep voice and the sensation of his body pressed against her. She twisted furiously in his hold, but her body slowly sagged. When she realized she was following Saint's order without conscious thought, her fury erupted.

"*God*, I hate you! How could you have done that to me?"

"I am what I am. If I could change my nature, I would in a second. You gave me no choice but to reveal to you the truth about why your dreams are merely that—the fantasies of a child."

Fury bloomed in her chest, feeling as if it would explode through the skin at any moment. "I told you the other night. I *knew* you weren't like everybody else. I didn't guess you're...whatever you are...a vampire?"

"Humans have called me that. The truth is a bit more complicated."

"Vampire or not, you're an asshole. Some things remain consistent across the species. Even the paranormal variety."

She braced her legs and twisted viciously to push herself out of his hold. She might as well have been trying to throw a mountain off her. His strength was effortless, as though she were being restrained by steel instead of flesh.

"Let *go* of me."

"When you calm down."

She tried to ignore the shiver of excitement that raced down her neck when she felt his voice rumbling from his chest to her back and his warm breath brushing her ear. She inhaled his familiar scent. As usual, it started an unstoppable chemical cascade of arousal in her body. Her lack of control over her reaction infuriated her further.

"I'm about ready to scream myself hoarse. Do you want to upset Aidan?"

"No. Do you?"

She twisted her neck around and glared up at him. "What's

that supposed to mean?"

"Do you think you're really doing the best thing by taking him away from Whitby?"

"As a matter of fact, I do."

"Who's making that decision? The loving mother? Or your battered ego?"

She went completely still. For a few seconds she thought she'd go stark raving mad if she didn't get to punch Saint Sevliss's gorgeous, smug face just once. He stared down at her with those amazing blue eyes while she panted and her breath burned in her lungs.

Using every ounce of her willpower, she forced herself to calm. She inhaled slowly several times, trying her best not to notice the sensation of Saint's arms enclosing her expanding and contracting ribcage.

"Let go of me, please," she said with as much dignity as she could muster.

When she felt him slowly release her, she gave full rein to her fury. She turned, stepped back, cocked her fist and swung. Two weeks of pent-up anger and frustration went into a well-landed right hook to Saint's angular jaw. His chin swung at the impact of the blow.

He slowly turned to face her. What she saw in his eyes made her take a step back in alarm. He halted her retreat by grabbing her upper arms and hauling her next to his body. Anxiety and anguish mixed with Christina's fury when she stared up at his face.

How can he feel so much and show so little? It was as if her punch had popped the lid off a tightly sealed container of frothing, scorching-hot emotion. A tear skipped down her cheek when he shook her.

"I didn't want to hurt you, Christina. I hate myself for having done it. But you gave me *no choice*, the way you were pursuing me."

His heat seemed to pour into her body. She experienced his inner turmoil clearly, felt his desperation, his need and his pain in equal degrees to her own. It was unbearable, the friction it caused inside of her. Without thinking about her actions, she struggled to get her right arm free from his hold. Much to her surprise, he released her. She grabbed a handful of soft hair at his nape and jerked fiercely.

"I would think you'd be glad we were leaving. Wasn't that little show you staged the other night precisely for that purpose?"

She sobbed as tears spurted down her cheek. Despite her unbridled fury, she couldn't stop staring at Saint's mouth for some god-awful reason, couldn't stop from pressing her body against his long, hard length, or rubbing her aching nipples against his ribs.

"I was trying to stop you from getting me into bed. I'm trying to keep you safe from me. Can't you see that? That doesn't mean I want you and Aidan to leave Whitby for good."

"Well, I guess your little plan didn't work too well, did it?" She jerked on his hair one last time for emphasis before she went up on tiptoe and pulled him down closer to her face. She didn't stop until she felt his warm breath brushing against her lips. "Why in the hell do I need to be kept safe? You must know by now I can read people's minds, Saint. I have *never* been afraid of you."

His upper lip curled; his eyes blazed. She cried out in surprise when he wrapped his hands around her waist and lifted her roughly until they were groin to groin, heartbeat to heartbeat.

"You *should* be afraid." He swooped down and took her mouth in a ravaging kiss.

A torrent of emotion and sensation surged through her. Christina dazedly realized Saint was right. A woman *should* be afraid she might drown in the deep, frothing well of carnal delight that suddenly submersed her entire being.

Nevertheless, she craned up for him hungrily, all vestiges of rational thought burned into a mist by her lust and need.

The first taste of Christina and he was lost. He felt like an addict who'd just fallen off the wagon face-first onto the pavement, a drunk who had acknowledged his addiction to watered-down wine and suddenly found himself drowning in premium bourbon.

Her potent vitessence flooded his cells, invigorating him like nothing else could. How could he have gone so many years without losing himself in her? He must have forced himself to forget the experience…self-imposed amnesia.

His body shook with need. This was all Christina's fault, dammit. He'd suffered in her nearness just as he'd gloried in it. He'd been able to keep himself from her, but barely, and only with monumental levels of restraint and willpower on his part.

But she was a mature female now, a woman who knew what she wanted. Gone were the days of her shyness, her uncertainty and hesitation in the presence of a more experienced male. He could no longer cow her with his silences or turn his back on her sweet, subtle invitations to share her bed.

Saint realized too late this was a whole new game, and he was back to square one.

He didn't tell himself to move, but suddenly he was sweeping the items off Christina's desk and lifting her onto it, bending over her as he continued to send his tongue deep in the honeyed cavern of her mouth, striking out again and again to capture her flavor, shivering uncontrollably at the sound and sensations of her whimpers as they vibrated her throat. His incisors throbbed with a need to extend, but he couldn't bring himself to stop feeding on the sweetest mouth in existence.

She pressed her soft mound against his erection, her hips rolling in tight, sensual circles against his straining flesh. The sensation of her pointed nipples thrusting against his chest made him lift his head and growl.

She stared up at him with desire-glazed green eyes. He had never known what the color green was—never known what color was *period*—until he'd first seen Christina. Pink was only pink because it was the sensation that had hit his brain when he first saw the bloom in her cheek and her lush, rosebud mouth.

Her lips were red now, not just from his ravening kiss, but with desire. His cock lurched furiously in his jeans, demanding its due. He saw only a pulsing haze of pure gold flickering with a rainbow of throbbing color and Christina's beautiful face at the center of it. He heard the rush of blood pounding in her veins even more clearly than he heard the thud of his own frenzied heartbeat. The aura of pulsating light surrounding her became tinged with red.

Against his will, his incisors elongated, the sensation excruciatingly painful and arousing at once. He *couldn't* do this.

He couldn't stop.

He was lost in a dream of pulsing color and blinding hunger. He ripped at her pants. Buttons clicked and skittered across the wood floor. He jerked her panties to her thighs and pierced warm, weeping, succulent flesh with his finger. Her head jerked up off the desk, her long, near-black hair falling like a silken cape down her shoulders and back. She bit her bottom lip, stifling a moan as he slid his finger in and out of her tight channel. It maddened him the way her sleek muscles squeezed around him, as though she never wanted him to leave her.

And the gods knew he never wanted to.

She clenched her teeth in an agony of pleasure. He was rough with her and he knew it, reaching high into her, kneading her tender cunt mercilessly. Her vitessence pulsated and sparked around her, looking like a rich, golden cloud spiked with flashing, colorful fireflies. He bathed in it, every cell of his being absorbing her energy hungrily. He flicked his forefinger rapidly across her swollen clit and watched her face tighten with pleasure while her aura surged, the tiny, living lights flickering more rapidly until they overwhelmed his vision.

He ripped at his own jeans, wanting...needing...to be fully embedded in her when her entire being exploded and the essence of Christina blasted into him.

Gods, he hurt. His hunger clawed at him. He fumbled wildly to free his cock as he continued to stimulate her, his eyes never leaving her rapturous face. His cock felt heavy and stretched to maximal volume when he finally took it in his hand and arrowed it toward Christina's tender cleft. He slid his finger out of her and replaced it with the head of his cock, hearing her gasp at the sudden invasion.

Then she was sinking her nails into his shoulders and shuddering in orgasm.

Her vitessence thundered into him like a tidal wave. His head flung back. His grunts mixed with Christina's whimpers of release. Her pussy milked the hypersensitive head of his cock. He snarled, his fangs fully bared, and leaned over her, held spellbound by the pulse throbbing at her throat.

He flexed his ass muscles in preparation to fully pierce succulent female flesh, but at the same moment, his tension amplified for another reason.

"Shhh...quiet yourself, beauty," he whispered harshly,

silencing Christina's mewls of anguished pleasure. She opened her eyes sluggishly and slowed in the eye-crossing little thrusts of her hips as she tried to seat his cock farther in her.

A second later someone pounded on the office door. With supreme effort, Saint drew in his incisors until they only barely protruded past his other teeth.

"Give me a minute, Aidan. Wait for me in the dayroom," he called over his shoulder, ascendancy flavoring his tone with authority.

"Okay," the boy replied from the other side of the door. Saint listened to the sound of Aidan's fading tread with a potent mixture of gratitude and regret. He met Christina's wide-eyed stare and withdrew his cock from her warm clasp.

Every nerve in his body screamed in protest at the cruelty of the resulting pain.

Her hands tightened in anguish on Saint's shoulders when he separated himself from her.

"How…how did you know it was Aidan?" Her voice sounded hoarse, like she hadn't used it in a week. It was the white-hot blaze of pure pleasure that had scored her throat, undoubtedly, just like it had the rest of her body.

Saint didn't respond. Her senses swam in a thick haze of arousal. He straightened and her eyes sprang wide. He'd shoved his jeans down to his thighs. Christina had frequently admired—well, salivated, in fact—over the manner in which Saint filled out his jeans. Seeing his full glory revealed left her brain vibrating with stunned lust. His long, beautifully shaped, golden-hued cock flushed with arousal was one thing. But his penis was erotically highlighted by a leather thong that encircled his lower hips and both thighs, just below his round, shaved testicles. She caught a glimpse of two leather straps tied tightly against his muscular left leg, a thin sheath of sorts, strapped to his outer thigh.

It figured. Saint couldn't just wear a pair of boxers like most guys.

He pulled his jeans over his hips, inserting his swollen cock down his right pant leg with a grimace. Reality crashed in on her as she watched him fasten his button-fly, wincing as he did so.

"You *called* him here with your mind," she whispered incredulously. "You *wanted* Aidan to interrupt us...to interrupt this," she said as she nodded to the juncture of her naked, spread thighs. His eyes flashed dangerously when he glanced to where she referred.

He turned his back to her.

Turned his back *on* her, Christina realized. A band seemed to pull tight around her chest, constricting her breath. Her lungs burned.

"Get dressed and meet us out in the dayroom," he ordered quietly.

But Christina remained spread-eagled and aghast for several seconds after he left. No human could engage in something so intimate and then just blithely turn and walk away.

Of course, Saint *wasn't* human, was he?

She blinked several times and looked around her office. The image of Saint's retreating back was superimposed on everything she saw.

Chapter Five

The first thing Christina heard, aside from a commercial for car insurance blaring on the television, was the sound of her son's voice.

Aidan had grown like a well-watered weed for the past six months. Christina was distantly surprised to see that the top of his head reached just below Saint's shoulders. It seemed like yesterday Saint towered over the boy like a giant would a munchkin. Aidan had grown up instead of out. She worried about his skinniness, even though she knew it was normal for boys to get that lanky, stretched appearance as adolescence loomed.

His thinness confused her all the more because she'd been flabbergasted by the amount of food the kid had been putting away for the past six months. Aidan's voice hadn't yet begun to crack and deepen like some of his eleven-year-old friends' had. Still, the coming of his manhood seemed to surround Aidan like a hazy glow before a fierce dawn.

She heard Aidan scold Saint. "Why did you have to go and have a fight with her? Now she'll never let us stay at Whitby!"

"Sorry," Saint said in his deep, resonant rumble.

"I'll say you are."

Both males looked around at the sound of her voice. Given the perversity of her mood, it gratified her to see that Aidan looked nearly as furious with Saint at that moment as she did. It'd confused her in the past sometimes, how she'd never become jealous while standing at the kitchen sink, doing the dishes and watching through the window as Saint and Aidan tossed a baseball in the yard, talking in brief bursts of what appeared to be some kind of mysterious, earnest male code that she couldn't quite break.

How could they say so little and make it *look* like so much?

Yeah, Saint and Aidan had always had a bond she couldn't touch. So the bunching of Aidan's dark brown eyebrows and accusatory stare at Saint especially gratified her at that moment.

"Mom, Saint didn't mean it. He didn't know what he was saying," Aidan stated immediately upon seeing her. He stepped toward her, his hands outstretched in a soothing gesture. "Saint wants us to stay at Whitby as much as I want to stay there. I'm *sure* he'll apologize for whatever he said or did."

Christina put out her arms toward her son, hating to see the wild, desperate look in his eyes. She threw Saint an acidic look that clearly told him, *this is all your fault!* His expression remained stony as he returned her stare, but she saw a muscle in his jaw leap with tension. Aidan remained by his friend and hero's side, despite Christina's beckoning gestures.

"Come on, Aidan. We'll go home in a while."

"To Whitby?" Aidan asked, his handsome, thin face transforming with triumph. His aquamarine eyes—a mixture of the sea and sky combined—gleamed hopefully.

"Yes. It's our home for now. It will be until the lease starts on the apartment in Old Town in two weeks. I've explained all of that to you," Christina said neutrally.

Her son's scowl cut right through her.

"Aww, Mom. Old Town sucks."

"Please don't use language like that, Aidan," Christina said, crossing her arms below her breasts.

"Where am I going to be able to skateboard? And Scepter is going to hate being caged up in an apartment!"

Christina's shoulders sagged. Aidan hadn't brought up this particular detail since she'd showed him the apartment yesterday and picked up the lease from the landlord. She'd been so busy enumerating all the advantages of moving and calming Aidan's doubts that the volatile topic of Scepter hadn't yet come up. She glanced at Saint nervously, wishing like hell it hadn't come up in front of his brooding, disapproving presence.

"Honey, we'll talk about this when we get home. I have some things I still need to do here at work. Maybe you can just watch television for a while and—"

"Mom?"

Christina mentally groaned when she saw the tightening of Aidan's focus on her. If only her son hadn't been born with her ability to read people...

"Scepter *is* going to be able to come with us if we move, isn't he?"

Christina clenched her back teeth when she saw Saint's eyebrows go up in a wry expression, as though he couldn't wait to hear her answer to this.

"Aidan...Scepter is half-wild. It'd be cruel to force him away from the woods at Whitby."

"I'm not going, then," Aidan said staunchly, crossing his arms across his thin chest in a stubborn gesture that was the mirror image of Christina's own. "There's no way I'm leaving Scepter."

"We'll talk more about it on the way home."

Aidan's mouth twisted into a frown, but he must have

recognized the finality in Christina's tone. "Can't Saint take me home on his bike?"

"No."

Both males' eyebrows cocked up at her harshness.

"We'll take the 'L' home after I'm finished working. Saint indicated he was in a big hurry to be somewhere else. We wouldn't want to keep him," Christina explained through stiff lips. She was quite proud of the fact that she'd controlled her anger at being abandoned in the middle of impulsive, hot sex sufficiently enough to sound only sarcastic instead of wildly furious.

Which she *was.*

Christina guessed it was true what they said. Hell hath no fury and all that crap.

Christina and Aidan paused in front of the Racine entrance to the "L" later that evening when they heard someone calling Christina's name.

"Christina! Wait up."

Christina was both glad and concerned to see that it was Alison Myers rushing up to meet her and Aidan. She hadn't been able to locate the girl following Saint's interruption of their conversation. Her roommate, Mirella, had told Christina that Alison had been to their room, but only to hastily grab her backpack and guitar. Christina's concern had escalated when Mirella held up a record album.

"Check it out, Christina. *The Pretenders* on vinyl."

"Isn't that Alison's?" Christina had asked.

"Yeah. She gave it to me before she left. Can you believe it? It's a collector's item," Mirella had replied, awe spicing her tone.

"Alison worships Chrissie Hynd. *The Pretenders* are her favorite."

The back of Christina's neck had prickled. The fact that Alison'd given Mirella the much-loved album was downright alarming. Years of experience working with disturbed adolescents and young adults told her it was a common gesture to give away cherished items before a suicide attempt. But Alison had been so adamant she wasn't suicidal, and Christina had sensed the truth behind her words.

She'd waited as long as possible for Alison to return home, but she couldn't keep Aidan at Altgeld House all night, especially when he had a baseball game in Evanston early in the morning. It wasn't like she didn't have a qualified staff, after all. She'd informed her night manager, Marianna, to page her without hesitation if there was any problem with Alison tonight or over the weekend.

Now the girl had finally shown up, but not to the safety of Altgeld House. Alison's guitar was strapped to her back and she looked as though she had every intention of getting on the "L" with them.

"Alison, I'm glad to see you," she told the young woman who jogged toward them.

"Yeah, you too. I know it's stupid, but I get a little nervous riding the 'L' by myself at night. Stupid, considering what I do, huh? Hey." Alison cuffed Aidan's head fondly with an open palm and ruffled his hair. Aidan smiled and blushed. Christina suspected her son had a bit of a crush on the girl. Alison grinned back.

For whatever reason, no matter how scarred and hardened a soul was, they found a soft spot in their heart for Aidan. All youth possessed a special spark, but Aidan had a steady, life-affirming flame that never seemed to waver. It was a fact of life

Christina had long ago ceased to question.

"You're not going out to play when it's so late, are you?" Christina asked, referring to Alison's profession as a busker. The girl must do pretty well street entertaining, because she had never failed to make her small donation to Altgeld House for food and sundries. When Christina had discovered Alison was performing her music at various subway stops and on Michigan Avenue without a city permit, she'd insisted upon purchasing her one from the Altgeld House funds. Alison had been disdainful of the mark of legitimacy at first, but Christina noticed she wore the permit proudly on a string around her neck at the moment. "I'm not so sure that's a wise idea, Alison. You remember the doors lock at Altgeld House at eleven-thirty?"

"I know, I know. But it's not even nine o'clock yet. I'll be able to get in over an hour at the Clark and Division stop. Good bucks from all those people coming down to party on Rush Street." She must have noticed Christina's doubtful expression. "Entertaining is what I do, Christina. And you can't lock somebody up for having a borderline personality disorder, you know."

Christina gave a disbelieving look before she saw the gleam of amusement in the girl's eyes. She shook her head and chuckled. Leave it to Alison to tease about something as serious as her psychiatric diagnosis in the middle of a disagreement.

Christina couldn't lock up her charges, no matter how concerned about their safety she was. She was hamstringed by any number of legalities. Alison was an adult and she lived at Altgeld voluntarily. Her wrist cutting had been alarming, but the wounds were superficial. The girl's psychiatrist and Christina agreed that, while worrisome, given Alison's history, her behavior didn't warrant hospitalization at this time. Alison wasn't suicidal. She had a long history of self-mutilation, but no obvious attempts at suicide.

"*Promise* me you'll get back in plenty of time, Alison."

Alison shrugged and flipped her raven hair out of her eyes. "Yeah, sure. No biggie."

The girl flung her arm across Aidan's shoulder and guided him over to the iron turnabout that led to the trains. "Hey, Aidan, you ever been to any shows at the Metro? *Dude*, you got to go," she admonished when Aidan shook his head, wide-eyed. "Awesome venue."

Christina gave a frustrated sigh, recognizing her dismissal as she followed her son and Alison while they animatedly discussed live music.

Ten minutes later, all three of them stood to get off at the Monroe Street subway stop. Christina hadn't really noticed how empty the train was as they traveled downtown and Aidan and Alison talked about everything from the best skateboarding parks in the city to tattoos—Christina giving Aidan a forbidding glance at the latter topic, which Aidan chose to ignore. Once the well-lit train rumbled away, however, Christina noticed they were the only three passengers to have gotten off at the stop.

She squinted as she glanced warily around the dim, empty platform.

"Some of the lights have been broken," Christina said, noticing the glass scattered across the painted concrete of the platform. She reached out to Aidan, putting a protective hand on his back. She peered north down the subway tunnel toward the Madison Street stop. Although there were usually at least a few emergency lights glowing along the subway tunnel, nothing penetrated the thick shadows tonight.

A shiver squirmed down her spine.

Someone was watching them. She suddenly knew it as sure as she knew her own name.

"Come on, you two. Let's go," she said, doing her best to

sound normal despite her rising anxiety. She urged the two young people toward the escalators that led to the block-long underground corridor connecting the Blue Line to the Red Line.

"Ah, crap. Why's the up escalator always out when the down always works?" Aidan grumbled as he noticed that the escalator in the distance was at a standstill.

"Hey, Christina. You know that guy that was in your office very well?" Alison asked, apropos of nothing. Christina sensed the intensity behind the girl's question, even though she seemed so casual asking it.

"You mean Saint?" Aidan asked. "My mom and I know him really well. You should listen to him, Alison."

Despite her sudden haste to get off the subway platform, Christina's feet faltered when she heard the very non-childlike tone of Aidan's voice. Her eleven-year-old pinned Alison with a preternaturally alert stare. She opened her mouth to ask Aidan about his strange steadfastness when something made her turn around.

Dread sank in her chest when she saw several silent figures emerging from the restricted area at the north side of the platform. The shadows seemed to cling to the figures like claws until they finally separated into long black coats that fluttered in the still air.

"Come on. I'll race you two to the top of the escalator," Christina challenged, her voice surprisingly steady.

There was enough of a kid left in Alison to make her dark blue eyes sparkle with mischief when they met Aidan's. They began to run, their high-pitched cries of excitement bouncing off the walls of the subway tunnel, Alison's guitar case thumping against her back as she ran. Christina unglued her gaze from the four dark, approaching figures when they, too, began to run.

She raced after Aidan and Alison.

"Keep going!" she yelled when she saw the two young people pull up short at the bottom of the escalator. Christina bumped into Alison's guitar case as she skidded to a halt. She looked between Aidan's and Alison's shoulders and saw why they'd stopped so abruptly.

"Saint?" she asked incredulously.

"No," Aidan said.

"Teslar," Alison murmured in a shaky voice. The girl tried to step forward, but Christina restrained her with a hand on her shoulder.

He sprawled on the immobile escalator as though he hadn't a care in the world. Supple black leather pants gleamed in the dim light when he pushed himself to a standing position, his movement graceful and sinuous as a panther.

Christina realized her mistake even before Aidan had corrected her. This man—this *creature*—was far, far from being Saint. His face may have been Saint's, but his luxurious mane of blondish-brown hair hung down his shoulders and back. While Saint wore a neatly trimmed goatee that was a shade darker than the burnished hair on his head, this man was clean-shaven. He wore a pair of circular, mirrored sunglasses that hid his eyes.

Christina saw the reflection of Aidan's pale, frightened face in them.

"Well, well, well. What have we here?"

His voice was very much like Saint's—resonant, rich, and mesmerizing. She felt his eyes on her even through the dark glasses.

Heat bloomed beneath the surface of her skin.

She glanced over her shoulder and saw three males and

one female standing behind them. All of them studied her with a glazed, manic expression in their eyes, each more rabid looking than the next. Two of the males had long, lethal-looking incisors protruding between their leering lips. The tallest male had a sculpted, classically handsome face and fashionably cut, mussed chestnut brown hair, but his eyes possessed the filmy quality of a corpse. The female's face was hideously pockmarked with circular, unhealed sores.

She began to tremble at the bizarre, frightening sight. This *couldn't* be happening.

Christina turned her attention back to the man who looked like Saint, knowing instinctively he was their leader.

"Let us pass."

Saint's look-alike slowly removed his glasses and latched a hungry stare on her. His shapely lips curved into smile that was awful to behold, not only because it reminded her of one of Saint's infrequent, much-cherished smiles, but because it connoted anything but warmth. When he shifted his gaze to Aidan, Christina pulled her son against her.

"Like a welcoming beacon...a never-ending font of vitessence," Christina thought she heard him mutter under his breath. The greed in his blue eyes alarmed her. She pushed slightly on Aidan's left shoulder, nudging him both physically and telepathically toward the down escalator. He could run up it to safety if she could distract these beasts long enough.

"Teslar."

Christina blinked when she realized it was Alison who called out. Her thin face seemed transformed by ecstasy. "Teslar," she repeated, this time more loudly. He finally tore his gaze from Christina, a scowl marring his handsome face.

"Here I am. Do you see? I told you I was capable of sacrifice," the girl said in a quavering voice.

He squinted at her as though he couldn't quite fathom how it was that a worm dared to address him. When Alison stepped toward him, he knocked away her outstretched hand with an impatient gesture. Christina took advantage of his fragmented attention and shoved Aidan toward the down escalator. Without pause, she spun around and slammed her fist into the ugly face of the creature nearest her son, the one with the six-inch-high Mohawk. Much to her shock, he squalled in agony. Christina had spent much of her childhood in an orphanage, and later in a series of foster homes. She was no stranger to dangerous situations or having to defend herself in a brawl.

But she hadn't expected *this*. A web of swollen red and purple veins spread on the foul creature's nose and between his eyes in the precise spot where Christina had hit him. The male backhanded her blindly, catching her jaw.

She reeled. Warm fluid filled her mouth.

"*Run.* You too, Alison," she shouted, although she saw from the corner of her eye the thin girl remained frozen on the spot as she stared fixedly at Teslar. At least she heard her son's rapid footsteps blending with the monotonous churn of the escalator engine.

The sight of the blood in her mouth caused one of the hideous males to let out a shriek of excitement. The tall one with the chestnut hair snarled, his handsome face twisted in fury. He barked an order.

The creatures tensed to pounce while their comrade continued to howl in pain and clutch wildly at his face. Christina braced herself, legs slightly spread, knees bent and fists cocked. She didn't stand a chance against the nightmare monsters and she knew it. She lived only for the fading thump of Aidan's tennis shoes as he leapt up the escalator. The creature farthest to her right—the one with a mouthful of pointed teeth and who wore what revoltingly looked like a necklace of human vertebrae—gave a throat-tearing snarl and sprang.

Christina prepared to die.

Something smacked into the monster midair with a dull thud. Her would-be-attacker fell to the platform floor several feet short of Christina, a large, dark gray wolf clamped around his throat. He writhed madly, trying to throw the animal off him. Howls of fury sliced through the still air as four more wolves launched themselves at the creatures, their pointed, gleaming teeth slashing and biting.

Christina turned away, knowing this was her only chance to follow her son.

"Alison!" she shouted again, trying to break through the young woman's trance. She followed the girl's rapturous stare. Teslar stood upright on the handrail of the escalator, a beautiful dark angel ready to take flight. He leapt and took to the air, his long coat billowing out behind him like leathery wings. He landed at the top of the down escalator. Aidan was just three steps away from him.

Teslar smiled at Aidan, his fangs fully bared.

"*No*," Christina yelled, launching herself up the escalator. Teslar reached out for the boy. Aidan threw up his hand, instinctively trying to block Teslar's grabbing fist. Teslar lunged back as though he'd been pushed, a look of surprise on his face. Christina paused, mouth hanging open when she saw a figure step behind and just to the right of Teslar—a figure that precisely matched Teslar's height and breadth.

"Back to your mother."

Aidan never hesitated when he heard Saint's order, scrambling back down the escalator toward Christina. She glanced around, seeing a writhing pile of wolves and—much to her amazement—what appeared to be a grunting boar and two dog-like creatures, all of them enormous and possessing hideous, blood-dripping maws and long, razor-sharp teeth.

The female still in human-form bit and slashed with her teeth as viciously as the animals. It revolted her to see the flesh and blood flying. The wolves appeared to be stalling her and the other creatures, if not conquering them, but the snarling melee was too close to the bottom of the escalator for Christina to lead Aidan in that direction.

Instead she treaded in place on the downward-moving escalator, holding out her hands until Aidan plunged into her embrace. Both of them peered at the top of the escalator. Teslar and Saint stood facing each other in profile, both entirely still. Christina was reminded of the eerie silence before a cyclonic storm.

Chapter Six

"Mom, what's Saint do—"

"Shhh." Christina quieted Aidan shakily at the same moment Teslar gave a lion-like roar, fangs bared in a grimace awful to behold. He lunged, making a slashing gesture with his arm. Saint moved and the sound of metal striking metal hit Christina's ears. She realized through a haze of shock that both men held unusual silver swords, both so short they might be better described as long, lethal-looking daggers. They began to parry so rapidly that both their blades and bodies became a blur of motion.

A heavy black boot landed in Saint's gut with a sickening thwack, only to be followed by a punch to the jaw. The blade sliced close behind, aimed at Saint's throat. Saint leaned back with inhuman flexibility and speed, avoiding the sharp metal without a millimeter to spare. He turned as if in slow motion, rolling into the air in an abbreviated cartwheel. One booted foot struck Teslar's head, then another, both kicks landing with brutal force.

Teslar reeled back, hissing in pain. Saint flew into him with the power of a charging locomotive, their swords clashing together, teeth bared in frightening snarls.

The rapidity and viciousness of their blows shocked Christina to the core. Teslar struck Saint in the chest with a rocket-like fist and Saint slammed into the railing, causing the entire escalator to shake from the force of the impact. When he didn't move, Christina made a sound of misery and surged forward on the moving stairs, only vaguely aware that her son also lunged toward Saint. She came to herself and stopped Aidan before he took another step.

Saint's long body remained draped over the handrail, motionless. The moving rail tugged at him, dragging his dead weight down a step or two while Teslar advanced, a leer on his handsome, bleeding face, the silver blade gleaming in his hand.

"Saint!" Aidan called out.

Teslar glanced down the escalator, his smile widening. He raised his hand and plunged the sword toward Saint's undefended chest. Christina's moan of anguish blended with the sound of metal striking metal. Saint blocked the blow as though his head wasn't flung over the rail and he'd perfectly seen Teslar's blade coming.

His long, lean body coiled up like a retracting spring. He flew at Teslar, the unexpectedness and savageness of his attack throwing Teslar off balance.

Saint advanced, while Teslar defended himself frantically. They moved so rapidly that Christina heard only the thumps of flesh striking flesh, the clash of swords and grunts of pain. At a pause in the storm, she saw Teslar's exposed chest. Saint slashed with his sword, but as soon as he made contact...

Teslar was gone. An enormous black and crimson bird with a vicious-looking beak and talons that looked like sharp bones rose into the air, the sound of its huge, beating wings echoing off the tunnel walls. She saw Saint crouch, preparing to leap, fangs bared in a snarl.

He paused when he saw Aidan surging out of her arms.

"Aidan," she called out shrilly. But Saint straightened and

calmly waited at the top of the escalator. Christina followed her son. Saint drew them onto the platform, his eyes running first over Christina, then Aidan, then Christina again. A long, thin cut oozed blood along his cheek. A deeper wound cut into the bulging meat of his right biceps. The ferocious quality of his gaze would have frightened Christina if it had belonged to anyone but Saint.

"Are you all right, Christina?" he demanded, his fingertips brushing her jaw. She realized blood must be smeared on her lips and wiped at her mouth hastily.

"We're fine, but Alison..." she trailed off breathlessly.

"Alison!" Saint's voice cracked like a whip in the silence. Christina turned around, stunned to realize she no longer heard the snarls and growls of the wolf-vampire battle at the bottom of the escalator. Only one casualty remained, sprawled on the concrete. Christina saw the wiry Mohawk and realized it was the male she'd punched earlier.

She blinked, trying to chase away the hazy sense of unreality that pervaded her awareness as she watched Alison jog up the escalator toward them. After she reached them, Christina saw the girl's face had been drained of every trace of color, her paleness made all the more striking by the contrast of her ink black hair.

"Did they bite you?" Saint demanded.

The girl just shook her head as she looked up at him in mute shock.

"Let's go then. We need to get out of the subway," Saint said. He prodded Alison until she walked zombie-like in front of him.

"Aidan," he prompted softly.

Aidan grabbed the girl's hand, murmuring to her in a calming fashion. Christina swung around to look at Saint.

"What the hell was *that* all about?"

"Not now, Christina."

"You can't expect us to just—"

"Do you think he won't come back, this time with more Scourge revenants?" He took a step toward her, his gaze so fierce that Christina clamped her jaw shut. He put his hand on her shoulder and pushed her toward Aidan and Alison.

"Let's go. Move. *Quickly.*"

This time, Christina sensed his tension and didn't pause to argue, despite all the questions and anxieties that spun in her head.

Christina knocked on the guestroom door, opening it after she heard Alison's soft, "Come in."

"Do you have everything you need?" she asked.

Alison swung her hair out of her eyes and nodded. She lay huddled in the double bed beneath the covers, her figure so slight that if it weren't for full breasts and the sad, knowing look in her dark blue eyes, she'd resemble a child more than a young woman.

"I've called Marianna at Altgeld House and told her you were here with me."

Alison's eyes widened. "You didn't tell her about—"

"No. I only told her we were attacked on the subway platform. I didn't say by what. Little hard to do when I'm not so sure myself."

Alison chuckled mirthlessly. "Yeah. I know what you mean." She swallowed convulsively as she studied Christina. "One thing I know for certain, that guy—Teslar. He's a psycho."

"You figured that out, did you?"

Alison sat up on her elbows. "Christina, you heard me telling Saint about how I met Teslar, where he would take me?"

She nodded. Saint had questioned the girl extensively after Christina had sent a protesting Aidan to take a shower after they reached the coach house. Christina hadn't wanted her son to hear. What Alison had reported had made Christina's stomach roil. While Alison had been upset about revealing some of the details of her and Teslar's twisted courtship, she didn't seem to *really* comprehend how correct she'd been when she'd called Teslar a psycho.

Christina thanked God the girl was still alive after spending time with that monster.

Alison leaned toward her and whispered intently, "What if Saint is just as bad? They're twins or something, right? How do you know he's not just as much of a nightmare?"

"I just know."

She gave the girl a small smile of apology for the fierceness of her reply. She stepped over to the closet and drew down a quilt, placing it at the end of Alison's bed.

"The air conditioning gets chilly at night," she explained.

"Christina, I think you're wrong to trust him. He says we're safe here, but how can you be sure?"

"I've known Saint for years, Alison. You can believe me when I say I'd trust him with my life."

Alison's expression was incredulous. "But he's some kind of a vampire or something. He's not *human*."

"I know."

"You knew what he was? Even when you agreed to live here on this property with your son?"

Christina closed her eyes and felt the burn of exhaustion.

"I knew he was different, yes. Truth be told, I didn't know about the…" She paused, hesitant to call Saint a mythological creature when she felt as though the label didn't quite fit. But even Saint had admitted that humans had labeled him thus. And Christina *was* human, after all.

"I didn't know about the vampire stuff until a few weeks ago," she admitted.

Alison sat up in bed, the bandages around her wrists making her look even more fragile. "Stay away from him, Christina. He's bad news. I can tell he has some kind of hold over you. Teslar did the same to me. He would look into my eyes and it was like his desires became mine. My own will vanished. I would have done anything for him…sacrificed my blood…died for him. Earlier in your office, I found myself telling Saint a few things I had no intention of ever revealing. He can control you, just like Teslar can." Alison shivered visibly. "And, Christina, it was amazing. Being with Teslar was like…nirvana."

"No. They're different. Saint was doing that to try to stop Teslar."

Still, it felt as if all the blood in her head rushed down in a torrent to her belly, bringing a wave of nausea with it. What if Alison was right? She'd long known Saint had the ability to command others to his will. Wasn't it beyond odd that she should trust him so completely after the things she'd recently seen? Yet her belief in the goodness of him, a goodness that she sensed had come from unimaginable suffering, had never wavered.

She managed a tremulous smile. "Try to get some rest, Alison. Saint has assured me his grounds are protected from Teslar and those…*things* that follow him."

The girl blinked heavily. "I hope so, because I'm exhausted."

Christina said good night and left the room, trying to erase the image of Alison's doubtful, frightened expression from her mind.

Saint didn't move, but his gaze trailed Christina as she came out on the coach house front porch. The light from the house reflected behind her, making her sundress translucent, highlighting the beguiling feminine curves of her hips and slender, naked thighs. He felt his cock stiffen, the sensation even more urgent than his typical reaction to her nearness.

Their interrupted mating earlier that day, the heat of battle, and his sharp anxiety for Christina's and Aidan's safety made his need for her swell dangerously.

She said nothing as she sat in a chair next to him. She'd showered and her dark, damp hair hung loose down her back and shoulders. Her clean, floral scent filled his nostrils, creating a potent chemical reaction that lit up every nerve in his body.

"What are you?"

Her soft question seemed to vibrate in the warm, still air between them.

"I am one of the Sevliss—the soulless ones. There are six of us in total, living in cities across the globe. Each of us possesses a clone. It's our primary mandate to keep our clone's hunger in check."

"What do you mean *mandate*? Who gave you this directive?" Christina asked, turning toward him.

"The Magian." Saint shrugged uneasily when he saw her questioning look. "We know very little about them. They form a council of sorts and monitor our activities. For the most part, they are invisible to us. They tell us little about our purpose, but we know they watch us...study us. They are similar to us in genetic make-up, but they possess souls. They were our creators."

"Creators?"

"I'm not like you, Christina. Kavya, the Magian who watches over me, told me Teslar and I were harvested in a laboratory. I have no memories of being young. When I came to consciousness, I was here on Earth, much as you see me now. Kavya reveals little about himself, but my brothers and I have formed our own conclusions."

"Brothers? You mean Teslar—"

"No. I mean the other Sevliss Princes. We communicate, exchange information about the best methods for controlling our clones. We have often discussed our origins and the Magian. The general consensus is that although Earth is the only home we have ever known, our genetic material is not *from* here."

"You're an alien."

His eyebrows went up at her droll tone. She smiled and shook her head.

"Believe it or not, I have less of a problem believing that than I do the whole vampire thing. You're not exactly *typical*, Saint. How can you possibly believe you're soulless, though?"

"I have no vitessence...no lifeforce. I have to feed off humans' vitessence in order to survive." He glanced away from her perplexed stare. "I'm not like Teslar, draining a human's vitessence—their very soul—until death. He's not only a soul-eater, but a fear-eater. The taste of fear is acid on my tongue. It's ambrosia to my clone."

"Saint," she said softly, leaning toward him. His nostrils flared when he caught a strong waft of her clean skin and the woman-scent beneath it. "You think Teslar is the Youngblood

Thief, don't you?"

He met her gaze and nodded once.

She exhaled shakily.

"How can you even begin to believe you're like him? He's a sociopathic killer...a rabid animal—"

"I *am* like him, Christina. I'm a parasite on your species. Humans have what I need, and I can't exist without it. I take, but I can't give. You'll do best to remember that."

He paused when he saw her flinch at his harshness. He closed his eyes tightly, but the image of her beautiful, confused face remained emblazoned on the back of his eyelids. He braced himself against the wave of pain that shuddered through his flesh.

It hurt him equally as much to consider her falling under his influence, however. He'd sensed his fate creeping up on him ever since she'd begun to pursue him more aggressively. He'd had to find a way to push her away, to demonstrate to her the impossibility of their union.

Once he'd done so, however, he'd discovered he was weaker than he'd ever imagined. The prospect of living without Christina left him breathless, like a powerful blow had just struck his heart. It had shamed him to have to try to convince her to stay and resume their platonic relationship, but he'd practically drowned in self-loathing ever since he'd fallen on her in her office like an animal. Now, because of Teslar's attack, she'd seen more of his vicious nature than he'd ever wanted.

What's more, now that Teslar knew of her and Aidan's existence, they were no longer safe anywhere except for Whitby's grounds. How was he going to explain that to her?

"Saint."

He opened his eyes reluctantly when he heard how close

she sounded. She'd moved and now perched on the edge of his Adirondack chair, near enough for him to see the light freckles sprinkled across her perfect nose.

"That's why you've been pushing me away? Because you believe you're soulless? Because you think you can only take from me and give nothing in return?"

"I don't *think* it, Christina. Kavya told me long ago that it's true, but even if he hadn't, I would have known it for fact. I am an empty vessel. I only feel full, energized...*alive* after I feed off another's vitessence."

"Saint, you're mistaken. You do possess a soul."

He was unable to speak temporarily when he saw the message in her green eyes. His hand suddenly appeared on her cheek, surprising him. He slowly stroked the silk of her skin.

"How is your jaw?"

"It's fine. My cheek is cut on the inside, but at least I didn't lose any teeth. Don't try to change the subject. How can you believe you don't have a soul? You do. I would know it if you were soulless."

"You possess such a singularly powerful soul that you cast your light onto everyone around you. Didn't you wonder why you were able to fell that revenant tonight—Jacob Crane—with just a touch of your bare skin against his?"

She looked confused and he shook his head, frustrated at his feeble attempts to describe the simple reality of his world. Who knew better than he how rich her lifeforce was...how magical?

Her mere touch could make a revenant burn.

"I may not be as foul as a Scourge revenant—" he noticed her confused expression at the term and added, "—those things in the subway, Teslar's followers—but I am still an empty vessel. The only thing you see in me is the reflection of your brilliance in my eyes. I have no more of a soul than the mirror that reflects your face does, Christina."

Chapter Seven

She leaned into his hand, the pulse at her throat throbbing into his palm. When she began to come toward him, her lips parted, her vitessence pouring into his cells, her scent filling his nose, Saint erected an energy barrier with an extreme effort of will. She blinked, and he knew she'd felt the sudden break in their connection.

"Don't," she whispered.

"Yes," he said softly before he removed his hand from her face. "We have to talk about Teslar. I'm sorry about what happened tonight. Alison told me she planned to meet Teslar at the Clark and Division stop, but I decided to follow her once she got off the Blue Line. I didn't expect you and Aidan to be with her. Now that Teslar has seen you two face to face, he won't rest until he has you. The two of you possess the strongest vitessences I've ever witnessed in my life, and that encompasses a good portion of recorded history. You shine like a thousand suns in my eyes. It's the same for Teslar and the Scourge revenants. You're not safe anywhere, save here at Whitby, where Kavya has provided me with a protective ward, of sorts. I can't allow you and Aidan to leave until I've thought of a way to protect you outside the grounds."

Her spine stiffened. "I won't live in fear, Saint. I'm sure if we call the police and let them know about the identity of the

Youngblood Thief—"

"We're not going to the police."

"Why not?" she asked, clearly aghast.

"Teslar and I share the same face. I can't afford to have the police watching me, possibly detaining me, when I'm the only one who can control Teslar. Besides, you've seen Teslar and the revenants. A jail cell won't hold them. They'd drain the life out of everyone in prison. Ten percent of the inmates would survive the Final Embrace, making a brutal addition to Teslar's Scourge army."

"*Army?*"

"Maybe I'm overstating it, but not much. Something has altered in him. He's been hunting with unusual fervor for the past six months or so. More killing equates to more humans turning Scourge. Only ten percent convert, but I have a feeling Teslar eats not only to empower himself, but to swell the numbers of his followers beyond my ability to destroy them."

"Why don't you just destroy *Teslar?*"

"I can't."

His answer clearly took her by surprise. "Why not?"

"The Magian's primary mandate has been both genetically and magically encoded into my blood. I can't kill Teslar, only try to control his bloodlust. That's why my heartluster—my short sword—couldn't pierce his flesh tonight. My power is such that I can destroy a Scourge revenant. I can battle Teslar, I can diminish his power, I can force him to flee and retreat. But I cannot kill him."

Christina shook her head incredulously. "*Why* would the Magian give you a mandate to control your clones and not give you the power to destroy them? It doesn't make any sense."

He forced a small smile. "I have almost as much

understanding of why the Magian act as a human being divines the logic of their God or gods. There are some things that are impenetrable. I only know my nature, Christina."

She sighed heavily. "Well, at least it's reassuring to know Teslar can't kill you."

"Teslar can kill me the second he pierces my heart with his heartluster. The Magian placed the mandate only in the Sevliss Princes' blood, not their Scourge clones'. There were originally seven Sevliss Princes. One hundred and twelve years ago, Shin was killed by his clone in Hong Kong."

"That's ridiculous! Why would the Magian do such a thing?"

He shrugged and glanced away from her outraged face. "Only the Magian know."

Christina bristled. "Well I'd like to meet this Kavya guy and let him have it. He sounds like a sadist to me."

He couldn't help but smile at her moral indignation. "Perhaps you're being a bit biased? Has it never occurred to you that a sentient being from another planet might say the same of humankind's gods?"

Christina crossed her arms in defiance, plumping her breasts. His gaze lowered to the sight of firm, creamy flesh swelling in the V of the halter sundress. His cock throbbed against his thigh, the magnitude of his need stunning him. How much longer? How much longer could he abstain from having her? It was necessary now more than ever for him to be as near to her as much as possible. No longer could he just stand up and walk away when his hunger became dangerous.

Fardusk, the chief of the Iniskium, insisted that Saint could control his hunger with Christina, but Saint had his doubts.

And with good reason.

He fought himself, just like he battled Teslar. The conflict was too sharp, too agonizing to continue much longer. Now that Teslar had seen her, Saint would have to be near Christina frequently in order to protect her. The thought of what Teslar would do to her, the fear he'd cultivate in her before he indulged in a bloodbath, was too unbearable for him to consider for longer than a second.

"I refuse to believe in a god who relishes seeing his creations suffer," Christina told him staunchly, green eyes blazing.

"Suffering is not pleasant, I grant you, but perhaps it serves a purpose we can't see."

"No!"

He was taken aback. He hadn't been prepared for her fierceness, so he couldn't defend against his reaction when she suddenly came down over him, straddling his hips with her thighs, her soft mound pressing against his aching cock. She placed her hands on his chest and pushed his back against the chair.

"I won't let you believe that it's your sole purpose to suffer," she said, her fragrant breath brushing against his lips. "I won't let you sacrifice what's between us to such an idiotic idea." She shifted her pelvis, rubbing her pussy against him. He couldn't stop himself. He grabbed her hips and ground her down against his erection rhythmically.

"I cannot have you, Christina," he growled. She lowered her face toward him. Against his will, he bit at her lower lip, scraping his teeth against the plump flesh until he felt her shiver.

"I can make you happy. You fed from those women. Why won't you let me sustain you?" He groaned as she ran her hands along his shoulders and back, dropping rapid, airy kisses along his jaw. Too late, he realized he'd dropped the energy barrier he'd erected between them when Christina made her surprise attack. Now his senses were inundated with her potent vitessence. He flexed his fingers greedily into her firm, round ass and rode her pussy along the ridge of his cock, gritting his teeth at the sensation of her heat penetrating his jeans.

"I never feed from a woman more than once. After that, I run the risk of taking too much of her vitessence and harming her. Christina—" She cut him off by biting his lower lip lightly and coaxing him to kiss her. For a few pleasure-infused seconds he ravaged her mouth. When he realized what he was doing, he lifted his head and swatted her ass.

"What...what are you doing?" she asked in amazement when she found herself in his arms. He didn't answer until he'd opened the screen door to the coach house.

"Taking you to bed."

She made a low, sexy sound of satisfaction and began kissing his neck hotly. He carried her up the stairs, knowing she occupied the solitary loft bedroom. He stared straight ahead, focusing on his wavering mission while Christina tormented him with her mouth and nibbling teeth.

He closed her bedroom door behind them.

She cried out in surprise when he tossed her down on the bed. He stared down at the vision of her, her midnight hair splayed across the pillow, her cheeks flushed pink, her full lips parted slightly, making them the sweetest, sexiest target for penetration Saint had ever seen.

Before he knew what he was about, he was sliding his first two fingers between those lips, into the warm, wet haven of her mouth. Her eyes went wide in surprise at his actions.

"You think you know what it would be like to bed a

creature such as me?" he growled as he thrust his fingers into her mouth.

She nodded and tightened her lips, sucking hungrily. He cursed under his breath but couldn't stop himself from penetrating her lush lips again and again.

"You're wrong. I have very little control once I become aroused, and you arouse me like no other, Christina. How are you going to react if I take you in the manner to which I'm accustomed? Are you going to like it when I replace my fingers with my cock and fuck your beautiful face?"

She mumbled an assent around his plunging fingers, her green eyes shiny with excitement as she gazed up at him. Trying to push her away with his crudity and threats of his feral nature was having the opposite effect—and not just on Christina, himself as well. His cock lurched against the confining material of his jeans, demanding he do just what he'd threatened.

He grunted in irritation at his inability to control his swelling desire. Gods, if he was so stupid as to allow himself to touch her, he should have at least done so in his subterranean bedroom, where he possessed various mechanisms designed to control his ravening hunger when he planned to pleasure a particularly attractive, powerful woman.

And there was none more so than Christina.

She made a sound of dismay when he withdrew his fingers from her mouth and roughly untied the halter of her sundress. Stretchy elastic around the back allowed him to drag it over her body and off her feet without difficulty. He tossed the dress aside and straightened as he stared down at Christina, who was wearing nothing but a tiny triangle of silk that barely covered the neatly trimmed black pubic hair between her thighs.

He placed his open hand on her belly, the sense of feral

possession that rose in him freezing his lungs for several seconds. His hand moved up and down as she panted.

He'd long admired the hue and sheen of Christina's skin. Her stomach looked strikingly pale next to his hand, although her long legs and lithesome arms were a shade darker. Her skin possessed an apricot hue, as though she carried the sunshine around inside of her. Her breasts were high and firm, the nipples large and succulent. He moved his hand slowly, entranced, and ran his fingertips along the lower curve of one breast. Her skin felt as soft as a dewy rose petal. Her nipples grew stiff as he stroked her. He looked into her face when she whimpered, pausing at the trust mixing with the lust in her green eyes.

"I can't, Christina."

"You *can*. You yourself told me my lifeforce shines brighter than anything you've ever seen. I can sustain you. Please...let me. Let me end your suffering."

Her words soaked into his lust-drunk brain. "The end of my suffering will mean the beginning of yours," he grated out miserably.

"*No*," she insisted. She sat up partially when he dropped his hand to his thigh. She looked incredibly beautiful to him at that moment, her cheeks stained pink with her arousal and indignation, her bare breasts heaving shallowly. Her vitessence sparked furiously around her. He smelled her blood as it tore like a torrential stream through her throbbing veins. The need to bury himself in her suffused every cell of his being in a potent rush, blinding him temporarily.

He barely resisted an urge to throw back his head and howl in anguish. When his incisors lengthened against his will, he turned and walked out of the room without a backward glance.

Afterwards, he realized how foolish he was to think he

could actually walk away from Christina for long when they were both primed to mate.

Chapter Eight

Christina awoke with a start. The trees outside her window thrashed frenziedly in the howling wind, causing eerie shadows to flicker against the drawn shades and the walls of her room. A summer storm was brewing.

She knew before she glanced at her glowing bedside clock that it was sometime between two o'clock and dawn. Sure enough, the dial showed that it was three-twenty-two a.m. She hadn't fallen asleep until a little over an hour ago, after she'd stewed in a vat of fury and helplessness when Saint walked away from her for the second time in twenty-four hours.

This time had been different, though. She better understood his bitter ambivalence about his desire for her. He wanted her as much as she wanted him. But he was afraid he would harm her.

He was wrong.

After she'd ranted at him both in her mind and out loud, with her mouth pressed against her tear-soaked pillow for over an hour, her anger had begun to fade. She kept imagining the naked longing on his handsome face as he'd stared down at her, his hand open across her belly. That longing tortured him, flayed at the soul he insisted he didn't possess.

Recalling Saint's anguish had altered her bitter tears of fury to tears of sorrow. It hurt her, like a physical pain, to think of him suffering so greatly when she had the power to comfort him.

Her anger had faded even more as she considered her and Aidan's situation. How were they going to function if, as Saint said, the only place they were safe was on Whitby's grounds?

And *why* was that, anyway? Christina realized with a burst of frustration she'd forgotten to ask Saint the question.

Alison had said she shouldn't believe him, Christina recalled as she turned anxiously in bed and thunder rumbled in the distance.

Not too surprising, since Alison trusted no one.

One thing was for certain, she wasn't going to be forced to be holed up at Whitby all summer long, although Aidan was another matter entirely. If Aidan needed to be kept at Whitby, she'd agree with that once she understood the terms completely. Aidan's safety was paramount.

Even though the coach house was situated on the farthest western side of Whitby, she thought she could hear the waves of Lake Michigan breaking hard on the beach as the storm built, the sound echoing her own restless spirit. With a grunt of irritation, Christina rose from bed, finding her discarded dress on the floor with the assistance of a bright flash of lightning. Thunder shook the night as she made her way down the stairs in the darkness.

She paused in the downstairs hallway, her heart freezing when she saw a flash of lightning reflected in a pair of gleaming eyes.

"Scepter," she gasped.

The huge, sinewy wolf rose without a sound. Christina realized he had situated himself halfway between Aidan's bedroom door and the stairs that led to her bedroom. Aidan must have heard Scepter scratching at the front door earlier, asking for shelter from the oncoming storm, and let him in. Christina hadn't initially approved of her son letting the half-wild animal into the house, but she'd quickly learned the wolf was the perfect guest—clean, silent, and gone quicker than either she or Aidan would have preferred.

She stroked the animal's soft fur as she passed and opened the door to Aidan's room. Scepter followed her as she checked on the boy. Aidan was already fast asleep after letting the wolf inside, his breathing even and peaceful.

She shut his bedroom door and checked that the front door was locked. When she turned from her inspection, she saw that Scepter stood in the hallway watching her, his ears standing up on his head.

"What is it, boy? Is everything all right?"

He made a plaintive sound in his throat, a mixture between a soft growl and a whine. She ran her palm along his neck, scratching lightly.

"It's the storm that's got both of us prickly," she whispered. "That and what happened tonight. I think I owe some of your brothers and sisters thanks for saving me on that subway platform." She frowned, realizing that the wolves and their strange behavior was something she hadn't gotten around to asking Saint about. She recalled that solemn, watchful half-circle of wolves blocking her way on Whitby's grounds. Her stroking fingers paused.

"Scepter?" she asked, her voice shaky with uncertainty.

The wolf looked up at her.

"I'm going to bed. Do you want to come with me, or stay down here?"

She got her answer when the wolf padded behind her up the stairs. He stood silently as she settled back into bed and drew the covers over herself. The wolf turned around once in a circle before lying on the floor next to her bed and resting his head on his paws.

Christina realized that her eyelids had gone leaden. She saw Scepter's gleaming eyes watching her in the darkness before she succumbed to sleep.

She dreamed she lay before a hearth containing a roaring fire, the heat penetrating and pleasant. Her body shifted in a sinuous stretch, her naked skin sliding against the softest, sleekest fur. An insistent pressure grew in her, a need for action, a biological imperative like thirst or hunger...but different. It took her dream-self several moments to recognize it as a sexual need unlike anything she'd ever recalled...

...although there had been once, hadn't there?

She groaned and turned belly-down onto the fur pelt. Her pussy felt enflamed and wet, her nipples hard and aching to be touched. She fumbled, her hands feeling clumsy, and grasped at one sensitive crest, squeezing lightly. She writhed in painful arousal, every silky hair on the pelt stimulating her prickly skin to even greater levels of excitement.

This wasn't sexual arousal, it was a wild, frantic mandate— the frenzy an animal must feel when it goes into heat.

Mate or die.

Thunder crashed in the distance as she squirmed in agony on the fur pelt. Her body felt like it wasn't her own, and yet she'd never before been so profoundly aware of every patch of skin, every pulsing nerve. In a fit of crazed lust, she threw her arms out and squeezed the fur against her, wishing she could surround herself in it.

The soft fur smoothed beneath her writhing body, becoming sleek, skin-gloving muscle. She pressed desperately, needing to feel that male strength against her soft, female flesh, her entire world narrowing until nothing existed but a blind sexual need.

"Restrain yourself, lovely. Do what I cannot."

Bright light flashed. Her eyes opened. She found herself staring up at Saint's shadowed form. Lightning illuminated the room. They were both naked, and Saint reared up over her, his erect penis throbbing against her belly, his full testicles pressing against her swollen, aching labia.

"Saint," she whispered anxiously. She licked her upper lip and tasted salt. The room lit up again and she saw they were both covered in a fine sheen of perspiration. She felt so hot...so aroused. She thrust against him, desperate for pressure. He flexed his hips, sliding his stony cock up and down between her sex lips, stimulating her aching clit.

She arched up in an agony of pleasure. He caught her wrists with one hand, pinning them down on the pillow. She cried out shakily when he leaned down and tongued the valley between her breasts with a wet, raspy tongue. He made a humming noise of satisfaction in his throat, as though he highly approved of the taste of her perspiration-damp skin. He lifted his head.

"If you won't control yourself then we're lost."

"Not lost. Found. You are my home. I'm yours, Saint," she murmured, saying the truth she'd always known out loud for the first time.

He growled and lowered his head again. Christina stared up at the ceiling blindly as he inserted the tip of a breast between his lips. His mouth was as hot as the rest of him. He lashed at her nipple with his tongue and then suckled until she squirmed beneath him in a frenzy of desire.

She felt his heartbeat throbbing in his engorged cock, heard her own pounding in her ears. She spread her thighs, desperate to fuse their desire. When she shifted her hips, trying to capture the thick head of his penis in her cleft, he cursed and lifted his head. Quicker than she could blink, he rolled her onto her belly. He came down over her, pressing his mouth to her neck.

"This is how an animal mates," he whispered darkly. Christina shivered uncontrollably as he scraped his teeth along her skin. His fist slid beneath her waist. He used his forearm to lift her. He braced himself on his knees, his thighs spread around her hips, and urged her bottom up in the air. She felt the thick, hard knob of his cock jutting against her tender slit. He pushed against her, parting her wet, aching tissues, insisting she take him.

"Ah, God, Saint!" she murmured in helpless bliss as he penetrated her, inch by steely inch. Every time her body resisted his possession, he pumped his hips, gently but firmly, working past the obstacle. Her vagina clenched around him tightly, hungering for his total penetration.

Her entire body trembled by the time he fully sheathed himself in her. He pressed deep. Christina felt him shaking just as greatly as she did.

He began to pump. Not just their bodies, but the bed, the room, her world seemed to quake as he fucked her while rain battered at the windowpanes and shadows from the wind-lashed trees made a frantic dance across the walls. She couldn't stop herself from crying out in bliss, the sound swallowed by a blast of thunder. Saint's loud groan outlived the crash and continued to rumble in his chest long after the thunder faded.

They slammed together again and again, as wild and violent as the storm. Her blood surged in her veins like waves pounding on a breakwater. His cock probed her so deep, stretched her, filled her, until she felt ready to burst. The sensation was sharper than a typical impending climax...far more volatile. She heard Saint groan in agony behind her, his hips striking her buttocks and thighs in a hard, merciless rhythm.

"Oh, oh...God help me," she mumbled into the pillow, not even sure what she begged for. She moaned when he paused, his cock fully sheathed, his balls pressing tightly to her moist outer sex. When he leaned over, her vagina tightened in a paroxysm of excitement.

"No god can help you now," he whispered in rough misery near her ear. He slowly withdrew his cock, the sensation of the thick, defined head sliding across her aching flesh, making her inhale through clenched teeth. He re-sheathed himself, half-staff.

She turned her head so that she could see the outline of his face in the dark room. A flash of lightning showed her his gleaming eyes and sharp white teeth. She also saw the essence of distilled agony on his face. She moved aside her hair, exposing her neck.

"You can, though, Saint."

She tightened her vagina around him hungrily. He snarled as though in pain and fell on her, sinking his teeth into a vein at the same moment he plunged his cock deep. Christina's eyes opened wide in shock. For a moment, she struggled. Human beings weren't accustomed to experiencing such a blast of pure sensation. At first, she thought it was pain, and then she realized it was previously unknown levels of pleasure that flooded her consciousness.

He spread a hand over one hip and buttock, making her a stationary target for his thrusting cock. He fucked her hard and relentlessly while her blood boiled and surged, as though every cell in her body rushed to be the one consumed by him. She opened her mouth, ready to scream as climax hit her, the blast shuddering not just through her body, but her very spirit.

His mouth covered hers abruptly, muffling her scream. He pounded his cock into her one more time, their flesh smacking together at the same moment thunder shook the night. He groaned roughly into her mouth. Christina whimpered in mixed pain and ecstasy when she felt him swell impossibly large inside her, then the exquisite sensation of his warm seed pouring into her.

Their lips fell apart, but they remained close as they gasped for air for several minutes. His cock remained embedded inside her, still erect, still stretching her hypersensitive flesh. The full, gravid sensation felt strangely familiar to her, although she couldn't think why...only that it had something to do with Aidan.

The feeling of his warm, fragrant breath striking her face in uneven bursts soothed her somehow...hypnotized her.

She closed her eyes as a feeling of delicious lassitude and profound rightness pervaded her awareness.

"Stina?"

His deep voice edged with anxiety made her blink her eyes open in surprise. He reared up over her, his hands on the mattress supporting his upper body weight.

"Yes?"

Lightning lit the room. For a split second she saw his handsome face framed by tousled, wavy hair, his brows pinched. Thunder rumbled in answer to the lightning, the sound softer than the previous shattering booms that had rent the night.

"Are you all right?" he rasped.

"I'm *so* good," she murmured drowsily. She wanted to remain with him planted deep inside of her, but she also needed to hold him in her arms. Her mixed desire made her shift her hips in a half-hearted manner.

"Don't," he grated out through clenched teeth. "I can't...I can't withdraw from you for a bit."

Christina's mouth fell open in wonder. She thought she understood what he meant. His cock not only felt iron hard, it felt even more swollen than before his climax.

"Why didn't you tell me you were a wolf?" she asked abruptly.

He just stared for a moment before he gave a bark of laughter. Christina wished lightning would have flashed at that moment and let her see his face. He smiled so infrequently, it was always such a gift when he did.

"When would you have had me tell you? Just after you learned I was what you would call a vampire, or maybe before?" He shook his head. "I told you there were so many things you didn't understand, Christina."

"I understand more than you think. I understand this." She flexed her muscles around his turgid flesh. He groaned.

"Do you?" he challenged after he'd recovered.

"I know it was right, Saint." She shook her head against the pillow. "Is Teslar a wolf as well?"

"No. Never a wolf. He can transform into any number of creatures, though. All of them foul."

"Like that huge bird he changed into tonight?"

She sensed his nod more than saw it. "Usually much worse, though—a blood boar, a canid, a stalker. But Teslar never becomes a wolf, while that is the only animal nature I possess.

"A blood boar—is that one of those things the Scourge revenants transformed into?"

"Yes. Javier Ash morphs into a blood boar. Javier was the tall one. He is very powerful, Teslar's first lieutenant in a rag-tag army. Crowbar is a canid—that huge dog-like creature. They were both on the platform tonight, along with Selena Constantine and Jacob Crane. It was Jacob left on the platform."

"So the Scourge are limited to one creature transformation while Teslar—"

"Can transform into all."

A tense silence ensued.

"All those times Scepter slept in this house...all those times *you* slept here with me. How could you not have taken what's yours?"

The room lit up briefly. He stared down at her, his nostrils slightly flared. "Do you think I wasn't tempted?" he growled. "I've allowed you a glimpse into my world, Christina, and yet you insist on staying in fantasy land."

"No, don't," Christina cried out when he withdrew his cock from her body. She gasped in slight discomfort.

"I'm sorry," he mumbled, wincing. She glanced back between them in fascination. Her eyes widened when she saw the outline of his penis jutting from his body. It looked blood-engorged and enormous.

"Is it...uncomfortable?" she asked awkwardly, referring to his still-swollen cock, when he lay next to her on his side. She pushed herself up and rolled on her side to face him. She scooted closer to him, stilling when her naked hip pressed against his damp erection.

"It's very sensitive," he muttered through a clenched jaw. "I shouldn't have withdrawn so quickly. I'm out of practice at this. Not that I've ever really had much practice."

She looked at his shadowed face incredulously. "Who are you trying to kid? All those women I've seen leaving Whitby over the years with a smile on their faces and a glazed look in their eyes? You've got a lot of nerve telling me you're out of practice."

She couldn't really see it in the darkness, but she sensed his mouth curving into a smile. "You wouldn't believe me if I say that it's very uncommon for me to actually mate with a woman?"

"You mean have intercourse? Why?"

He didn't answer immediately. He spread a hand on her hip and pushed her into him. Christina couldn't help but touch his engorged penis. She sensed the tension in his body when it pressed against her belly. She tried not to breathe to save him from more uncomfortable stimulation.

"Breathe, Christina, it's okay," he murmured with a chuckle when air began to burn in her lungs. His hand slid along the sensitive sides of her torso and over her shoulder, making her shiver. He delved his long fingers into her hair, his fingertips rubbing against her scalp. "Run your hand up and down on it," he ordered gruffly, referring to his penis. "It will help to desensitize it a little."

Her clit pinched in painful re-arousal when she wrapped her hand around his warm, damp cock. There must have been a good inch-long gap between her encircling fingers, he was so thick. He groaned deep in his throat when she began to slide her hand up and down his length.

"I have told you that I don't feed from a woman more than once. The more...intimate the joining, the more painful it is when I..."

"Refuse to see her again?" Christina finished for him when he faded off.

He nodded. She wondered if his penis was sufficiently desensitized. Should she let go, so they could press their bodies close? She didn't want to stop stroking that hard, dense column of flesh, however, so she kept pumping him with her fist. It was exceptionally exciting, stroking what might have been the phallus of a god. For several long seconds, silence stretched between, both of them motionless with the exception of her moving arm.

"Intercourse is very...intimate. I try to avoid it. If I do choose to mate, I usually use certain equipment that helps me to maintain my control," he explained gruffly after a moment.

She paused at that, running her thumb over the ridge below the fleshy, arrow-shaped crown of his cock, finding the slit and rubbing the liquid she found there into his skin. He hissed and grabbed her wrist.

"You're not soothing me, you're readying me to mate again."

"I'm sorry," she murmured as she began to stroke his entire length again with slow, firm strokes, purposefully misunderstanding him. She felt the tension rise in his body and continued in a tone of mild interest. "Will I become a vampire now?"

"Of course not," he growled. "I didn't take anywhere near enough of your vitessence for a Final Embrace."

"Final Embrace? You mean death?"

"The end of mortal life. Yes."

"Do you have to bite me three times or something?"

"No, that's legend and Hollywood stupidity," he murmured distractedly. Despite the darkness, Christina sensed he watched her hand with a tight focus as she stroked his cock. His fingertips continued to massage her scalp in a motion she found both relaxing and arousing. A troublesome thought suddenly wriggled its way into her awareness.

"We didn't use anything."

His fingers didn't pause in their delicious massage. "I can't get a female pregnant. I don't have a soul."

"Yes, you do."

He grunted in irritation.

"Believe what you want, it doesn't change the fact. Both the Sevliss and their Scourge clones are sterile. We cannot create, unless you consider what happens with those who survive the Final Embrace, and that's a twisted, unnatural creation," he mumbled bitterly.

"But—"

"Don't you think if one of us could impregnate a human female, it would have happened at least once after half a dozen centuries?" he asked sharply.

Christina scowled at him in the darkness. If the Sevliss couldn't impregnate a woman, there must be some genetic reason for it, but the cause certainly *wasn't* because Saint didn't possess a soul. She didn't want to argue with him right now, of all moments, so she leaned forward and pressed her nose into a hard pectoral muscle, inhaling his scent, never ceasing her stroking of his cock.

When her lips touched his chest, his hand tightened in her hair, pushing her closer against him. For a few seconds, she nibbled at smooth, thick skin.

"Saint?" she asked huskily, her lips hovering over a flat, stiff nipple.

He grunted in response.

"You were wrong about losing control if you made love to me."

She immediately wished she hadn't spoken when his fingers froze in her hair.

"I didn't this time."

"You'd never harm me. You yourself said you didn't take anywhere near enough of my blood for the Final Embrace."

"You don't *get* it, Christina. I didn't just take some of your blood. Vitessence is concentrated in your blood, sweat and sex juices—yes—but it surrounds you as well. I let down my guard. I absorbed enough of the powerful energy that exudes from you to make me drunk." He grasped her wrist and roughly jerked her hand off his erect penis. Christina cried out in protest when he stood abruptly, pausing by the bed.

"Drunk and stupid," he added.

"Saint—"

She stared in rising disbelief as he stalked toward the balcony doors. He opened them and disappeared. Christina realized with a jolt that she was alone.

"*Saint?*" she called. She hurried out of the bed and rushed to the open patio doors. The rain had slowed to a steady downpour. Lightning struck, and Christina caught a fleeting image of a wolf running through the yard.

Chapter Nine

The earth muffled his howls of torment, but the planet's powerful soul could offer him no solace. Kavya watched dispassionately as his charge writhed, his agony so intense, it was as though a frantic serpent twisted inside of him in the midst of a death agony, contorting his body. When Kavya saw the blood-tears that stained his face, he finally stepped forward and touched a bunching, rigid shoulder muscle.

Saint collapsed on the luxurious carpet of his bedroom, panting wildly. He squinted up at Kavya through eyes veiled by misery.

"Why do you make me suffer?" he rasped when he'd caught his breath sufficiently to speak.

"No one makes you suffer but yourself, Saint."

He slowly rose to a sitting position. "Christina thinks you're a sadist. I'm beginning to think she's correct."

Kavya chuckled and sat in an upholstered chair, smoothing his slightly soiled and singed orange robes. He spent much of his time isolated in his laboratory and often forgot the niceties, including clean robes, when he wandered back out into this blindingly lovely alien world. "I would say that Christina is spirited, but that's a monumental understatement, as we both know."

Saint said nothing and stood. He blinked and stared

around the luxurious subterranean bedroom, as though wondering how he'd gotten there. Kavya suspected the memory of what led up to his misery struck him, because he shuddered visibly. He walked over to a table that held a pitcher, water and towels. He dampened a towel and wiped the blood-tears from his face.

"Where have you been for the past ten years?" he asked Kavya.

"Has it been so long?"

"Longer. I have been in need of your advice," Saint said, his tone accusatory. "I have called you repeatedly with my mind."

"Yes. In the matter of Teslar. He has found a means to grow more powerful."

"He is harvesting fear in young, vulnerable humans. I believe he is convincing them to give their life freely to him. It makes their vitessence more potent."

Kavya nodded. "Wise of you to realize it, Saint. Yes, Teslar's discovered an ancient truth. The life given willingly offers the magician more power than merely stealing what is not his to take. Add to the mixture great fear, and an even more potent alchemical cocktail is created. Great magic is released when a being feels such overwhelming fear in the act, and yet still chooses to sacrifice their life willingly."

Saint's upper lip curled in disgust. "So, that's what he's doing to gain strength."

"That...along with one other factor that you will have to discover for yourself."

"Always speaking in riddles to me, aren't you?" Saint asked bitterly.

Kavya shrugged. "It's your journey, not mine."

Saint closed his eyes briefly. Kavya sensed him trying to

chase away his bitterness and grief so as to attend to what must be done. When he stared at Kavya a moment later, he felt the return of his charge's normal tight focus.

"We are ready to stop Teslar, especially now that I have a means of finding him. The young woman who sleeps at Christina's—Alison—I believe she knows the location of Teslar's hideout in the tunnels. I have been training regularly with Strix, Isi, and Fardusk. Their skills have improved greatly. I can give one of them my heartluster," he said, referring to the special silver sword that both he and Teslar carried. "But it would be better if you supplied me with another to give them."

"The heartluster has been specially designed for the Sevliss princes and their clones," Kavya said mildly, unfazed by Saint's rising fury.

"Teslar has never been this blatantly methodical in his bloodlust. He forever hunts, but the Iniskium and I have curbed him through the centuries so that he resembles a natural predator. But he no longer feeds like an animal; he's become a sociopathic murderer. How can you stand by and allow him to terrorize and kill those young people? How can you continue to refuse to let me finish him?"

Kavya picked at a chemical burn on his robes thoughtfully. "Have Isi, Strix, or Fardusk battled Teslar yet?"

"Isi has faced off against Javier several times. Isi only lives to kill Javier for turning Jane Farrant, his lover, into a revenant several years ago. Isi and Javier are well matched. Odds are, Isi will eventually kill him. He nearly did so in the subway tunnel tonight."

"But Javier Ash is not Teslar," Kavya said calmly. "Have any of your Iniskium warriors confronted your clone, Saint?"

"Only in a few brief tunnel skirmishes."

"And?"

"If only you would allow *me* to destroy him!" Saint raged, and Kavya had his answer as to whether or not Saint's three strongest Iniskium warriors were powerful enough to finish Teslar.

"Saint, we have discussed this too many times to count. There is a means of vanquishing Teslar, but only if you first acknowledge that the two of you are joined."

"I acknowledge it daily," Saint exclaimed, looking insulted. "Who knows better than I that we share the same parasitic nature?"

Kavya continued as if he hadn't been interrupted. "Teslar and you are two sides of the same coin. He is evil, yes, but he is your dark self. Your shadow. If you cut him down, you destroy something in yourself. There is no telling what will happen to you. If you are weakened or killed in the process, who will keep the Scourge revenants in check?"

"Huh, let me see... How about you?" Saint bellowed.

"I'm afraid that would not serve my purpose. Controlling the Scourge is not a mandate that has been set in my blood, after all."

Kavya smiled pleasantly in the face of Saint's low, dangerous growl. "How is the boy?"

"He grows strong. He is much like his mother," Saint muttered after several seconds.

Kavya leaned forward in his chair. "Is that all you have to say on the matter?"

Saint scowled. "What more *should* I say?"

Kavya leaned back and sighed. "If you don't know, it's not for me to put it into words."

Alison and Aidan devoured the breakfast of homemade waffles and bacon while Christina watched them broodingly and sipped her morning coffee. She didn't move when someone knocked on the kitchen screen door, already knowing who the visitor was. Aidan leapt from his spot at the oak table, syrup leaking from the side of his mouth, in order to answer the door. Saint followed him into the sunlit kitchen a second later, wearing jeans and a dark blue T-shirt and carrying a motorcycle helmet. His light blue eyes met Christina's briefly before he glanced resolutely away.

"Want a waffle, Saint?" Aidan asked.

"Nice of you to offer my services," Christina said wryly. Aidan grinned at her before he attacked his waffle again.

Saint shook his head. "No, I came to get Alison."

Alison's fork clattered to her plate. She stared up at Saint, flabbergasted.

"You came to get *me*?" The girl's gaze flickered over to Christina and then back to Saint.

"If you'll come. I was hoping you could show me where Teslar has taken you in the tunnels. Teslar and the Scourge revenants are day-sleepers. It should be safe, as long as we don't get too close."

Aidan also set down his fork, his waffle forgotten. "How come sunlight doesn't hurt you like it does Teslar?"

Saint's shapely lips—which in Christina's opinion, were made almost indecently sexy highlighted as they were by his trim goatee—twitched with grim amusement. Thoughts of how his mouth had moved over her hungrily while his cock plundered her in a deep, thorough possession swamped her awareness, the power of the memory so realistic and intense that her cheeks flamed and her sex heated.

She blinked away the sensual haze imposed by the mere

97

sight of him. She was still angry at him for running away again last night, but she'd grown pensive as well, trying to think of the best way to cut through his stubborn hide.

"You're being influenced by stories, Aidan," Saint said. "Teslar can go out during the day. It's just that, for the activities he prefers, the night suits him better."

"What kind of activities?" Aidan asked. "Stuff like attacking people on the subway?"

Christina cleared her throat loudly, throwing Saint a warning look when he glanced at her. Aidan was too young to know about Teslar's twisted nighttime activities.

"Yeah. Stuff like that and a lot worse," Saint replied.

"Like what?" Aidan demanded.

"You let Saint worry about that," Christina said abruptly.

"But, Mom, I want to know! He's dangerous. Saint told me last night he wants to kill us."

"You told him *that*?" Christina accused Saint furiously, standing from the table.

"He has a right to know if he's in danger. He has a right to know if his mother's life is threatened. Do you think Aidan didn't recognize the truth last night? You put yourself at a grave disadvantage by burying your head in the sand," Saint stated impassively.

Christina glared at him before she turned around and dumped her coffee in the sink, hissing a curse when some of it splashed onto her white shorts.

"So I guess I still can't go to my baseball game this morning, huh, Saint?" Aidan asked.

"No."

Aidan sighed in disappointment. His little league team was in the midst of playoffs for the championship and Aidan was easily their most valuable player.

"You and your mother aren't to set a foot outside of Whitby's property until Teslar can be contained. Alison, will you show me where Teslar is holed up in the tunnels?" Saint asked.

Alison stood, her eager nod surprising Christina a little, given how down she'd been on Saint last night.

"Wait a second! If it's so dangerous for Aidan and me to leave Whitby, why's it okay for Alison to go?" Christina demanded.

"Alison is different than you two. She'll be safe with me. I regularly hunt the revenants in the underground, usually during the day, when they're relatively inactive. You two aren't safe anywhere but here for now...and *especially* not in the tunnels."

"I don't get it," Aidan said. "My mom and I take the subway all the time and Teslar has never attacked us before."

Saint considered first Christina and then Aidan with his enigmatic gaze.

"The subway tunnels are relatively shallow compared to where the revenants reside."

"Yeah," Alison whispered, her enormous eyes fixed on Saint. "He took me down on an elevator real deep, into places I never knew existed under the city."

"The planet itself possesses a soul," Saint said. "The deeper one goes into the earth's mantle, the more it can be felt. For us, it is a constant source of nourishment—like a human breathing the purest air and drinking the freshest water. We could live off the earth's vitessence alone for a week or longer. We are creatures of the underground...of the earth."

"But that doesn't explain why it's okay for you to take Alison down into Teslar's hellhole," Christina said fiercely.

"It's okay, Christina," Alison murmured. "I want to help if I can."

"It *does* explain it," Saint told Christina as if Alison hadn't spoken. "If you or Aidan were to go that deep into the earth, the vibrations of the earth's energy and your powerful vitessences would amplify one another's. It'd be the equivalent of a crashing gong going off in Teslar's sleeping brain. A clanging dinner bell," he added harshly when Christina opened her mouth to argue. "The relative shallowness of the subway tunnels is the only reason I've allowed you and Aidan to use the subway in the past."

"The only reason you've *allowed* us," Christina repeated in mixed amazement and outrage. This was really too much. The guy refused to even commit to being her bedmate and yet had no problem masterminding her life!

"We can talk about it when I get back," Saint said, jerking his head at Alison in a *let's go* gesture.

Christina felt like she had no choice but to watch helplessly as Saint handed the motorcycle helmet to Alison and both of them headed out the door.

Chapter Ten

The metallic whine of the hydraulic crane bounced off the walls of the limestone shaft, the echo making it necessary for Alison to shout in order to be heard.

"Where in *hell* are we going? Or, don't tell me—my question contains the answer, right?" She glanced nervously below the steel grating on which they stood. They'd started out in an empty water reservoir that was already two hundred and fifty feet below the surface of the ground. By the time the crane reached the bottom, they'd be far, far down in the bowels of the earth.

"Chicago Deep Tunnel. Close to a hundred miles of tunnel and reservoirs used for water runoff. All of the tunnels have been mined at this point, but only some of them are currently in use. The project has been going on for several decades. According to my sources, some of the tunneling equipment is mysteriously being utilized at night, although they haven't been able to figure out the precise location of where, or who's doing it."

"Teslar?"

Saint nodded. "I'm guessing he's been burrowing below the deep tunnel."

"Even *farther* down?" Alison exclaimed. "Why didn't we just use the elevator Teslar took me on? I said I'd be able to show you the location."

Saint shook his head. "Teslar would make it impossible for just anyone to access that elevator. Even if we did access it, he'd be alerted to the fact. I guessed from your description where the elevator must have been located. You got off in the deep tunnel before you transferred to a chamber where you went farther downward, right?" Alison nodded. "We'll use this entrance and hope one of the chambers looks familiar to you. You can lead me from there."

"He did key in a code to call the elevator," Alison mused, her brow wrinkled in memory. She stepped closer to him. "So, how do you rate, just walking into this pumping station and being allowed to come down into these tunnels? I thought that guy up there was going to lick your boots, he was so happy to do whatever you asked."

"I happen to know the President of the Water Reclamation District," Saint murmured.

Alison snorted. "More likely you *own* the bastard." She stumbled and almost fell when the metal platform reached the bottom of the shaft and came to a halt with a shudder. She scurried off the platform quickly, casting a suspicious glance at the hydraulic crane.

"You've got an awesome bike, but your twin's got one up on you in regard to the transportation to hell department."

Saint didn't reply, just walked over to the MinerMobile that would quickly take them to the first giant maintenance chamber five thousand feet away. Alison perched on the side of the vehicle and he steered them to the entrance of the thirty-foot-high limestone tunnel.

"It's weird down here. I noticed it when I was with Teslar," Alison murmured in a hushed voice after several minutes, glancing around the dark, circular tunnel. The flashing lights on the MinerMobile cast her pale face in crimson light. "Do you think I'm sensing some of those energies you were talking about back at Christina's—the earth's soul, or some shit like that?"

Saint shrugged. He doubted it. "What do you hear?"

"Hear? I hear this little car-thingy moving and nothing else. That's what's so weird. It's like we're insulated from every sound on earth down here. Why? What do you hear?"

"The earth singing," Saint said simply. "What you're experiencing is more than likely your imagination. Only the rarest of humans can sense such things."

"Rare humans like Christina?"

He gave her a hard look when he heard her snide tone of voice. Alison swallowed heavily. He noticed the rapid throb of her heartbeat. He instinctively set up an energy barrier when the girl leaned closer to him, her eyelids sinking heavily over her huge eyes.

"It's possible I'm just as special as Christina," she said huskily.

Her eyes fixed on his mouth. He leaned back deftly, avoiding her seeking lips.

"You know, if you weren't so busy trying to fuck everyone before they fuck you, you might notice most people aren't half bad," Saint said.

"Oh, is that right? Such an angel, aren't you, *Saint*? You don't fool me, even if you have turned Christina into your number one cheerleader."

Saint stared straight ahead and continued to drive. He knew the girl was taunting him. She existed by quickly gauging other people's weak points, and Christina was certainly his. Good thing he possessed no vitessence, or a human like Alison could drain him to exhaustion in five minutes flat. As things stood, his admiration for Christina deepened for putting up with little energy-suckers like Alison around the clock.

He drove into a sixty-foot-tall chamber filled with emergency backup generators, metal staircases, and maintenance equipment. He shut off the vehicle. Alison remained seated when he stood. She still scowled at his rebuff of her advance. Saint sighed, not particularly wanting to put up with her sulks at the moment. He needed to find Teslar and lead the Iniskium on a surprise attack as quickly and efficiently as possible. The longer Teslar had to fade back and retrench, the worse it was going to be for Christina, Aidan, and any number of innocent humans in Chicago.

"I'm not Teslar, Alison," he said wearily.

"I'll say you're not," she countered, her tone disdainful.

"Did you come here to help me or to act like a spoiled brat?"

She jolted in shock at his harshness before she rolled her eyes and made a disgusted *phffing* sound. She glanced up and gasped.

"What the—"

"Alison, meet Fardusk and Isi," Saint said evenly.

Fardusk stared impassively at the slight girl from his lofty height. "I have seen her before."

"Yeah. When you've been shadowing Teslar, no doubt," Saint said.

"She's one of his future entrées," Isi said, his expression disdainful as he looked Alison over. "Or, wagering from the size of her, one of those tasteless, low-fat appetizers."

"Fuck you, Chief *Head Up His Ass!*" Alison shouted as she leapt off the MinerMobile, looking fully prepared to take on a skilled Iniskium warrior who was twice her weight. Isi's dark eyes widened in surprise before he cracked a grin, his white teeth flashing vividly in his dusky face.

"Actually, *he's* the Chief." Isi hitched his thumb at Fardusk, who watched the exchange without twitching a muscle. Isi pointed at Saint. "And he's our leader, seeing how he made us what we are. So why'd you bring the tiny morsel, Saint?"

"Stop your teasing, Isi. It's obvious Saint wants her to lead us to Teslar's new den," Fardusk said.

Alison refused to back down, however, edging toward an amused-looking Isi with her hands balled into fists.

"Alison, thicken up the skin a bit, huh? Isi rides everyone. It's nothing personal," Saint chided, although in truth, he was thinking just the opposite. The warrior's sense of humor had grown dark since Javier Ash had turned his lover into a revenant several years ago. But presently, Isi's manner was almost playful.

"Does this chamber look familiar?" he prodded, trying to distract Alison. She glared at Isi balefully before she glanced around as though she'd just noticed where they were.

"Yeah, maybe."

"Which way?"

Alison pointed to the right corner of the huge, concrete-reinforced chamber, still glowering at Isi. When they got there, she nodded to the floor. The three males removed several coiled hoses and wheelbarrows filled with concrete reinforced bolts. A few seconds later, Fardusk knelt and tried to lift the metal grate on the floor.

"Is it nailed shut?" Alison asked.

Fardusk's massive biceps flexed, stretching the fabric of his white T-shirt. Metallic popping noises echoed off the high concrete walls. Several nails skittered onto the concrete pavement.

"Not anymore," Fardusk deadpanned as he set aside the grate. The fringe on his leather vest flew up when he lightly sprang into the black hole he'd just revealed. Fardusk's boots struck the ladder with a dull, metallic sound, his head and shoulders poking out of the hole. Alison made a squeaking noise of shock.

"You guys aren't *normal*. What...you're all vampires, right?" Alison accused as Fardusk lowered the ladder and Isi dropped blithely into the dark hole, grabbing the ladder with inhuman speed and ease.

"We're the Iniskium," Isi told a disgruntled Alison with a brash grin. "And since you're here with us in the underground, you'd better thank your lucky stars we're not *normal*, tiny morsel."

Saint thought he was going to have to shove Alison down the hole when he ordered her to follow Isi.

The woman's drunken, high-pitched laughter was amplified by the crystal-lined chamber. It interfered with Teslar's appreciation of the earth's harmonious, soothing song. He was becoming so powerful by feeding within the chamber that he hardly required sleep anymore. He could have never fed again and remained strong; the crystals amplified the earth's vitessence to an exponential degree.

Of course, it was ridiculous to think of never feeding again. He had only two aims in life, to feed and to defeat Saint. After he slaughtered his annoying clone, he could devote himself full-time to his one true love. Teslar'd thought the discovery of the crystal chamber was the most important discovery of his life.

But last night had changed his mind.

The woman and the boy were even more significant. Kavya had told him long ago that some day he would encounter something that he would want so much, he would be willing to sacrifice everything in order to obtain it. When he'd seen the woman, he'd recalled Kavya's prediction. But the riddle-speaking Magian had ignored him for centuries, and Teslar's respect for him lessened as his own sense of self-worth grew.

He longed to possess the woman, but there was no need to sacrifice anything. Teslar did not sacrifice; he was too deserving, too supreme. She would be his, eventually. A creature of such power and beauty—like life itself distilled—*must* belong to him.

And to think his sanctimonious clone had been hoarding her all to himself.

Teslar would actually be amused by his clone, if he weren't so busy hating him with blistering intensity. How Saint managed to continually deny what he was, to choose suffering over the potential magnificence of his existence, was the most flabbergasting, annoying riddle Teslar had ever encountered.

The woman laughed shrilly once again.

"Get her out of here, Marcellus. She annoys me," Teslar ordered impatiently.

Javier Ash paused in the activity of running his extended fangs across a nude female's shivering naked torso. Teslar met his first lieutenant's gaze across the chamber. At least Ash's evening meal had the courtesy not to annoy Teslar with her braying laughter. Ash was used to his preferences. Teslar rolled his eyes in a long-suffering manner. Ash gave a small smile and sunk his fangs into the female's hip, the action so effortless, he might have been biting into melting butter.

His latest prey's hand paused in stroking Teslar's chest.

Teslar gave Elliot a warm smile when he realized the beautiful young man had been put off by the sharp tone of his voice. Elliot resumed petting him worshipfully.

Marcellus's expression had frozen in the midst of manic mirth. The Scourge slave's face was pockmarked and hideous, as Teslar had used the Iron Maiden on him for the Final Embrace when he was still in the beginning stages of learning how best to create fear in his victims. That had been several decades ago, before Teslar had perfected and refined his methods.

Marcellus stared at the human woman who knelt before him, wearing nothing but a thong, as if he'd never seen her before. The woman's hand paused mid-shaft on Marcellus's thick, glistening cock. Her smile trembled, and her eyes widened in dawning horror at the abrupt change in her companion's countenance.

Ash lifted his head, a thin rivulet of blood dripping from a fang to his chin. The woman he'd been biting writhed and moaned in protest at his withdrawal.

"Marcellus, *don't* you dare," Ash said, his tone resembling a dog owner who saw his pet start to lift its leg in a public place.

Marcellus hissed, bearing a mouthful of spiked fangs. He ripped out the woman's throat so abruptly that he ate her scream. She fell over onto the floor with a dull thump, her blood soaking Teslar's rare oriental carpet.

Teslar made a sound of weary disgust.

"You moron!" Ash shouted, springing off the couch where he'd been lying with the female. He charged across the room, back-handing the Scourge revenant hard across the face. Marcellus spun around and flew into the wall. Blood spurted across the crystals.

"Get it out of here, now!" Ash roared, pointing at the

woman's corpse. "You can come back later and clean up the mess you've made."

Marcellus staggered to regain his balance. He turned around slowly, blood smearing half his Iron Maiden-kissed face.

"But...she displeased the Master," Marcellus fumbled.

Ash bared his fangs. "The Master hates a mess even more, idiot. *You* displease me at the moment. Shall I show you the same treatment?"

Marcellus moved quickly to follow Ash's orders.

"Thank you, Ash. You may leave now as well," Teslar said after Marcellus had clambered out of the chamber.

He sensed Ash's gaze shift from him to Elliot. Elliot snuggled closer in his arms. Teslar couldn't say he was surprised by the young man's reaction. Ash evoked terror with just a glance.

When he wasn't inspiring blind lust, that is, Teslar acknowledged with distant amusement as he watched Ash sweep across the room and lift the naked woman into his arms. The female stared up at the handsome revenant, completely at his mercy.

Well, at least she'd die happy on this night, Teslar thought in an off-handed fashion. It was a wish most humans were never granted.

"I'm glad he's gone, Master. Javier Ash scares me," Elliot admitted after the chamber door had closed with Ash and his prey on the other side.

Teslar sighed. He noticed the deathly pallor on the boy's face as he stared at the pool of blood on the carpet. Well, maybe Marcellus's idiocy was not completely without purpose.

Teslar casually whipped off his shirt and dropped it into a chair. Lust mixed with the fear in Elliot's expression as he stared at Teslar's bared torso.

"You shouldn't think twice about Ash. I don't," Teslar murmured quietly as he sat on the couch. "He is merely a slave. I care nothing for him aside from his beauty and skill at giving pleasure. You yourself have enjoyed those skills on occasion, pet."

Elliot flushed and Teslar knew he recalled the other night, when he'd shared Elliot with Ash. He'd sent Ash on a mission to plot some new tunnels he'd discovered near the Chicago River. As a result of his mission, Ash hadn't had the opportunity to take nourishment. Since Teslar had been in an indulgent mood, he'd allowed Ash to fellate Elliot while he watched.

Despite his stark fear of Teslar's first lieutenant, Elliot had managed to have an explosive orgasm in Ash's mouth, satisfying the revenant's hunger.

"Is that...is that really how you feel about Javier Ash?"

Teslar glanced up sharply when he heard the hesitancy in Elliot's voice. "Of course. What makes you think otherwise?"

"Well, it is only that..."

"Yes?" Teslar prompted, pushing Elliot's shoulder, encouraging him to lie back.

"That one revenant—Crowbar. He hinted that you and Ash had once been...you know—a thing."

Teslar chuckled as he lay down next to Elliot, sliding the bare skin of their bellies together. He stroked the young man's face soothingly and thought of the moment when he would separate Crowbar's head from his body.

"My pet shouldn't be preoccupied with meaningless rivalries on his special night, should he?"

"No, Master," Elliot whispered.

"That's right," Teslar said. His ascendancy over the young

man was such that it would be a waste of time to defend himself more, and Teslar never made excuses unless there was something to be gained by it. "Now, let's get you out of these pants, shall we? Your blood is calling to me, pet, and so is your cock."

Chapter Eleven

Elliot Birch trembled when he heard Teslar say those words. He was scared to the point of numbness at the thought of the Final Embrace, but Christ, if there was even a ten percent chance it would mean being with Teslar for an eternity, it would be worth it.

Teslar got up on his hands and knees and helped him out of his pants. Elliot watched, mouth agape, when Teslar immediately spread his legs and dove between them. His eyes rolled to the back of his head as Teslar vacuumed his cock into his warm mouth.

"Ah, *God*," Elliot mumbled incoherently. It would be worth risking death if there were even a *one* percent chance he could experience the nirvana of Teslar giving him head for an eternity.

Before he'd met Teslar, his life had been miserable, barren...and worst of all, boring. His parents had rejected him after he'd told them he was gay. His many boyfriends had only been interested in one thing, treating him like a disposable boy toy. What did he have to lose by sacrificing himself?

And he had *so* much to gain.

His eyes opened into slits. He panted as he watched Teslar swallow his cock whole again and again, his hunger so voracious, his method so precise, it stunned Elliot anew every time he experienced it. He resisted an urge to put his hand on

Teslar's head, to thread his fingers through his beautiful mane of hair.

But Teslar wouldn't allow that. He'd explained patiently to Elliot that his cock aroused him so much that he didn't want to be distracted while he sucked it. Teslar's revelation about how much he adored Elliot's cock had brought tears to his eyes. But even if Teslar hadn't admitted to his weakness, Elliot would have known. All he had to do was take one look at the sublime expression on Teslar's face as he sucked him forcefully to know that Teslar did, indeed, love his cock as much as he loved Elliot.

Elliot's body shook in ecstasy as he climaxed down Teslar's throat. After a moment, however, Teslar moved him so that he could run his tongue greedily over the spurting slit of his cock. Elliot grunted and moaned uncontrollably. He watched, mesmerized, as Teslar's neck muscles convulsed again and again as he swallowed.

"Hmmm, delicious cream," he praised, his voice made sexy and husky from taking Elliot's cock so deep.

Elliot shuddered in bliss as Teslar took his penis into his mouth again. He didn't know if it was Teslar's astonishing lovemaking skills, some effect of his supernatural powers, or both, but he typically sucked Elliot to climax three times in a row, sometimes more, before it became necessary to pause before resuming again. It was Elliot's greatest wish—besides to survive the Final Embrace, of course—that Teslar would allow him to return the favor. But Teslar only laughed every time Elliot tried to reach for the long, stiff ridge that ran along Teslar's left thigh, pressing tightly to his leather pants or jeans.

"I think we'll wait for after the Final Embrace for that, pet," Teslar had explained once after he'd rebuffed Elliot's attempts to get into his pants. Then he'd surprised Elliot by standing next to the couch where Elliot reclined naked. As usual, Teslar had worn his pants during their lovemaking. He'd ripped at the button fly of his jeans and slid them down to his thighs. A few seconds later, he'd stood over a dazed Elliot, holding his erection in his hand. He'd stroked his length slowly while Elliot stared and saliva pooled on his tongue.

"My cock will rule your world some day. It will be your sole job to pleasure it," Teslar had whispered. "Would you like that, pet?"

Elliot had nodded, speechless, unable to unglue his eyes from that long penis with the fat, mushroom-shaped, succulent crown. Teslar's cock and balls were highlighted to erotic perfection by the leather harness he wore. The fleshy spear was the same golden color as the rest of Teslar's skin, with an added rosy hue.

"I hope you like it in the ass," Teslar had said huskily.

Elliot had looked up at him, a plea in his eyes. "Oh, yes, Master."

Teslar had smiled. "Then that's where you'll get it once we're together forever," he'd murmured before he'd tucked his big cock back into his clothing, climbed back onto the couch, and expertly attended to the erection Elliot had acquired while staring at the most magnificent cock Elliot had envisioned in his wildest fantasies.

Yeah, *anything*, Elliot thought as Teslar's firm lips bumped against his shaven testicles in an insanely rapid rhythm. Who *wouldn't* risk death if there was even the slimmest chance of living in this carnal heaven with this beautiful God forever? He bucked his hips and cried out as his seed poured into Teslar's throat once again.

Christ, a one in ten shot was excellent odds, when Teslar's singular brand of love was the prize.

Teslar slid his tongue over the crown of Elliot's cock, hungry for the taste of his vitessence to spread on his tongue. When the full flavor of it penetrated his brain, he scowled around the young man's cock.

Flat. Too much lust. Too much adoration. Too much need.

Not enough fear.

He hadn't prepared him adequately for the Final Embrace. True, he'd described the process in detail in the past, licked Elliot's sweat and tears hungrily while he'd trembled in anguish and fear.

As always, Teslar had longed to take blood then. At this point in his victim's preparation process, it was excruciatingly difficult to abstain. He failed one out of two times and drained his victim completely with his mouth. But now that Teslar knew about the powers of the combination of the crystal room, the willing sacrifice, and the automatic pneumatic exsanguinator, he became increasingly disappointed with himself when he succumbed to blood too soon. When he did so, he felt no better than a callow human boy, spilling his seed after a woman touched his cock for ten seconds.

It made him proud to know he could abstain when he chose. Saint wasn't so superior to him after all.

Teslar needed the extra edge of power now that he'd witnessed the miracle of the woman and the boy. Something strange had happened to him in the moment when he'd looked into the female's green eyes and bathed in her powerful vitessence.

He'd glimpsed his destiny.

Since then, Teslar had become consumed with one thought—he needed to grow strong enough to take Saint's prizes for himself.

Elliot grunted in misery when Teslar abruptly popped his cock out of the tight seal of his lips.

"What... Why do you look so sad?" Elliot asked.

"I am doing you an injustice. You don't understand the full impact of the sacrifice that you are making, Elliot. There is a ninety percent chance you will be *dead* after tonight."

Elliot sat up on his elbows, obviously wild with concern when he saw the paroxysm of grief on Teslar's face.

"I know how much you worry about losing me, Master."

Teslar grabbed Elliot's wrist when the young man tried to reach to touch his hair. He forced a smile to hide his abrupt halting gesture. If there was one thing he couldn't stand, it was to have a slave touch his mane. Unlike humans, his hair was alive. It made him shake with pleasure to have it stroked.

It seemed so indecent, somehow, to allow a slave to control him if only for a moment; to let a subservient see him shudder in bliss.

"I want to take the chance, Teslar. More than anything. I'd die inside knowing I'd been too much of a coward to risk being with you."

Teslar endured as Elliot used his forefinger to tenderly wipe a tear from his cheek. Why did humans always mention this nauseating concept of *dying inside*? How ludicrous. It made him want to laugh every time he heard it, which would have been a most unfortunate loss of control at such a crucial moment.

Luckily, Teslar secreted tears as easily as blinking. For him, it was a matter of simple muscular control. It had always amused him, those first years on Earth that he'd spent with Saint, to learn that his clone could not produce tears. Only the blood of his prey ever escaped his eyes.

Pitiful.

Teslar sighed regretfully. "I suppose if you are determined to continue, we should proceed then." Elliot's hand froze in his hair and Teslar knew precisely what he was thinking. He'd hoped that Teslar would bring him to climax several more times before the Final Embrace.

The greedy little bastard.

But Elliot's semen had gone flat, and Teslar was anxious to move onto much richer, tastier fare. He'd harvested Elliot so carefully after all, and he was impatient for his feast.

He smiled and kissed the young man's muscular abdomen. It would be all right if he survived the Final Embrace, for he was a handsome one. He sensed Elliot's veins constricting with fear, heard the desperate thumping of a heart that knew it was about to beat no more. Teslar urged him off the couch. Elliot stumbled as they walked across the room, but Teslar steadied him before helping him up onto a medical table.

"Now, I've told you how this works several times," Teslar murmured as he rolled the pneumatic exsanguinator closer and chose a cuff from one of the drawers, setting it beside a trembling Elliot. "But, before we begin, you must look in my eyes and solemnly swear once again that this is what you choose. If you mean to sacrifice yourself willingly, declare it now."

"I swear that I sacrifice my life willingly if it means there is a chance I will be with you forever," Elliot said shakily.

Teslar resisted an urge to lick the tears flowing down Elliot's cheek. Instead, he smiled and tenderly ran his fingers through the young man's hair before he opened a drawer and removed the captive bolt. He would insert it into Elliot's brain, keeping him immobile and paralyzed. Elliot would be very much aware of what was happening as he watched Teslar collecting his fear-infused blood.

Just as he was about to pierce the base of Elliot's skull with the captive bolt, Marcellus and Crowbar barged into the crystal room.

"Get *out*, you idiots," Teslar snarled.

"But Master...it's Saint and the Iniskium. They've found us."

Teslar hissed in disgust as he tossed the captive bolt onto the table.

Why must Saint insist upon ruining *everything*? Why had he been so cursed to forever be plagued by his uptight, party-crashing clone?

"Marcellus, get Ash to evacuate everyone through the south tunnel. We'll re-group again in the LaSalle Street freight tunnels. We'll need a diversion. Crowbar, you take Cyrus and...whatever that new girl's name is—"

The whites of Crowbar's eyes showed up starkly in his face. "Jane Farrant? But she and Cyrus are both practically new to the immortal life. They've never engaged in a battle, let alone one where Saint was present—"

"Which is why I'm sending you," Teslar said briskly as he pulled a dazed-looking Elliot down off the table. "I want you to face my clone, Crowbar."

Crowbar's face stiffened in fear. Of course he knew Teslar had just signed his death warrant. Well, that's what the loud-mouthed fool got for flapping his mouth in front of the meal Teslar had been harvesting, telling Elliot about his former lovers. If Saint didn't separate the fool's head from his body, Teslar would when he had a spare moment.

He shoved Elliot toward the crystal room's escape tunnel, but he'd apparently cultivated the young man's fear too well. Elliot stumbled on rubbery legs and fell hard to the floor. Teslar started to shout at him in rising frustration when he noticed that Marcellus and Crowbar hadn't moved. He turned up his ascendancy to maximum levels.

"Did I not just give you two orders?"

They scurried out of the room. Teslar gritted his teeth in mounting outrage as he glanced around the crystal chamber. He'd never valued anything so greatly in his life...save the woman. Damn, Saint. This was *his* special place, and now his clone had gone and ruined it all! He was going to treat that girl, Alison, to a slow, tortuous death for betraying his location.

A shout erupted out of his chest and he kicked the only object available to him. Elliot grunted in pain and looked up at Teslar in shock.

"Fuck it." He kicked Elliot again, this time in the face, before he leapt fifteen feet to the escape chamber.

Chapter Twelve

Fardusk and Isi's flashlights flickered off walls as they made their way down the circular limestone tube.

"So what *are* the Iniskium?" Alison asked Fardusk. She and the tall, somber chief of the Iniskium walked in front, Saint and Isi behind. Alison had to skip and trot to keep up with Fardusk's long strides.

"Iniskium was the name of an ancient tribe of people who once lived in this area on the banks of what you call the Chicago River. Today, it refers to the survivors of that tribe," Fardusk said, keeping his gaze trained down the tunnel. The passage that had been dug by the Scourge revenants under Teslar's command was much narrower than the tunnels dug by the city. It hadn't been reinforced by concrete and was crumbling in spots.

"But *what* are you? *He* said Saint *made* you." Alison tilted her head back toward Isi. "Does that mean he turned you into vampires?"

"We have many of the characteristics of our sire, although we are not as strong. Vampire is a word used by humans, as is werewolf. But we think of ourselves only as the Iniskium warriors who help Saint hunt the Scourge revenants. We must fight hard, because our numbers have decreased over time while the revenants' numbers grow," Fardusk said.

"Werewolf. Wait...was that *you* guys on the subway platform? Were *you* those wolves who fought off Teslar's followers?" Alison asked.

"As I said. We share the same characteristics as our sire. A wolf is always the animal nature of the Iniskium, while the Scourge revenants resemble their creator—although Teslar can transform into any number of beasts, while the revenants can usually transform only into one fixed form."

With his powerful hearing, Saint heard Alison whisper to Fardusk. "Did you *ask* Saint to turn you into what you are?"

Fardusk didn't respond.

"It's all right," Saint said, startling Alison.

"No," Fardusk continued now that Saint had given him permission to reveal one of the most painful secrets of Saint's past. "Saint attacked our village many centuries ago, when he was new to this Earth...before he had learned to control his bloodlust."

Saint met Alison's stare when she glanced back at him speculatively. "Don't you hate him for it?"

"No. But he hates himself," Isi supplied drolly.

"*Quiet*, Isi," Fardusk commanded. Isi immediately looked contrite. Fardusk didn't exert his authority often, but when he did, it carried absolute weight amongst the Iniskium.

Saint tried to focus on the soothing sounds and sensations of the earth's vitessence. He wished they'd change the subject, but Alison was a leech for information.

"But he stole your *soul*," Alison hissed at Fardusk as they resumed down the tunnel.

"He *gave* us our wolf-souls," Fardusk intoned. "The Iniskium revere the wolf as a teacher, its hunting prowess, its great spiritual power, its ability to survive in the most difficult of circumstances. Saint allowed us to embody all those qualities and more. We are thankful to him and will forever be in his debt."

Alison once again peered at Saint over her shoulder. This time, she didn't bother to lower her voice. "He could be brainwashing you into thinking that."

"No one can brainwash a wolf," Fardusk said with a tone of curt dismissal that even Alison didn't dare to question.

Saint stopped abruptly and turned around. Isi followed his lead, crouching slightly in the balanced stance of a warrior waiting for an attack. Saint knew that Fardusk was poised and ready for a threat in the opposite direction.

"Reveal yourself," Saint shouted at whomever or whatever was in the tunnel behind him. His ears had picked up a slight scuffling noise, but whatever was following them was not near enough for him to yet catch their scent.

"What's going on?" Alison asked anxiously.

"Quiet," Saint ordered. They waited tensely. The figures of a thin, wiry male and a female slowly appeared out of the darkness.

"What is it?" he asked tensely. Saint and Isi turned, knowing that if Strix and Bena—their Iniskium rear guard—approached, a threat was coming from the other direction.

"We have been observed," Strix said calmly. "They are coming."

"Wha...? I thought you said they wouldn't know we were here," Alison accused Saint.

He drew his heartluster out of the leather sheath tied to his thigh. He pushed her back against the curving side of the tunnel in order to cover her, hearing her gasp when Fardusk, Isi, Strix, and Bena transformed into their wolf-selves. He saw several figures emerge out of the shadows—a boar leading several other Scourge creatures. The boar's eyes glistened with bloodlust, its maw dripping thick saliva. Saint thought he recognized Crowbar, but he couldn't make out the identity of the others in the dim light. No telling how many were obscured in the darkness of the narrow tube. The blood boar let out a shriek of fury as it caught their scent.

"Put out the lights," Saint ordered, knowing it was better to go on instinct and scent where shadows and darkness played deadly tricks on a warrior in such a confined space.

"You're fucking nuts!" Alison shouted.

"You'll be fucking dead if you don't shut your mouth," Saint replied quietly as the lights blinked out and the Scourge closed in on them in the darkness.

Shrieks and snarls echoed off the tunnel walls, the sounds amplifying until it seemed hundreds of creatures fought tooth and nail in the darkness. Saint moved through the blackness, his sense of smell sharpened until it became more acute than his sight. When the scent of sulfur, blood, animal and fetid breath filled his nose, he reached and found the boar's matted fur and corded neck. A razor-shop incisor cut into his biceps, but he'd long ago learned to dissociate himself from pain. Saint twisted viciously and heard the sound of cracking bone. He tossed the dead weight onto the floor.

The earth itself shook as the battle raged around him and bodies were hurled against the limestone tunnel with great force. Saint slashed with his heartluster, finishing Crowbar.

When Isi clicked on his light less than a minute later, silence reigned. A canid and a prowler lay motionless and bleeding from deep wounds at the neck and belly. A beheaded Crowbar had transformed back to his human-form.

"So few," Isi said.

"Teslar sacrificed them," Saint commented as he knelt and wiped the blood off his heartluster onto Crowbar's coat.

"Crowbar must have done something to piss Teslar off if he ordered him to fight you," Strix agreed. His lean, scarred face looked like it'd been carved from wood in the dim light. Saint watched as he raised his bowie knife and finished what he'd begun in his wolf-form, hacking the canid's head from its body. Alison started and cried out in mixed disgust and dismay when the hideous animal transformed into a beheaded bloody man in his early thirties.

Bena stepped over to the prowler, ready to do the same as Strix, her long blade gleaming in the dim light. Her slender, powerful muscles flexed.

"No, wait!"

Alison clutched Saint's waist in fear when Isi lunged in the shadowed tunnel. He reached for Bena's slashing arm, but he was too late.

Isi let out a howl of pure misery that caused crumbling earth to fall into the tunnel. Saint started instinctively toward the grief-stricken warrior, but Fardusk was there before him. Isi strained to look over the shoulder of the Iniskium chief, his eyes trained on the gruesome sight of the beheaded female.

"What is it? What the hell's *wrong?*" Alison asked wildly as she peered around Saint's chest and Isi continued to moan as though he were being tortured.

Alison tightened her hold on Saint's waist and shook. "What is going on? What is wrong with Isi?" she seethed.

"That revenant was once Jane Farrant, Isi's lover. A powerful revenant named Javier Ash took her in the Final Embrace, transforming her into a Scourge revenant. Ash did it to spite Isi."

Alison strained around him, taking in the long, lithesome

limbs and the golden hair of the beheaded corpse.

"How awful. That woman just killed Isi's lover right in front of him?" Alison whispered in a choked voice.

They both watched as Isi suddenly collapsed in Fardusk's arms. Alison started toward the tableau of misery, but Saint stopped her, understanding that nothing could penetrate the warrior's agony in that moment.

"Bena didn't kill Jane Farrant, Alison," Saint corrected quietly. "You must understand. Javier Ash murdered her two years ago. Isi has lived in anguish every day of those years knowing that a monster inhabited his lover's body, making a mockery...a sacrilege of everything she was."

Alison didn't say anything for a moment. Isi sobbed harshly and shoved himself out of Fardusk's arms.

They all watched as he staggered like a newly blinded man down the dark tunnel.

"He loved her," Alison breathed out, her tone tinged with awe.

"The Iniskium can love," Saint said in a hushed tone.

Saint slid his heartluster back into its sheath, knocking Alison's clutching hands off him. He glanced back at her. She'd plastered herself against the wall of the tunnel. He saw where she stared fixedly. He kicked aside Crowbar's severed head, clearing the path for her.

"It's not pretty, but it's the only way to kill a Scourge revenant," Saint explained. His tone softened when he saw how pale the young woman was as she stared at Crowbar's remains. "Crowbar died more than seventy years ago, Alison. What you see is the remains of his walking, talking, eating corpse. Now, come on. Teslar and his followers will have fled by now. I want you to show me his den."

Alison glanced up and met his gaze. Her hand shook in his as he led her away from the carnage.

Ten minutes later, Saint stepped into the crystal chamber alone. The sound of the earth's singing escalated a hundred-thousand-fold, the vibrations making his flesh quiver like a stroked harp string. A young man with dark curly hair and a bloody face appeared to be the only occupant of the furnished chamber. He rushed toward Saint.

"I am *not* Teslar," Saint said distractedly, easily reading the man's mind in his vulnerable state.

"I...I don't understand," he said shakily, wiping his bleeding nose on his sleeve. Saint barely noticed the man's eyes studying his hair and goatee. He was too stunned by the power of the earth's energy infusing him with life to be aware of much of anything else.

"What's your name?" Saint asked.

"El...Elliot."

"How long ago did Teslar leave, Elliot?"

Elliot shrugged. "I'm not sure. Five minutes ago? Ten?"

Too much of a head start, Saint thought in rising frustration. He glanced over at the medical table. The chief of the Chicago Police Department had been keeping him updated on the Youngblood Thief case and he'd seen the grisly photos of the corpses. He recognized the captive bolt Teslar used to paralyze his victims.

"You just narrowly escaped being the Youngblood Thief's next victim." The young man swayed on his feet. Saint caught his arm, steadying him, and guided him over to the couch. He saw what appeared to be his pants lying there and laid them in Elliot's lap, covering him.

"I don't understand. If you're not Teslar, you must be his

twin. If you see him, will you ask him to give me another chance?'" Elliot grabbed at his waist and looked up at him pleadingly. "Why is Teslar angry at me? Please tell me where he is. I have to apologize for whatever I've done."

Saint grimaced and moved back from the young man's desperate clutch. He was saved from having to reply when Fardusk entered the chamber. He stared, open-mouthed. Saint realized it was the first time in more than half a millennium he'd ever seen Fardusk stunned. Strix and Bena followed. Bena gasped loudly in wonder.

"Do you know what this means?" Bena asked, referring to the miraculous chamber.

Saint nodded. He thought of Christina—Christina laughing, the way her face softened when she looked at Aidan... Christina staring up at him with green eyes glazed with desire.

"It means never having to feed from another human again."

Elliot's confused expression segued to dazed wonder when he saw Saint break into a smile.

Chapter Thirteen

Christina caught the baseball Aidan tossed her and looked around at the sound of Saint's motorcycle approaching. She and Aidan left the yard and reached the patio at the same moment as Saint and Alison.

"The wound on your arm's re-opened," Christina said immediately when she saw the mixture of dried and wet blood on Saint's biceps. She charged across the patio and lifted the sleeve of his T-shirt.

"Actually, I think it's a different wound," Saint said mildly. He caught her hand and Christina looked up into his face. When she saw the heat in his blue eyes, she stared, open-mouthed.

Alison cleared her throat loudly. Christina realized several seconds had passed as she gaped at Saint and breathed his scent.

"Are you all right?" Christina looked first at Alison and then back to Saint.

"I'm fine, but I can't say those three Scourge revenants down in the tunnels are doing so good. Not that they'd notice, without any heads," Alison mumbled.

"Scourge revenants? Were you attacked *again*?" She searched Saint's long, whipcord lean body for wounds before she went back to examining his bleeding arm. Saint stopped her just as he had before.

"I'm okay. Were you two about ready to eat?" he asked, nodding at the smoking barbecue.

"Yes, but that'll wait—"

"Go ahead and start your dinner," Saint said. He glanced over at Aidan, who was listening in on the conversation. Christina knew he didn't want her to make a big deal about his wound and worry the boy. "I'll just go clean this up and be out in a second."

By the time Saint came out of the coach house, Aidan had finished his second burger and was starting on a third. Christina wished she knew where he put it.

Alison had seemed quiet and distracted at first, but had rallied. She now ate with as much gusto as Aidan. Christina longed to ask the girl what had happened in the tunnels, but guessed from the girl's pale face that it wasn't something that should be discussed over supper.

"Do you want to eat?" Christina asked Saint when he straddled the picnic table bench next to her. For some reason, she blushed when she met his gaze. She glanced away, only to notice Alison watching them steadily as she chewed her hamburger.

"Yeah, I'll get it," Saint replied. "I want you three to stay up at the main house tonight," he said when he came back with his food.

"Why?" Christina asked. "I thought you said it was safe here."

"It is." He stepped over the bench with his long legs and sat. Christina noticed he'd neatly bandaged his upper arm. "It'd be even safer up at Whitby. I'd rather you were close to me."

Christina's eyes went wide when she once again saw the

undisguised heat in his gaze as he regarded her. What had happened? He'd been so guarded against her when he left earlier with Alison.

"Can we, Mom?"

Aidan's excited question brought her back from the depths of Saint's eyes. "I...I think..."

"It'll be better, Christina. I promise."

Christina forced her gaping mouth shut as Saint's underlying meaning struck her consciousness. A simmering sensation rippled from her lower belly to her sex. She clamped her thighs tightly together. "All right, if you think it's best."

She avoided Saint's blatantly erotic gaze for the rest of dinner, feeling as self-conscious about looking at him while Aidan and Alison were present as she would had he sat there naked. That's how transparent, how raw...how undefended she was when it came to him.

If anything, staying up at Whitby should give her the opportunity to get Saint alone to ask him what had happened in the tunnels today.

And to find out why he'd so drastically changed his opinion about them being lovers.

They stared at each other from opposite sides of the elevator, the silence broken only by the low hum of the motor. Aidan had been asleep now for well over an hour. He and Alison had watched a comedy in Saint's high-tech entertainment studio while Saint and Christina sat outside on the balcony. Neither of them spoke as the sounds of the movie and Aidan's and Alison's laughter filtered through the opened French door. In fact, Christina and Saint hadn't said more than three words to each other since dinner...not out loud, anyway.

But the air between them seemed to crackle with unspoken emotion. Just when he thought he couldn't stand the unbearable tension a second longer, Christina had reached out and taken his hand. He'd felt her trembling. It had been hell to wait until Alison and Aidan went to bed, but it had been delicious too, surviving the last minutes of what he'd once thought would be a never-ending torment.

Knowing that torture was about to come to a glorious end.

"Why did you change your mind?" she asked softly as the elevator sped them down to his subterranean bedroom.

"I found something today in the deep tunnels after Teslar and the Scourge revenants fled. Actually, Teslar discovered it before me, during all of his digging—a crystal chamber deep within the bedrock." He shook his head, still amazed by the discovery. "I've never known anything like it. A crystal chamber within a layer of limestone bedrock? That limestone used to be the floor of the earth's ocean, ages ago. That chamber is more ancient than I can even begin to imagine. Who knows how deep it was inside the earth when it formed? Those crystals amplify the earth's vitessence to incredible levels."

The elevator slowed and stopped. He reached and grasped Christina's upper arm when she started to walk out the opened doors. "The strength of it is such that I could live off that energy alone, Christina. Do you understand what that means?"

Her green eyes looked enormous in her face as she looked up at him. "That we can be together?"

"I will never again have to feed," he whispered, awe flavoring his tone. "I can metabolize the earth's energy alone and survive. I no longer need to be a parasite on human beings."

Her full lower lip trembled as she stared up at him.

"And...and that's what you want?"

"Yes. Gods, *yes.* It means I will be able to control my hunger when it comes to you. I can touch you...bring you pleasure, and not submit to my need to feed. We'll still need to be careful—I don't want to harm you—but the crystal chamber will help me with my control."

"I don't believe you'd ever harm me, Saint. Making love isn't about always being in control."

"It has to be for me, Christina."

The elevator door started to close. He braced it open and pulled her into his bedroom. He could count on one hand the number of women he'd invited into his private sanctuary since he built Whitby one hundred and nineteen years before. Saint couldn't have recalled any one of their faces if he tried while Christina stared up at him with a mixture of desire and uncertainty in her green eyes.

His need swelled, confusing him for a moment. The energy he'd absorbed in the chamber had satisfied him greatly. It wasn't the equivalent of bathing in Christina's vitessence, drinking her blood, or plunging his cock into her last night, but he had felt energized after standing in the crystal chamber for only ten minutes.

"I want to be clear. I can't be what you want, Christina... I can't fulfill your fantasies. We're still far too different to be a normal couple. I can't feel the same way a human man could for you. I can't give you what you deserve. But if you choose it, we can give one another pleasure. Is that what you want?"

Her lower lip trembled, but her gaze looked hot and wanting when she stared at his mouth and then dropped her gaze to his chest.

"That's all you're willing to give me? Sex?"

Something tightened in his chest. He stepped toward her

and cupped her cheek. "I would give you everything if I could. But I'm hollow...empty. If you refuse my flesh, then I've nothing else to offer you."

"Saint," she said in a choked voice. She shook her head and a tear spilled down her cheek.

"Shhh, don't cry," he whispered. "I never allowed myself to hope for the possibility of being your lover, not just for one night...but for many nights to come. For me, it's nothing less than a miracle." He leaned down and touched her only with his mouth, rubbing their lips together softly, languorously. The tip of his tongue traced her lower lip, glorying in her singular flavor. Her tongue met his in a questing, sweet caress. His mouth closed over hers.

"There has never been a day since I laid eyes on you that I haven't burned for you," he said gruffly when they separated to draw air.

She encircled his waist with her arms and pressed close. Not only his nose, but every cell in his being absorbed her singular essence.

"I'll say yes to having sex, but I'm not sure when I'm going to forgive you for ignoring me."

He smiled as he cradled her jaw with both hands. "Accuse me of what you will, but never believe for a second that I ignored you. As easy for a fish to ignore water." He leaned down over her. "You entranced me from the moment I first saw you."

"Past time you surrender then," she whispered.

His nostrils flared greedily to capture her scent before he fell on her mouth. He lifted her body against him and carried her to the bed. Her eyes blinked open and she started.

"What is that?" she whispered in confusion as she stared at the complicated leather harness and pulley system above the bed.

"I told you that I have to use special equipment to maintain control."

Christina said nothing. The troubled expression she wore faded as he undressed her. When she lay before him completely naked, he just stared at her for a long moment. As he had last night, he laid his hand across her abdomen, experimenting with the idea of cherishing her without absorbing her vitessence. It felt strange to be so intensely sexually aroused and yet not feel the building compulsion to feed.

"Saint," she whispered, holding up her arms for him.

He blinked and lowered himself, pulling her up to the head of the bed and lying beside her. She ran her hands over his shoulders and back. She threaded her fingers through his hair and pressed the tips to his skull. When she pulled up his T-shirt and slid her palm along his bare skin, he shivered and grabbed her wrist, pushing it down next to her head.

"I want to take off your clothes," she protested.

"Not yet," he muttered gruffly. He leaned down and brushed his cheek against the exquisitely soft skin of her lower breast. He tilted his head and ran his closed lips over the succulent curve. She groaned and delved her fingers into his hair. He continued to nuzzle her fragrant skin, entranced by the sensation of her flesh. When she took the shell of his ear between thumb and forefinger and squeezed rhythmically, he growled and sat up.

"What are you doing?" she asked when he dove for a bedside table and pulled open a drawer. He pulled out a long, red silk scarf and came up to a kneeling position.

"I'm going to restrain you. I want to touch you everywhere and your hands are driving me crazy."

She looked doubtful, but he saw arousal in her eyes as she considered the red scarf. He coaxed her by sliding the silk in a sensual caress against the side of her waist, along her belly and over one beading nipple.

"All right," she agreed shakily. "But I still don't think making love is all about maintaining control. Even for you, Saint."

"*Especially* for me," he corrected grimly.

Chapter Fourteen

He arranged her arms over her head and bound her wrists together, then tied them both to the wooden posts on the headboard. Once he'd finished, he lay beside her and ran his fingertips along the side of her torso, from hip to just below her armpit. She gasped and shivered. Her nipples pulled tight. Unable to stop himself, he leaned down and enclosed one of the hard crests in his mouth.

She writhed beneath him, but he spread both hands on the side of her ribcage and kept her captive while he rolled his tongue over her beaded flesh and suckled her. Never was there flesh sweeter than Christina's. The sound of her blood pounding in her veins swelled in his ears. Even though he wanted to suck on her breasts more, he forced himself lower, tasting the skin at the sides of her body and nipping lightly at her waist and belly.

When he lowered to her slender, lithesome thighs, she squirmed. He held her hips immobile, kissing and tonguing the satiny skin between her legs. She cried out in rising excitement when he flicked his tongue just inches away from her pussy, capturing her flavor on his tongue.

It was a dream come true, Saint thought as he spread her thighs and drank in the sight of Christina's glossy, exposed pussy. How many nights had he lain in this bed, alone and suffering, and imagined what she'd look like naked, restrained and spread wide for him. A shudder of excitement went through him. He came up on his knees and grabbed for one of the leather harnesses, drawing it downward.

"Saint?" she whispered in confusion when he slipped a leather loop over her foot.

"Shhh, it's all right. I'm just going to restrain your legs. It'll be more comfortable for you. You can just relax and give into your pleasure," he explained as he slid the other loop over her foot. When he'd finished restraining her in the harness, her legs were spread wide, her feet suspended several feet off the bed. Her dark pink, glistening pussy made a striking contrast to her pale thighs. His cock lurched furiously at the sight.

He gave a guttural groan and dipped his head between her legs. He inhaled the scent of her desire.

"Oh God, please...please don't torture me," she begged hoarsely.

He glanced up and saw the desperation in her eyes, her vividly pink cheeks, her flushed breasts, and distended nipples. The sight was so compelling he couldn't stop staring as he leaned down and worked his tongue between her juicy labia. He growled low as her sublime taste flooded his awareness.

How could she think he wanted to torture her? The only thing he ever wanted to see on her beautiful face was happiness, contentment...and profound pleasure.

She cried out sharply as he became more demanding in his stimulation, making her clit his captive, gently sucking her and then moving his head slightly from side to side, vibrating the sensitive kernel of flesh. She pulled against her restraints, her body going rigid as she strained for climax. When her cries became an unceasing keen, he released her and lapped at her, wanting to savor her desire.

He noticed that she watched him. He heard her heart

beating frantically with his powerful hearing, knew the instant it perfectly synchronized with his own. The only other sound that could be heard in the silent room was the moist, clicking noise of wet flesh against wet flesh.

Christina groaned in torment and lifted her hips off the bed, trying to increase the stimulation. Saint raised his head and clenched his teeth. Before she knew what he was about, he'd sat up to a kneeling position. He spread his hands on her ass and lifted her to his mouth. He plunged his tongue into her slit again and again, his arms flexing as he brought her against his mouth in a rhythmic fucking motion. She screamed and went rigid. He lashed her clit with his stiffened tongue, hard and ruthless, and she broke in orgasm.

Centuries of experience and a preternatural knowledge helped him to know every female's unique physiology, assisted him in gleaning what to do to prolong her orgasm. He instinctively reached for Christina's bare feet, scratching the soles lightly as he continued to tongue her. Her feet jerked in his hands as she climaxed, but he continued to stimulate her. She screamed louder, her body shuddering even more forcefully.

"That's right," he whispered next to the skin of her belly when he'd finally worked every last orgasmic tremor out of her body and she'd sunk to the bed in exhaustion. "That's how I always want you to give yourself to me." He felt her shiver when he scraped his teeth against her ribs. He came up on his hands and knees, working his way up her body, tasting her flesh as he went along, before he lowered to her lush mouth. "Taste how sweet you are."

She lapped at his lips, which were moist from her juices, then sunk her tongue into his mouth, kissing him hungrily.

Saint groaned as her essence flooded his awareness. He

tore at the button fly and shoved his jeans down his thighs. His arousal was so sharp that he didn't even pause to remove the soft leather thong that held his sheathed heartluster next to his thigh. He took his cock in his hand and arrowed it toward Christina's wet cunt. At the last second, however, he reared up over her and reached for the mechanism above the bed. He turned two separate wheels and watched as her thighs spread even wider and her hips rose off the bed. He studied her face carefully for any signs of discomfort.

Instead, he saw only undiluted lust in her green eyes.

He palmed his cock and pressed it to her slit, holding her hips steady for his penetration.

"You're dripping wet for me, aren't you?" he murmured before he flexed his hips and drove into her. She screamed. He snarled at the cruelty of the pleasure of being fully encased in her tight, warm clasp. He grabbed her suspended hips and pushed her back even as he drew his cock out of her. Then he flexed and slid deep once again.

A sort of wild, carnal fury overcame him as he fucked Christina and watched her vitessence spark and flash around her beautiful body. He used his arms to optimally maximize the friction of his thrusting hips, pulling her onto his cock as he pounded into her again and again.

Their combined heartbeat throbbed so loudly in his ears that he heard Christina's cries and screams of pleasure as if through thick insulation. Her muscles constricted and liquid heat surged around his cock. He clamped his eyes shut and endured the exquisite torture of being surrounded by her spasming pussy. He thrust forcefully, their smacking flesh signaling the moment when he released the energy barrier he'd erected, allowing her powerful energy to surge into his cells.

He fucked her as if he'd find salvation at her furthest

reaches. Time stood still as he agonized and gloried in Christina's fires yet again.

"Saint."

Christina's plaintive cry pierced the haze of his rabid lust. He blinked, focusing on her face. He paused with his aching cock thrust halfway into her.

The ugly realization hit that he'd been wild...even more out of control than he had been last night, during the storm.

"Fuck," he shouted hoarsely. His flesh shuddered when he withdrew. He collapsed on the bed next to her, panting like he'd just run uphill for miles.

What had gone wrong? He couldn't comprehend it. He'd absorbed his fill of the earth's powerful vitessence. The need to feed shouldn't come again until tomorrow.

But he'd been consuming Christina's energy just now. True, he hadn't felt compelled to drink her blood, but he'd lost control while her sublime sex juices had been covering his tongue and sliding down his throat. The next thing he knew, he'd been crazed and fucking her like a madman.

"Saint?" Christina asked shakily. The volume of her voice rose when he remained with his eyes shut. "Saint, what's wrong?"

He slowly opened his eyes and pinned her with his stare.

"I'm sorry. I was taking from you. I didn't mean to. I don't know why..."

She craned up with her head, her dark brows knitted together on her damp forehead. "Of course you were taking from me, Saint. We were making love. That's what it's about." She glanced down at his thick erection. "Besides, I gave you nothing compared to what you gave me. Saint... Stop looking at me like that. I'd sure like to talk to this guy, Kavya, if he's the one who taught you about making love. That guy's got a real screw loose."

"Kavya's got nothing to do with it. I've been having sex for five hundred and ninety-six years, Christina. I would think I know a thing or two about it," he said irritably as he panted, trying to get a handle on what had just happened. He couldn't comprehend how he could have lost control when he was so *sure* he wouldn't have. Why had he felt the need to absorb Christina's vitessence when he wasn't even hungry?

She tugged in rising frustration on the silk scarf. "Will you untie me, please? I want to touch you."

He just studied her for several seconds while his mind churned. Despite his mental turmoil, he couldn't help but appreciate the flush on her naked skin, her heaving breasts, and spread, suspended legs. *Gods*, it'd felt so good to drown himself in her.

His cock lurched up from his thigh.

"Saint?"

"All right," he said finally as he reached for the knotted scarf. "Maybe you're right. I'm the one who needs to be restrained here, not you."

As soon as Saint unbound her, Christina reached for him. The fact that he restricted her worship of his lean, muscular body and smooth skin made her exponentially more excited every time she touched him. This nonsense he kept uttering about regretting the hot, soulful manner in which he'd been making love to her made her want to scream.

How could he regret something so elementally beautiful?

She massaged the corded muscles of his neck and ran her fingers through the sweat-dampened hair at his nape. He must have expended a thousand calories, the way he'd been fucking her with so much delicious exuberance. It'd made her feel like a goddess to have him grow so wild at the experience of merging their flesh. If the sensation of his long cock probing deep, secret flesh hadn't been enough for her to come repeatedly, she thought she might have climaxed from just witnessing his profound need.

"Wanting someone...needing them...isn't a sin, Saint," she whispered as she met his fierce, blue-eyed gaze. She felt her heart sink, however, when he glanced away.

"Maybe that's true for you. For me, it's the polar opposite of truth. Do you want to continue having sex, or not?"

A pocket of restrained air flew past her lips. "Of course I want to continue. You make it sound so...*mechanical*. You're not a robot. Stop acting like one!"

His facial muscles pulled tight as he pulled back from her embrace. He sat at the edge of the bed, removing his boots and socks. He stood to shove his jeans off his long legs. Christina's mouth went dry when she saw the two thongs that fit snugly beneath his muscular ass cheeks. She watched, mesmerized, as he untied two well-worn leather straps from a thigh dusted with golden brown hair. He moved with brisk economy—the actions performed by a man day in and day out until they were second nature.

He turned in profile and Christina groaned. For some reason, the sight of the leather next to his naked skin and in such close proximity to the glistening, stiff rod of his cock, caused her clit to pinch in painful arousal. After he'd loosened the sheath from his left leg, he pulled the thong down his thighs and stepped out of it. He set the sheathed short sword on the bedside table and turned toward her.

He seemed entirely unaware of her stunned state as she

gawked at his magnificent body. He knelt on the bed to remove her ankles from the restraints. Christina bit her bottom lip, trying to still her mounting lust. It'd been so dark last night, she hadn't really been able to savor him with her eyes. Seeing him like this—all that delineated muscle gloved by smooth, golden brown skin, his long, swollen cock, the weight of the head pulling down the stalk, his large, shaven testicles hanging like lush, ripe fruit—made her feel like she was in bed with a pagan fertility god of old.

Too bad Saint's strange ideas about sex seemed to parallel that of the wildly different nature of gods and humans.

He once again sprawled across the bed and dug in his bedside table. This time she wasn't quite so shocked when he extracted two leather wrist cuffs with sturdy-looking metal buckles and hooks attached. She sat up slowly as she watched him kneel on the bed, buckling a cuff around each of his wrists.

"Saint..." she mumbled doubtfully when he tossed aside the pillows and sat at the edge of the bed, his back against the headboard.

He glanced up at her before he resumed pulling two heavy straps up from the end of the mattress. Christina whimpered in rising arousal when she saw him matter-of-factly shift his penis from one thigh to the other while he affixed one strap at the top of his thigh. He did the same with the other. After he was done, she couldn't unglue her eyes from the erotic site of the restraints highlighting his full testicles and swollen cock in a V of black leather. He stretched his arms out to the side.

"Now attach my wrists to those," he said, using his chin to indicate the metal hooks in the wall. He'd been so businesslike about the whole ordeal that Christina couldn't help but be irritated.

"What if I don't want to?" she asked testily, even though it was a moronic question. She wanted to all right. She'd have to be brain-dead not to want unrestricted access to his beautiful body.

His face fell. "Does it turn you off? The idea of restraining a male? I'm sorry—it's not my thing either, really, but I have to keep control, Christina. It's such a trial, wanting you as much as I do."

Her mouth had been open in preparation to protest until he said that last sentence, and she saw the uncertainty in his eyes. She told herself that the sight of his beautiful cock and balls cupped in supple leather had nothing to do with it. She'd never been into any type of bondage before and couldn't figure out why the concept lit up all sorts forbidden pathways of excitement in her body. The idea of restraining Saint for her own personal consumption was just as exciting as it had been to have Saint tie her up and do the same to her.

When she saw his questioning look after she'd restrained one muscular arm, she added, "It's not that it turns me off. In fact, it's..." She swallowed thickly as her gaze flickered down over the divine specimen of male flesh she'd just finished restraining to a sitting position on the bed. Downright triple-X hot, she couldn't help finishing in her head.

"You said you wanted to touch me, didn't you? You'll be able to bring us both pleasure this way. I won't be as likely to take from you."

"Saint." Tears of exasperation sprung to her eyes. "Whatever I give you, I give you freely."

His angular claw clenched, and she knew instinctively he didn't want to argue with her. She shook her head, but her eyes remained glued to the awesome sight of his naked abdomen. Before she knew what she'd planned, her lips were rubbing against a fascinating landscape of delineated muscle and smooth skin. Her lips and cheeks became her instruments of knowledge as she explored him slowly, her eyes closed in suspended sensual gratification. When she tasted his skin with the tip of her tongue, running it over a ridge of taut muscle, he groaned roughly.

Her hands joined in her mouth's discovery. She found that he shivered when she scraped her front teeth against the sides of his ribcage and that he growled dangerously when she suckled his tiny copper-colored nipples to taut erection. The taste she gathered on her tongue with more and more frequency as she toured his chest and nibbled at succulent shoulder muscles and dense biceps was salt.

She loved that she made Saint sweat.

Her absorption was so complete that at first she didn't hear him calling to her.

"Stina!"

His shout finally pierced her intoxication. She blinked heavily and looked up at him. He pulled tight on his wrist restraints, making every muscle on his arm, shoulders and chest bulge. She shivered. His eyes seemed to glow preternaturally in the dimly lit room, a blatant reminder that she was definitely not in bed with a human male.

"Suck on my cock."

Christina blinked, realizing she was bending down to his lap when she'd never told herself to move. She glared up at him.

"Don't you dare pull that thing on me."

"What *thing*?" he asked blandly.

"That mind-control thing."

He shook his head slowly. "As if it'd do me a bit of good to use my ascendancy on you."

Christina swallowed thickly, unsure what to make of the

rich resonance of his tone.

She rose to a kneeling position and straddled his hips. She brought her face to an inch of his and rubbed her breasts against his chest, using the light coat of sweat on both of their bodies to slide their nipples together. When he curled his lip, she expected to see an elongated incisor. The evidence of his restraint caused her to seal her belly to his ribs. She moved her hips in a tight, circular motion, writhing against him, her opened pussy perched just inches from his lap. His nostrils flared and she wondered if he could feel her heat on his cock. She thought she got her answer when his erection batted her on the bottom.

"I have made myself vulnerable to you. This is how you would treat me?" he accused, his brows arching up wryly.

"You're about as vulnerable as a caged lion. Are you saying you're not enjoying this?" she whispered.

"As much as anyone enjoys torture," he replied gruffly, his gaze glued on her mouth.

She leaned down and brushed his lips with her own in a whisper-soft caress. His penis popped against her ass again.

"It's only torture if it doesn't end," she whispered. He leaned in to consume her mouth, his arms stretching behind him. But Christina moved quickly, dropping her head to his lap. He hissed a curse; his body jerked against the restraints. She might have been teasing him, but in truth, his expression of profound need left her heart sore.

She picked up his swollen erection and studied his naked length in fascinated lust. A stream of pre-come leaked from the slit, wetting the succulent cap. She licked it hungrily. Her tongue traced a few blue, turgid veins. She stretched her jaw wide and vacuumed him into her mouth.

His indrawn breath across his teeth made a hissing sound.

Chapter Fifteen

Saint watched her head moving in his lap through narrowed eyes. He groaned as she slid another inch of his cock along her tongue, her jaw creating a strong clamp around him, her suck sublime. Fellatio being the primary manner in which he took sexual satisfaction, Saint immediately recognized innate talent for the skill. Christina possessed it in as much abundance as her other gifts.

When she fearlessly worked past her gag reflex and squeezed the tip of his cock into her throat, he felt his incisors lengthen. He clamped his eyes shut. It infuriated him that he had so little control. Christina began sucking him long, rapid, and deep, her exuberance making it impossible to focus on anything but the dizzying, electrifying thrill-ride she treated his cock to.

Gods, it felt *good*. He imagined their positions being reversed, saw her restrained to the bed while he plunged his aching cock between her lush lips again and again. It was his preferred manner of oral gratification...to be in total control of his pleasure. What had he been thinking giving up what little power he had in this situation?

She sucked even harder, pistoning his aching, throbbing flesh between her lips at a pace that made his eyes roll back in his head. She'd desensitized her throat sufficiently to take the tip of the head of his cock into the narrow, clasping channel on each forceful down stroke. He strained up wildly, the leather restraints biting at the flesh of his thighs.

"Christina, stop."

When she continued to consume him like he was her last meal for weeks, he repeated his instructions with the full force of his ascendancy. It was true that his ascendant function worked inconsistently on her, but when she was distracted, he'd often been able to nudge her actions one way or another.

He inhaled raggedly when she paused mid-staff on his cock. He sensed a sudden caution mixing with her pitched arousal.

She resumed her relentless pace.

He cursed and jerked viciously at his restraints. A crunching sound and a slight give in his right arm told him he'd just cracked the concrete-reinforced bolt. Christina flipped her long hair back and looked up at him with one wide, green eye, her red lips spread wide just beneath the head of his cock. She'd heard the concrete break as well.

"I asked you to stop," he growled.

It shamed him to have to reveal to her that his incisors were extended in preparation to feed. Gods, this wasn't going the way he'd hoped. *Why* did he *still* want to take from her— consume the essence of Christina—even after his hunger had been satisfied?

Christina merely shook her head slightly and gave the head of his cock a few healthy swats with her tongue. He clenched his teeth in a mounting fury of need and flexed his hips, stretching the leather restraints on his thighs taut. Christina's nostrils flared. She shifted slightly, the tight clamp of her lips bending his cock forward an inch or two. She maintained eye contact and slid his cock into her mouth slowly, knowing full well he watched every detail of his penis sinking between her stretched, reddened lips. Her tightly clamped fist followed the path of her pistoning mouth.

"You little..." He growled and lunged mightily. The bolt gave in the cracked concrete. Christina paused in her torture. He saw her through a red and gold haze of pulsing, sparking vitessence.

"Getting nervous?" he rasped between pants. A drop of sweat rolled down his abdomen. For a split second, regret flooded his awareness when he saw the anxiety in her gaze.

But then he felt that brief shake of her head again. *No*. Her lips sunk.

He roared and jerked his straining muscles. The bolt popped out of the wall. Again Christina paused. He barely could see her beautiful face through a red-tinged blur of lust, but he felt perfectly when she vacuumed his cock into the narrow channel of her throat.

The haze completely overcame his vision.

Christina's heart pounded so loudly in her ears she distantly wondered if she'd have an aneurysm. Her excitement was sharper than it had ever felt, the sensation like a blade in her spirit, a sharp ache in her womb. She watched Saint's bulging muscles flex yet again as the other bolt popped out of the wall, bringing a patch of drywall with it. She had no choice but to slide the head of his cock out of her mouth. Her lungs burned so badly from panting in arousal, she couldn't catch her breath by merely breathing through her nose. Her cheek fell to his flexing thigh.

She whimpered in anxiety and lust as she watched Saint hastily release the wrist cuffs and then the leather straps holding his thighs. She glanced up, catching a glimpse of the inferno raging in his blue eyes, before he lunged. He put his arm beneath her waist and, for a second, she was airborne. She barely had time to put her hands down, bracing herself to prevent a face plant on the mattress.

He spread her thighs roughly and parted her buttocks. A cry of surprise popped out of her throat when he held one cheek tightly and spanked it several times. The brisk smacks on her flesh caused warm juice to surge out of her vagina.

"Saint—" she began to protest. She was confused by the acute arousal she experienced from being spanked. But, he interrupted her by grabbing her other bottom cheek and landing several concentrated swats on it.

"That's what you get for teasing me, Christina," he muttered once he'd made that buttock sting and tingle.

She gasped when his long erection pressed between the crevice of her ass cheeks and along her spine. It felt like a hot, heavy, iron-hard poker sliding along her skin. He grabbed her hips and pressed her to him tightly.

"How dare you?" he seethed. "You're a little girl playing with fire."

"No," she retorted between pants of burning air. "I'm a woman giving pleasure to her lover. What's wrong? Can't you take a challenge?"

He didn't move or speak for an eternal second.

His cock lurched in the crack of her ass. "Challenge? You want a *challenge*?" he roared. He shifted his hips and pressed his cock to her slit. Air exploded out of her lungs when he thrust into her. Before she had time to recover from that fierce possession, he was pounding his cock into her pussy. She keened shakily as wave after wave of sensation crashed into her.

He pressed the back of her head, forcing her down so that

only her bottom remained sticking up in the air. She turned her hot cheek onto the comforter as he grabbed her hips and served her flesh to his ravenous cock again and again. The strident smacks of their crashing bodies, the bang of the headboard against the wall, and Saint's grunts of pleasure all blended into a rich carnal symphony in her lust-addled brain.

Her facial muscles tightened in a convulsion of pleasure. She didn't need to strain for climax because Saint's forceful possession was giving her no other choice but to accept it. A whimper of shock popped out of her throat when he suddenly thrust a thumb into her asshole while he continued to drive his cock into her pussy. Her eyes sprang wide.

"That's where you deserve to get it for being such a tease. That's where you'll get it the next time you pull something like this too."

Her rectum tightened around his thick thumb. Her vagina writhed and contracted around his pounding cock. His growl sounded ominous. She cried out at the sensation of his penis swelling inside of her. Every nerve in her body lit up as climax tore through her flesh.

She lost herself for a few seconds...a few minutes? Wave after torrential wave of pleasure battered her consciousness, leaving no room for anything else.

The next thing she was aware of was Saint panting near her ear. He nuzzled her cheek with his nose. Christina gulped air. Her vagina tightened reflexively around his huge, swollen cock. He grunted.

She clamped her eyes shut and tried to calm her body after its plunge into the storm-battered realms of ecstasy. Eventually, she found the strength to turn her head so that their faces were less than an inch apart. His fragrant breath hit her face in puffs. She tried to read his expression, but when she couldn't, she read his mind.

"Don't. Don't flagellate yourself, Saint. I loved it," she whispered. She rubbed her lips against his open mouth.

"You love to have your soul sucked until you're empty?" he asked dully.

"I hardly feel empty." She tightened around him for emphasis, liking the way his eyes sparked. But then his face transformed into stone.

"Teslar took a young man to the crystal chamber tonight. We found him after Teslar abandoned it. His name was Elliot. Elliot told me that Teslar had been treating him so sweetly for the past month. What he didn't tell me, I guessed. He bought him expensive gifts, whispered how special he was into his ear, gave him more sexual pleasure than he'd ever dreamed possible.

"The Iniskium and I interrupted a special little ceremony Teslar had planned for Elliot tonight. He'd been about to pierce his supposed one and only love's brain with a captive bolt. It would have kept Elliot conscious, but paralyzed, while Teslar proceeded to methodically drain every last ounce of blood from his body for his consumption. Do you want to know what Elliot said to me, Christina?"

Christina felt dizzy with horror, but he continued ruthlessly.

"Elliot wondered what he'd done to make Teslar angry with him. You must be his twin, he said. If you see him, will you ask him to give me another chance?"

"Oh my God," Christina managed through rubbery lips. "How awful for him. How awful for *you*. Teslar is a monster."

He reared up, bracing himself on his hands. "Teslar is my clone. Do you know what that means? Not only do we come from the same bloodthirsty race, we share the same genetic material. We are one."

Christina felt a tear slip out of her eye when she sensed his wild desperation to make her understand a truth that she had no capability of comprehending. He struck his chest with his fist, the force of his blow alarming her.

"*That* is what you taunt. A ravening animal. You are blind when it comes to me. You see a reality that isn't there. You were wrong to tease me when you saw I was losing control...when you *knew* I would take from you!"

"I think it's you who's blind, Saint," Christina retorted, bracing herself up on her elbows. "You didn't drink my blood. I hardly feel diminished by the experience. In fact..." she twisted around and met his gaze defiantly, "...I can't wait to do it again."

His rigid face convulsed when she dipped her hips, sliding his engorged penis out of her an inch, only to push it back in. She studied him intently as she shifted her hips and rocked him inside of her. At first, he stayed immobile, but she could tell that, like her, his entire consciousness had focused on the tiny tongues of flame caused by her bobbing hips.

"Christina." He closed his eyes tightly. After a moment, he leaned on one hand and grabbed her wrist. He pushed it to the bed over her head and then switched, doing the same to her other hand. Christina's face fell into the mattress. He pressed his mouth near her ear.

"You want me to prove to you that I'm an animal, is that it?"

"No. I want to prove to you that you're *not*," she whispered.

He placed his hands next to her shoulders and began to fuck her. Christina whimpered in slight discomfort and intense arousal. The head of his cock was still swollen from his previous climax, although not as large as it had been minutes ago.

While their previous mating had been uncontrolled and boisterous, Christina thought they both held their breath for the first minutes of this joining. Only the sounds of flesh slapping flesh entered her ears. She felt hyperaware of him behind her, knew that he watched himself as he fucked her steadily. Thoroughly. She tried to twist her head so that she could see him, but he pressed a hand to the back of her skull gently, keeping her face on the mattress...blinding her from the powerful sight of him.

Then he nailed their flesh together again and again with a precision that stunned her. Her face contorted in an agony of pleasure. She mindlessly bit into the soft comforter. His cock rubbed her deep. Even though neither of them grunted or moaned, she could hear the arousing, wet sounds of him moving so forcefully in her slippery flesh, the smack of skin against skin.

"Come here," he said after a minute or two more of this exquisite torture. Even though he'd verbally made a request, he was the one who moved her, sliding her across the silk comforter until her thighs fell off the edge of the bed. He stood with one foot on the ground while the knee of his other leg remained on the bed.

He spread his big hands over her hips and ass, lifting her as he straightened. A shaky cry burst out of her throat as he began to use his arms to slide her pussy up and down his cock. Christina's mouth sagged open. She stared blindly in the face of the crashing pleasure. He was eerily focused as he drilled into her, creating a nearly unbearable friction. She felt helpless and small as he used his powerful body to completely control the movements.

A moment later she gripped the silk comforter and

screamed in orgasm. He continued to fuck her as she came, hard and mercilessly. Jesus, she was going to be sore tomorrow, but she couldn't care less today, as her vagina clamped madly around his plunging cock and pleasure tore through her. She was so lost in the delicious sensations that it took her a moment to hear him speaking to her as he shifted her limp body yet again.

"You've got such a hot little pussy. You burn me every time you come," he rasped from behind her as he lifted her sagging body. "Up on your knees, baby. Face down on the bed."

Then he was fucking her again. He had both feet on the floor now and was plunging his cock into her at a downward angle. She moaned in mixed shame and excitement when she realized he'd pushed her ass cheeks wide. She felt the cool, air-conditioned air on her slick perineum and asshole. He held her buttocks tightly, making her an immobile target. He made free with her. When his strokes became more choppy and short, she knew he was about to explode.

He reached between her thighs and rubbed her clit. Christina shouted hoarsely and detonated with him.

This time, he didn't scold her or try to push her away with blatant reminders of his clone's evil nature or his bestial race. Instead, he remained standing behind her while the swelling in his cock subsided. He stroked her bottom and back soothingly while her breathing returned to normal.

After he'd calmed her, he reached around her and used his fingers to bring her to climax yet again. The utter precision of his actions stunned her. Certainly she'd never given herself such powerful orgasms, and never so rapidly in succession. It was as if he coaxed reactions from her body she hadn't known existed.

"You're magic," she whispered when he finally withdrew his

cock from her body and they embraced on the bed.

"Elliot mentioned something similar in regard to Teslar," he murmured, his chin on top of her head.

Christina clamped her eyes shut. "You're not Teslar, Saint."

She squeezed him and pressed her face to his chest. His arms tightened around her. She felt the kiss he placed on the top of her head in every cell of her body. A feeling of lassitude weighted her eyelids and limbs. She still sensed Saint's turmoil, but it seemed distant...a storm brewing on the horizon on a lazy, sunny day. She reminded herself to take heart in the fact that he hadn't walked away this time.

That was progress, wasn't it?

But she wondered about that when he tensed and gently pried her arms from his body. Christina's heart froze.

"If you walk away from me again, I can't be responsible for what I might do, Saint."

He grimaced as he glanced back at her from a sitting position. "I'm sorry. It's not what you're thinking. Kavya is here at Whitby. He's speaking to me with his mind...asking me to meet him."

"What's wrong?" Christina asked as she watched him lunge off the bed. "You seem upset. Surely he's requested a meeting before, hasn't he?"

"Yes. But never once in my living memory has he indicated the summoning was urgent." He froze in the action of reaching for his heartluster.

"What is it?"

"Kavya indicates you should come as well," Saint said warily.

Chapter Sixteen

Whitby was a three-story, granite, Romanesque-style mansion. A fifteen-foot-wide balcony stretched along the length of the front of the house, couched between two cupolas. Mahogany French doors opened to the balcony from a library, the dining room, and the entertainment studio.

Saint led Christina by the hand through the entertainment studio and out onto the balcony. Her eyes caught movement. It was as though the shadowed granite wall had shifted and sprung to life.

"Christina. It is my greatest honor to meet you."

Christina shivered when Kavya took her hand. She didn't think it was from fear...more like awe. His hand felt cool and dry when he squeezed her hand in greeting. Wonder reverberated through her flesh when she realized she touched a being from a different planet.

An *alien.*

"Yes, in the truest sense of the word," Kavya responded immediately. *"I'm forever bumbling about your lovely planet...forever an interloper. We are much more similar in genetic make-up to humans than different, but alas...the difference is telling."*

"You're not telling me anything new," Christina replied with her mind. It somehow didn't seem strange at all that she carried on the conversation with Kavya telepathically. She'd always possessed the skill, but without the company of truly adept telepaths, her talent had never been prodded into full expression. Aidan and Saint were both mind readers, but Kavya's sharp, blazing clarity of thought was like nothing she'd ever experienced before.

"Saint is so strange, sometimes. I can't believe other humans don't notice it," she said.

"Humans don't notice many things. The richness of their planet, for instance. The vibrancy of their souls. They are forever wasting their vitessence—allowing others to rob what is theirs by right. They respond to the theft by draining another's energy, and the cycle proliferates. Shame, really."

She peered at Kavya's lean, angular features in the dim light cast from the entertainment studio. The strange hat he wore covered his hair, but his thick sideburns were light brown in color. His face was arresting—stunning, even. It was so perfectly proportioned, so elementally masculine, that she had the impression she gazed at a god. She stilled when she looked into his striking blue eyes. She turned her hand in his hold, gripping his wrist, absorbing his energy more fully.

"You're Saint's father."

He laughed aloud, the joyful sound making Christina start in surprise. He'd been so sober before, so formidable. To see two sets of lethal-looking fangs set amidst that genuinely beautiful smile certainly underlined the *difference* of Kavya to an exponential degree.

"Yes. Saint has my genes, in addition to those of a particularly fierce human-wolf shapeshifter I once knew."

"Human shapeshifter? You mean creatures like that actually exist outside of Hollywood—I mean, aside from Saint and the Iniskium, of course," she finished awkwardly.

"Oh, yes," Kavya replied matter-of-factly. *"Many things exist here on Earth that apparently only a few chosen humans can see. But, in regards to Saint's true creation, you are as much responsible as I."*

"Excuse me?" Christina whispered out loud.

"What are you two talking about?" Saint asked, his tone sharp with irritation. Christina realized he was even more perplexed by what was going on than she was. Kavya must have blocked him from their telepathic exchange.

"I need to speak with you both about the boy," Kavya said aloud.

Christina slowly withdrew her hand from Kavya's.

"Do you mean Aidan?" she asked warily.

"The time has come. I must explain about—"

But Kavya's words were cut off by a loud crash and then the sound of tinkling glass. Christina grabbed for Saint in alarm, but he was already moving.

"That sound came from Aidan's room," she heard him growl. Much to her disbelief, even though she'd seen him do it once before, he vaulted over the balcony and just...dropped.

"*Saint*," she shrieked. She ran to the stone railing and peered into the darkness. When she saw nothing, she turned around and raced for the French doors. She gasped when Kavya reached out and grabbed her arm, pulling her up short.

"Let Saint deal with it."

Christina jerked her arm, but Kavya had a grip as unbreakable as his biological son's.

"Saint told me we were safe here from Teslar and his revenants," Christina muttered as she tried wildly to get out of Kavya's hold.

"He's correct. Teslar cannot enter. My magical ward is

intact. *That's* got nothing to do with Teslar," Kavya said, nodding toward the stone railing where Saint had dropped out of sight a moment ago.

"Let go of me," she seethed telepathically. Several more loud bangs and a whimper emanated from below.

"He should be fine," Kavya said. The sound of wood splintering was followed by the howl of a dog in pain. Kavya shook his head regretfully. "Damn tortuous process, growing up."

"Let me go to my son, dammit," she shouted furiously. Much to her surprise, Kavya released her. Fear-saturated blood rushed in her veins as she raced down the stairs to the first-floor bedrooms. More sounds of chaos followed—yelps and growls, the sound of items being knocked to the floor, and furniture being moved violently as bodies crashed into it.

"Aidan," she screamed as she flew into the bedroom. She couldn't see anything clearly in the moonlit room but the white curtain billowing inward from the opened window and shadows writhing on the floor.

She reached for the light and flipped it on. It took her a second to recognize Saint in his wolf form. He stood rigid, his mouth clamped on the back of the neck of a smaller wolf. The other animal lay on its side on the floor, writhing and struggling against Saint's hold.

"Scepter... Saint, where's Aidan?" she demanded. She looked desperately around the room. The bed was mussed, but there was no sign of her son. She ran to the attached bathroom, but it was empty. The smaller wolf continued to snarl and whimper as it struggled in the hold of Scepter's jaws. She whipped back the curtains.

"Aidan!"

The snarling wolf went quiet. She froze.

Christina turned around slowly. For several seconds, she just stared at the two wolves. Horror crept over her slowly and then swelled when the smaller wolf tried to rise off the floor, but Saint held it down firmly.

"Let go of him," she screamed.

Scepter's eyes were on her as she charged across the room. When she was several feet away, he unclamped his jaws. Christina pulled up short when he growled at her through bared fangs. The smaller wolf began to writhe and convulse as though it were having a seizure. Its body jerked against the wooden footboard of the bed, causing the bed to lurch several inches on the wood floor.

"Aidan?" she whispered incredulously, tears splashing down her face. As before, the smaller wolf paused in its agonized writhing when it heard her voice. She started toward the fallen animal. Scepter stepped in to her path, teeth bared ominously.

"You *bastard*. What have you done to my son?" she asked, horrified panic nearly stealing her voice. The wolf that Christina sickeningly believed to be Aidan gave a high-pitched bark of pain and growled. She lunged past Scepter, desperate to give comfort. The next thing she knew, Saint was wrapping his very human arms around her. He lifted her off her feet. Christina kicked furiously, but he swung her around his hip until her feet thrashed in the air.

"Put me down!"

"I can't let you near him. He might hurt you unintentionally while he's struggling."

Her mind went numb for a suspended moment. Was this really happening, or was she caught in some kind of horrific nightmare? She needed to get her son and get out of here. Saint sat her down on the edge of the bed. Through the haze of her rising panic, she noticed he was naked. As soon as he released her, she stood and tried to get past him, slugging him in the ribs when he didn't get out of her way. He grunted.

"Dammit, Christina." There was a ripping sound. Saint grabbed her thrashing arms and shoved them behind her back. She realized he'd torn a length of decorative braid off the bedspread. He tied her wrists together. She screamed and kneed him in the groin.

"Ouch!" He shoved her onto the bed. Christina fell back and stared up at him. His breathing was harsh and his eyes flashed fire.

"I need to go help him. You're not making this any easier," he said as he picked up a pair of jeans from the carpet and hastily donned them.

"Why should I make this easy? You attacked my son. You changed him into a...*whatever* you are. How *could* you?" she accused. Tears soaked her face.

Saint blanched visibly. "*I* didn't do anything. When I came into the room, he'd changed into a wolf. He was frantic, fighting the transformation. It usually happens that way the first few times and—"

"You were *biting* him," Christina accused.

"I was holding him so he didn't hurt himself. I don't know any more about this than you do, Christina."

"You *liar*. How can you claim not to know anything? He's a wolf—like you." Something caught her eye and she struggled to a sitting position.

"Kavya," she said through numb lips when she saw the Magian's impressive figure sweep into the room. He said nothing, but approached the whining wolf at the foot of the bed.

He drew a small rectangular box from the pocket of his

robes. He uncapped the end and Christina saw a needle. "No, wait...*don't.*" She started to stand again, but Saint held her on the bed with his hands on her shoulders. "Don't you touch my son!"

Kavya knelt. The pleated fabric that draped from the top of his odd hat fell onto his sculpted features. The ornate mahogany footboard blocked her vision, but a few seconds later, the wolf went quiet. Kavya stood.

"I can explain, Christina. I was going to earlier, but then...well, better late than never I suppose." He bent and lifted Aidan into his arms effortlessly. Christina whimpered when she saw he carried the familiar figure of her eleven-year-old son. She'd suspected Aidan had been that thin, suffering wolf, but seeing the evidence firsthand caused a wave of fear and nausea to sweep through her.

"We need to get him to bed. He'll have a fever tonight. It's always that way for a first change." Saint helped her stand to make room on the bed for Aidan. He kept his hands on her shoulders, but she shrugged him off, staring at her son's face while Kavya settled him on the bed. Aidan's cheeks were unnaturally flushed and perspiration gleamed on his face.

"I need to take him to the hospital," she said hoarsely.

"Have you forgotten you can't leave Whitby?" Saint asked from behind her.

"Are you planning on keeping us prisoner here?" she challenged.

"If need be." The fury in his gaze confused her. What right did *he* have to be angry?

"What the hell have you done, Kavya?" A chill went down Christina's spine at the violence she sensed in Saint as he asked the question with lash-like intensity.

Kavya sighed. "You accuse me of making the boy a

shapeshifter? Well...I suppose you might. The wolf possesses a pure, dignified animal soul. I deemed it best for my experiment."

Saint moved so quickly that Christina didn't even have time to blink. He wrapped his hand around Kavya's throat and squeezed. "You were doing experiments on that boy?" he roared.

"Please...Saint... Calm down. Let...me explain," Kavya grated out through a constricted windpipe. He inhaled raggedly when Saint lessened his hold slightly. "I haven't *experimented* on the boy. I suppose you could argue that I am partially responsible for the boy's wolf genes, but *you* are as much so."

"Are you mad? I never would bite Aidan, let alone *embrace* him."

"Of course you didn't take Aidan in the Final Embrace. But you are responsible for his wolf aspects, nonetheless."

Saint went still as he met Kavya's intense stare. Christina sensed a message pass between them, but couldn't comprehend its content. Saint's grip on Kavya's throat slowly released.

"That's not...that's not possible," Christina thought she heard Saint mutter hoarsely under his breath.

"Silly to deny the obvious," Kavya said as he smoothed his rumpled, dirty robes.

"What's going on in here?"

Christina turned to see Alison standing in the doorway, wearing her jeans and a half camisole that revealed a silver ring in her bellybutton, her hair sticking out at various odd angles.

"Hey...what's wrong with Aidan?" the girl asked. Her gaze transferred to Kavya. "Who's he?"

"Saint, untie me," Christina demanded.

Saint looked around. He seemed disoriented...dazed.

"I haven't got time for all of this now," Christina hissed. "My son is ill. I need to take care of him. *Untie me.*"

She saw his muscular throat convulse as he swallowed thickly. He nodded and moved behind her, loosening the knot he'd made in the silk braiding from the bedspread.

As soon as he'd released her wrists, Christina started anxiously toward Aidan. He felt hot beneath her fingertips as she stroked his hair back from his face. He moaned in his sleep. "Alison?" she asked without turning around. "Will you go to the coach house and get a few items for Aidan's fever, please?"

"Sure," Alison replied dubiously.

"The fever will break by morning. There is little we can do until it runs its course. He is not in any mortal danger, Christina." She realized that Saint stood near her.

"I still want Alison to get the things," she said shakily. She felt like her world had just completely tilted off its axis and she was floundering, falling through empty space, desperate for something to grab onto. She turned when Saint put his hand on her shoulder. A rogue tear spilled down her cheek.

"He's going to be all right," he said.

"So you say."

"So I say," Saint said.

"I don't know what to believe. All I know is Aidan's life just changed forever and you two are somehow to blame," she said, giving both him and Kavya an accusatory glance. "I also know my son is burning up with fever. If you have something relevant to say about making him well, say it now. Otherwise, I'd appreciate it if you two would leave us alone. Alison?" She beckoned to the girl, effectively dismissing the two males.

Saint straightened. His face looked like it'd been carved from stone. "I know you're upset, Christina, but I'm not going to allow you to leave Whitby's grounds. Not until Teslar has been eliminated as a threat."

"It would seem things are pretty damn dangerous for us at Whitby as well," Christina replied, refusing to meet Saint's gaze.

Chapter Seventeen

Kavya didn't flinch when Saint slammed the door to the library. He sat calmly on one of the twelve armchairs that surrounded a large, square, polished cherry table. Various books were stacked on it, in addition to several rolled maps. His expression was that of polite distraction as he watched his charge stalk into the room, his eyes broadcasting a message that would have made even the bravest of humans quaver and run. Saint placed his fingertips on the table and leaned across the corner.

"Explain yourself," he bit out.

"I am sure you read the gist of my message while we were downstairs just now. What part would you have me elaborate upon?"

"How about the part where you suggested Aidan was my son?" Saint seethed.

"Hmmm, yes," Kavya murmured. He placed his elbows on the arms of the chair and made a steeple of his fingers as he considered Saint thoughtfully. "I take it from your manner you're still unbelieving?"

"It's not possible!" Saint bellowed, shoving his upper body weight off the table. He began to pace back and forth before the marble fireplace, a coiled spring of sinew and muscle. "The Princes and their clones have no souls. We are sterile! You

Beth Kery

yourself have told me so, and none of us have fathered a child in almost six centuries on this planet."

Kavya shrugged. "If there is one thing I know as a biological alchemist, it's that change is inevitable. In the process of evolution, it's a given that what is true today will be false tomorrow."

Saint paused in his restless pacing. "Aidan's father is Richard Fioran. You can't be serious in claiming I fathered him."

Kavya leaned forward in his chair. "Surely you're not suggesting that it's an impossibility? The opportunity occurred, did it not? Christina may believe that she first met you eight years ago when her new boss at LifeLine told her about the coach house for rent at Whitby, but you two *had* met before that. It's a foregone conclusion, even if I hadn't read your mind in regard to the matter. I'm sorry for the intrusion, but the incident was much more important than you might expect. You and I both know that you knew of Christina years before she and Aidan moved to Whitby. You encouraged the manager at LifeLine to hire her. In fact, you suggested to her boss that he mention the coach house to her and the extraordinarily good rent."

Saint's heart pounded in his ears. He stared at Kavya with a mixture of incredulity, outrage, and shock. Shame shuddered through him at the idea of another witnessing his weakness. His lips felt like rubber when he opened his mouth. Nothing came out at first. It was as though his body instinctively denied putting into words the memory—a memory that he regularly tried to avoid as ritualistically as the recollection of his bloodthirsty attack on the Iniskium.

The memory of what he'd done to Christina.

She'd been more than willing on that afternoon so long ago.

168

He'd been deeply in contact with her unconscious mind. But maybe if she'd been fully aware of what he *was*, she wouldn't have agreed.

She'd been twenty-one years old when he'd first seen her...first *experienced* her. She'd been fresh out of college and interviewing for a case manager position at LifeLine. He'd been dropping off a check at the downtown facility. He'd just left the office of the president of LifeLine when he saw Christina being led down the hallway by Michael Moorhead, one of the managers.

He'd stared in blank shock as color infused his gray world in a vivid flash. For a blinding, senseless moment, he'd become a savage, primitive creature, like the one who had attacked the Iniskium.

He'd known only a vast hunger, a wounding need.

Then he'd blinked and his bloodlust had cleared. He'd watched Christina walk down that hallway, wearing a conservative gray suit, her vitessence sparking around her at incredible speed. She drew him like a powerful magnet. He'd fallen back against the wall in the empty hallway when he realized he'd been heading toward the room where she'd disappeared with Michael Moorhead. To do what, exactly? Attack her while she was in the midst of an interview? he'd thought incredulously.

For almost six centuries he'd tamed his bloodlust and repented for his sins, only to have his control melt to mist at the sight of a young woman.

He'd struggled against his need for nearly a month. But, in the end, he'd lost his battle.

How could he not crave the very essence of life when he was one of the walking dead?

Kavya watched him intently. Saint clamped his eyes shut,

wishing he could shut the powerful Magian out of his mind, wishing he could purge the memory altogether.

But, of course, he would never have done that, because despite his shame, despite the horror of what he'd done, he clung to the beauty of the recollection of seducing Christina.

He knew he'd never let that memory go.

Twelve years ago

He only saw vibrant color when Christina was present, so Saint knew for the first time in his life why they'd named the huge flowers after the blazing sun that gave life to this planet—sunflowers.

His skin warmed under the yellow star's rays—another new experience. It'd never imparted its enlivening heat before. He'd never been cold, like someone might imagine a soulless creature. But he'd certainly never known the comforting kiss of the sun until Christina entered his sterile, shadowed world.

He approached her still figure silently. He'd watched over her for the past month, seen her coming and going from her Lakeview apartment, observed her from a distance as she waited for the "L" train to take her to work, or to meet a friend for a drink or dinner. He'd seen her with a dark-haired, good-looking young man who Saint instinctively didn't trust. By then, he understood that Christina's brilliant, powerful vitessence conferred her with special powers, including the ability to read other peoples' minds.

He couldn't comprehend why she refused to see the falseness behind the man's white-toothed smiles.

She was sleeping with him. He easily caught her scent on the man—Rick was what she called him—when he left her apartment after spending the night there. The odor of her arousal intertwining with the cocky human's odor nearly sent him into an animalistic rage every time he smelled it. Not a bloodlust, but a fury of violence. He shook with a need to share his profound pain with Rick.

He'd refrained, and eventually nature had set things to right. Christina's luminous smiles were less and less in evidence when she was with Rick. They fought once in front of a restaurant, Christina accusing Rick of sleeping with a woman who they'd unexpectedly encountered while dining. Rick had denied it, but Christina's telepathic powers were no longer dulled by the flush of first infatuation.

Saint had watched over her afterwards as she'd taken the "L" and walked home alone. He'd gotten a savage satisfaction from hearing her tell Rick to go to hell and never come back. But Saint'd become tense and restless as he watched her solitary figure walking down the darkened street, her vitessence still brilliant, but muted.

It hurt, seeing her sad. Hurt like when he considered the Iniskium villagers he'd wantonly murdered before he understood his nature, pained him like when he'd considered damning the few Iniskium, his trusted companions and friends, to a life of near immortality, but also emptiness and strife. Saint had responded in the only way he knew, ceaselessly trying to atone for his sins by helping those in need.

He wanted to make it up to Christina, too, wanted to make her smile again...somehow.

He'd stayed outside her apartment all night in his wolf form, hidden by the shadows of a tree. His gaze never left the window he'd learned was her bedroom. The next morning, she'd left, carrying a beach bag, looking pale and exhausted, as if she'd slept fitfully, if at all.

He'd followed her to Lincoln Park, to the outdoor gardens of the arboretum. She'd been the only occupant in the thousand-square-foot clearing surrounded by thick, seven-foot-tall hedges, trees and prairie-growth perennials. With his preternatural hearing, Saint could hear two males tossing a Frisbee in the near vicinity, and farther off, several people having a picnic. But Christina and he might have been the only two creatures on the entire planet when he approached her sleeping form.

His cock felt leaden and heavy as he stared down at her. The sunflowers and lavender danced in the soft breeze, creating a moving, colorful background that mimicked her vibrant lifeforce.

He'd never been this close to her before. Her face looked young and innocent in sleep. His gaze traced her flushed cheeks, lush, sweet mouth, the light sprinkling of freckles on her nose. Her dark hair had been pulled back into a ponytail, but a few strands flicked across her cheeks. She'd been reading a paperback before she fell into a sleep of exhaustion. The pages flipped lazily in the breeze against her relaxed fingers.

She wore a patterned, floral sundress that tied in a halter around her neck. Her skin looked dewy and sun-kissed. Saint's eyes lingered on the swells of her pale breasts in the V of the fabric. The thought of her curving, succulent flesh filling his hands, the satin of her skin sliding along his cheek and lips, made his cock surge painfully.

He thought he was hallucinating when her nipples suddenly pulled tight against the clinging fabric. Without telling himself to move, he rubbed his thick erection through his jeans, needing the friction to stop the sharp ache of desire.

He burned. He'd never known a hunger like it, never imagined a need that could score you from the inside out. Looking back on the incident twelve years later, Saint realized he hadn't been that different on that sunlit, golden day with

Christina than he had been on that gray dawn when Teslar and he had attacked the Iniskium village. Both times, he'd been overwhelmed with a blinding hunger, incapable of controlling his need because it was so new to him...so raw.

Having no experience with standing face to face with the essence of beauty, he had no ready defenses against it.

He reached out to her with his mind, the action as instinctive and natural as a wolf calling to its mate. Wolves knew the dream world intimately. He called to her soothingly, seductively. Her lips parted and a soft moan escaped her throat. Her hips shifted and, as connected with her as Saint was at that moment, he knew she tried to get friction on her swelling sex.

He recognized the answer to his call and came down on his hands and knees over her.

The sounds of the two men shouting and laughing on the other side of the thick hedge didn't faze him as he untied the halter around Christina's neck. He was entranced. Nothing existed for him but her singular, intoxicating scent, her sparking vitessence...the soft, sweet body where he would find release from this unbearable tension soon...soon.

But he wished he could make this last forever.

He spoke to her while she slept, keeping her in the cocoon of the sunlit dream. Wolves often communicated using dreams, especially with their mates.

"Do you want me, Christina?"

"Yes, more than anything. Who are you?"

"A dream," Saint replied before he kissed her parted lips.

He lowered the fabric carefully below her breasts, going still for a moment as he stared. He suppressed a groan when his cock lurched. With his mind, he praised her beauty. Her blood sung an answer, surging hot and fast in her veins.

He reached for the hem of her dress and brought it up to her waist. She whimpered when he drew down her tiny, white bikini underwear over her sandals. He came back over her on his hands and knees, his nostrils flaring to catch the exquisite scent of her arousal. He tossed aside his shirt, letting the warm summer sun beat down on his skin, and spread Christina's pale thighs. He could have as easily stopped himself from eating her pussy at that moment, from drowning in the sweet juices she gave him in such abundance, as he could have single-handedly changed the direction of the earth on its axis.

She moaned and thrashed in her sleep. He stilled her hips with his hands, adamant about not being denied her delicious, vitessence-rich cream, her soul-infused juices. He drank hungrily, bringing her to climax again and again. When an object struck the hedges, Saint blinked, rising slightly out of his carnal entrancement. He heard the young man talking and laughing as he retrieved the Frisbee out of the bushes just feet away.

Saint plunged a forefinger in and out of Christina's sleek vagina and rubbed her clit vigorously with a stiffened tongue.

She went rigid and shuddered as she came once again. He subtly kept her in the dream with his mind while he milked every last delicious tremor out of her body and lifted his head. He licked his lips, still hungry for her, but hurting, too.

Hurting so much.

The muscles of her lithesome thighs felt supple in his hands when he pushed them wide and eyed her glossy, vividly pink cunt.

"I could drink your cream forever." His voice was soft and low, but somehow Saint knew Christina heard him, that she focused on him, heedless of the sound of the men bantering and laughing just feet away, the muted noise of traffic in the distance, even the warm, beating rays of the sun on her skin. She'd gone entirely still except for the pulse fluttering wildly at her throat.

He unbuttoned his jeans, his eyes never leaving her face. He cupped his aching balls and resituated them over the leather harness he wore to secure his heartluster to his thigh. His face tightened in a grimace when he fisted an erection so tight, so full, it felt ready to burst through the skin. He came down over her and kissed her lips lightly. He groaned at the sensation of his sensitive cock-tip next to her warm, juicy slit. He pressed.

It took some effort to work his way into her tight channel. By the time he was sheathed completely, he sweated and panted from the energy he expended not to blast his seed into her in what felt as if it would be the most powerful orgasm he'd ever experienced.

She gloved him like she'd been tailor-made for his cock—sleek, wet, tight. Her vitessence vibrated wildly around her, flowing into him...energizing him, enlivening him. It must have given him the strength he required not to give in to his almost overwhelming desire to give her his seed then and there.

He gritted his teeth as he began to pump.

He lost himself in Christina, lost himself in the rich, golden minutes that stretched into another dimension. A cocoon of sunshine and the essence of Christina encapsulated him. His desire was so raw, so painful, it felt like an open wound. But, just when it became unbearable, Christina's vitessence filled him, soothed the emptiness...magicked his flesh to life.

He drank her in greedily. Her vitessence crackled and sparked as he fucked her—hard now, demanding. He braced himself on his hands and stared at her face as he drove into her again and again. He took and he took...more than he'd ever taken...more than he'd taken from his Iniskium victims, who he'd drained of all life. Yet, her energies continued to flow into him in pounding waves.

She clenched his cock as she climaxed. Her vitessence slammed into him with the strength of an energy tsunami. He fell on her in mindless need. Her blood was rich...so sweet. He drank it while his cock jerked viciously inside her tight sheath, shooting his seed to her farthest reaches.

He became conscious by slow degrees that everything had gone fuzzy, like he experienced the world through an insulating barrier. Sweat rolled into his eyes, the salt burning him. He blinked in rising awareness and slowly withdrew his fangs from Christina's throat.

Her face had gone pale beneath her sex-flushed, pink cheeks.

"Christina?" he asked shakily. But she didn't stir from her deathly stillness.

He groaned in misery. He'd drained her. Not completely— but he'd harmed her nonetheless. He fell on her in desperation. His mouth fastened on her parted lips. It was a kiss only in the strictest definition. He poured energy back into her, transfusing her with the vitessence that he'd stolen.

Eventually, he felt the steady glow of her vitessence once again. Her color returned and her breath became soft and even.

He lifted his head. He'd nearly murdered the most exquisite thing he'd ever experienced. His cock was still swollen inside her. He couldn't run, couldn't escape the evidence of his foul deed.

He stared at her while he steeped in horror and regret. When the swelling of his cock dissipated sufficiently, he withdrew from her, his face tightening in anguish at the reawakening of his hunger.

After he redressed her, he waited covertly outside the entrance to the clearing, ensuring that she wasn't bothered while she finished her nap. When she left a half hour later, she wore a dazed, uncertain expression that cut at him deeply. Saint recalled how he'd wanted to make her smile last night when she'd seemed so sad after her breakup with her boyfriend.

He hadn't made her happy, maybe, but he'd brought her pleasure. Sexual gratification was one of the few things a parasitic creature like him could give a human.

But he could never again give Christina sexual pleasure. Perhaps next time he wouldn't be able to stop taking from her...and taking...and taking.

Chapter Eighteen

Alison paused in the process of searching in Christina's bathroom vanity cabinet for Children's Tylenol. She turned around abruptly, her hand flying to the back of her neck. She looked around nervously, but saw nothing out of the ordinary.

She was completely alone in the coach house. The sensation of air flowing across the skin of her nape must have been her imagination. She'd felt so secure up at Whitby earlier, but now all the frightening memories of what had occurred in the tunnels came back to her in graphic detail.

She turned around and grabbed a bottle. Christina had requested the liquid form of the fever reducer, concerned that Aidan wouldn't wake up sufficiently to swallow a pill. Alison was still confused by what had occurred in Aidan's room tonight, but Christina had said she would try to explain later. Alison agreed that getting something from the coach house to help Aidan needed to be the priority.

She really liked that kid, she thought regretfully as she walked out of the bathroom.

"You betrayed me, little songbird."

The bottle of Tylenol thumped on the wood floor in Christina's bedroom.

"I didn't. I wouldn't, Master."

She began to shiver uncontrollably in the empty, dead silence that followed. Alison clamped her eyes shut when a pain lanced through her skull. Teslar's voice sounded rich and clear in her mind. He'd never spoken to her telepathically before and she was shocked when she instinctively responded in kind. She didn't know for certain if he'd heard her, but she had a funny feeling he had.

Something swelled in her breast and it took her a moment to recognize the feeling as pride. She could read minds, just like Christina. She *was* special, regardless of what Saint said.

"I suppose it's impossible for you to have intentionally betrayed me, weak human that you are. But you allowed yourself to be swayed by my clone's ascendancy, and I'll have to punish you severely for that," Teslar said, his tone irritated and slightly bored.

"What are you doing?" he snapped.

"I was...I was getting some Tylenol for Christina."

"The woman?" Alison stiffened when she heard the greed that laced his tone. *"Tell me where she and the boy are. What's my annoying clone doing? Tell me everything, little pet."*

Several pain-filled minutes later, Alison left the coach house. She gave a sharp shriek of alarm when a large hand wrapped around her upper arm and jerked her around.

"What's the hurry, tiny morsel?"

She gasped at the sight of Isi staring down at her from his great height. The moonlight showed his one black eyebrow raised in a mocking expression. His dark hair fell forward on his brow. Even though he technically looked only five or six years older than her, his lancing stare and rigid features made her feel like a child. The knowledge that he was really centuries older than his face revealed intimidated her.

"Let go of me, you animal," she seethed. But, instead of

179

releasing her, he urged her closer. Alison felt his heat penetrate the exposed skin of her belly.

"You don't know the meaning of good sex until you've had a wolf," he taunted softly.

"You don't know the meaning of good sex until you've had Teslar."

"Too bad the price of it is your life. Are you really that stupid?"

Alison laughed. "Maybe I'm that *smart*. Maybe not one of you paranormal superjocks knows a *thing* about me."

He squinted at her in the darkness.

"I know something about you."

Something lacing through his deep, low voice made her pause. Had he just dropped his head closer to her upturned face?

"What do you know about me? That I think you're an asshole? Brilliant deduction."

He continued as if she'd never spoken. "I know your scent. I know you were afraid just now in the coach house." His voice dropped a decibel. She found herself straining up to hear his quiet words. Her bare belly brushed against the fly of his jeans. He was hard. She swayed closer, liking the tickling, burning sensation in her lower abdomen.

"I know you're getting turned on right now," he added.

Her head snapped back.

"Dream on," she replied caustically.

For a moment, he didn't speak. Alison heard her blood pounding loudly in her ears in the tense silence. She gasped in surprise when he suddenly shook her. Hard. Her hair flung into her face and her brain rattled in her skull. Her groin batted repeatedly against his hard thighs, his cock thumping against her abdomen.

"What were you doing in the coach house for so long?" he seethed. "I saw you standing up in Christina's room like you'd been frozen."

"Let go of me, you spaz!"

He stopped shaking her and leaned down until their mouths were only inches apart. "If I discover you've been conspiring with Teslar or have betrayed Saint...if I find out that you've been playing the fool by sacrificing your life wantonly, I'll make you regret it. I don't know why the hell I should care one way or another, but I'm personally insulted by the idea," he snarled.

Alison strained for air when she saw his extended fangs.

"Let go of her, Isi," Saint growled.

Alison stumbled out of Isi's hold when he suddenly released her. She didn't know how Saint had gotten there all of a sudden, but she was thankful for his powerful presence.

Wasn't she?

"You've got a bunch of *whack-jobs* for followers, Saint," she said before she passed his tall, forbidding shadow and ran like hell for Whitby.

Christina's muscles tensed when she heard someone enter Aidan's room. She didn't want to see Saint right now. She was so disoriented by what had occurred, still existing in a numb shock that Aidan had transformed into a wolf. Her heart kept insisting that Saint would never harm her son, but if that were the case, what the hell had she just witnessed? Even if Saint weren't directly responsible, he'd *somehow* tainted Aidan.

She breathed a sigh of relief when she saw it was Alison

who entered the room, carrying a bag with the items she'd requested. Her brow furrowed in concern as the girl drew nearer.

"Alison, what's wrong? You look like you just saw a ghost."

Alison gave a bark of laughter and shook her head as if to clear it. "I didn't see a ghost, but these grounds are dark at night...and...and creepy."

"Thanks for going," Christina murmured as she opened the bag.

"Do you want me to fill that up with water for you?"

"Yes, please," Christina said gratefully, handing the girl the large plastic cup with a lid and straw. "The kitchen is on the opposite side of the hallway from the entertainment studio."

Alison nodded, her eyes looking huge in her pale face. Christina regretted the girl's involvement in all this drama and danger, but there was no way to resolve it for the time being. She brushed Aidan's damp hair off his brow.

For now, the only thing she could consider was her son.

"Christina, why did you act like it was something Saint did that made Aidan sick?" Alison whispered hoarsely a half hour later. They both sat at the edge of Aidan's bed. Christina had lifted his head and managed to get down most of the Tylenol. Aidan's eyes had fluttered open when she'd poured a little ice water into his mouth, but he'd almost immediately fallen back into a deep sleep.

Christina closed her eyes, making them water and burn. She didn't think she could put the truth of Aidan's transformation into a wolf into words. Maybe she was afraid if she spoke it out loud, it would make it true.

"I don't know if he's responsible or not. He says he isn't."

Alison glanced warily at the closed door. "Are you having

second thoughts about trusting him? You guys were all hot for each other earlier this evening. If pheromones had weight, you would have been swimming in a sea of them."

Christina couldn't suppress a groan when she thought of her and Saint's impassioned lovemaking. How could something so horrific follow so closely on the heels of something so wonderful?

"I'm getting creeped out by staying here, Christina. It's like Saint is keeping us prisoner or something." Alison leaned toward her and whispered conspiratorially. "I think we should try to escape Whitby."

Christina sighed and grabbed Aidan's limp hand. "Aidan's not going to be going anywhere for a while, Alison. And that means I'm not."

Later, Christina cracked open a gritty eyelid.

"*What the—*"

She flung herself off the bed, glancing around the dawn-infused bedroom.

"Aidan is with Fardusk."

She spun around to a corner of the room, following the direction of that low, resonant voice. Saint sat in an upholstered chair, his long legs bent at the knee, his thighs spread. His eyes seemed to glow in the shadows as he watched her.

"His fever?" she demanded

"Broken."

He uncoiled his long body from the chair and stood. He wore a pair of jeans and a gray T-shirt. Even though she was angry at him, and wary of his intentions, Christina couldn't help but admire the sleek, animal-like grace of his movements as he came toward her. When he got several feet away, she stepped back.

He planted his scuffed, black leather boots on the spot. A ripple of emotion went through his face at her defensive gesture.

"Fardusk has begun teaching Aidan about his animal nature and how to safely shift."

Tears burned her eyes. It hadn't been a dream. Her son really was a wolf, in addition to being a boy. Strange, but what had seemed impossible in the night—terrifying even—seemed somehow graspable in the morning light.

She had always known Aidan was special. Now she knew he was unique beyond her wildest dreams. Anxiety filled her chest cavity for what the future would bring, but she no longer felt overwhelmed with fear for her son.

"Who is Fardusk?" she asked Saint flatly.

"He is the leader of the Iniskium. A friend... Someone to be trusted."

Christina straightened her spine and thrust out her chin. "I'm so glad there are those you can trust. It's not a luxury I share."

His face stiffened and he stepped toward her. Again she took a step back.

"And will Aidan be a vampire as well?" she asked shrilly.

Saint spread his hands in front of him and shrugged in a helpless gesture. "I wish I knew. Aidan's nature is unique. Not even Kavya knows precisely what strengths he will possess, what parts of him will manifest as wolf, what parts human, what parts Magian.

"I asked Kavya to examine him this morning before Fardusk took him for his lessons," Saint continued. "He says that Aidan is the healthiest child he's ever seen. His unique biology will make him exponentially stronger. He won't get ill, as other children do. His immune system has strengthened way beyond human capacity. From what I've observed, his eating habits haven't changed. He ate half a pound of bacon and ten pancakes for breakfast, but you have to admit...that's not too far off his usual quota for the past six months."

When she didn't return his small smile, he added, "We will watch him closely, Christina. If he does show signs of craving vitessence, we will teach him how to control his hunger, have little doubt of that. I would rather Teslar gained ascendancy over me than allow Aidan to burn in the same fires of remorse that I have suffered."

The irksome tears once again stung her eyes when she sensed Saint's earnestness in trying to alleviate her anxiety, even when he himself was far from certain. The knowledge that he floundered in these bizarre circumstances as much as she did made her angrier for some reason. He might not have bitten Aidan, like she'd accused him of last night, but he *still* was responsible. He was the one who was supposed to be super-powerful. He didn't have a right to be worried or anxious or...was that *guilt* she felt swirling around amongst his other emotions?

"How could you let this happen? How *did* it happen?" The words burst out of a throat that was constricting with emotion.

His blue eyes looked shiny as he regarded her. Did Saint actually have the ability to cry? she wondered dazedly. He entreated her with his gaze. She took another step back in her rising confusion, then found herself stepping toward him when she sensed his desperation. Their gazes held. A feeling like hot, flowing, molten metal began to spread in her belly.

She realized tears were pouring down her face. She stood

there stupidly as Saint came closer. One arm encircled her, his scent enfolded her, causing a flood to spill from her eyes. He gently dried her cheeks with his fingertips, patiently continuing when more fell to replace them.

"I have no excuse for what I've done, Christina. I couldn't resist you. The gods know I tried, but it was like ordering myself not to breathe."

His gruff voice rumbled close to her ear, causing shivers to race down her spine. She leaned forward, placing her forehead on his solid chest.

"Aidan is ours?" she whispered. It was really more of an incredulous statement than a question.

"Yes. I only just learned of it last night, after he shifted. Kavya told me. I was as shocked as you."

She lifted her head and gazed up at him solemnly. After a taut moment, she blinked.

"I was going to ask you if Kavya somehow created Aidan in his laboratories like he did you, but he didn't. Did he?" she whispered.

Saint's mouth fell open. She could almost feel the words scalding his throat and tongue, his guilt infusing the truth like an acid.

"You don't have to say it. I already know, Saint."

He looked taken aback. "Since when?"

"Since just now. I saw the truth in your eyes." She took a deep breath. "But I think I knew before as well. Maybe the truth was never fully in my consciousness. It was like a shadow I'd see out of the corner of my eyes. Something I couldn't fully understand. I remember it now."

She glanced up at him when he stiffened.

"Maybe not in the same way you remember it," she

continued, her quiet voice shaking. "But it was the most realistic dream I'd ever had. And when I woke up, I wasn't convinced at all that it *had* been a dream. Your scent was still on me. I was wet from you...wet with you." She saw his cheek muscle twitch and his eyes glistened even more than they had a minute ago. "I had felt so full in those moments, so alive...so complete. And when I woke up in that field, I was alone. I don't think I'll ever forgive you for that."

A spasm of emotion tightened his face. "I don't expect you to forgive me for it, Christina. But I want you to know my mind was joined with yours. We were joined in the wolf dream. I had your consent."

"I never said you didn't."

"Taking you while you slept was an unpardonable sin. I don't *think* I used my ascendancy on you to get your consent, but I wanted you so much in that moment. I might have pushed—"

Christina made a sound of disgust and moved out of the haven of his arms. She felt his gaze boring into her as she stared out the curtained window onto the new day. When she thought she'd gathered herself sufficiently, she turned around and met his stare.

"I wasn't accusing you of making love to me without my consent. Waking up in that park was the worst experience of my life because I was *alone*. I'd felt what it was like to be with you, only to wake up and know on some deep level the experience had been ripped away from me. That's what I'm not sure I can forgive you for, Saint. It was damned selfish of you."

Christina had to admit that it felt wonderful in those rare moments when she saw Saint at a loss for words. He could do things that were beyond her ability to comprehend, he possessed super-human strength and speed, he could enslave with his will...love like a god.

But he was such a child when it came to understanding the heart of a simple human woman.

He stood there, his stark, handsome face still frozen in disbelief at her words. The need to go to him in that moment nearly overwhelmed her.

Instead, she shook her head and headed for the door. She didn't know who she felt more disgusted with at that moment—herself, for getting so much satisfaction out of seeing him floundering when it came to what was as obvious to her as the sun in the sky, or Saint himself for being such a frustrating puzzle. Weren't men in general a conundrum?

Leave it to her to have fallen for an alien who was even thicker than human males when it came to matters of the heart.

She paused in the process of reaching for the door handle.

"I guess you were wrong about that whole infertility thing," she said archly over her shoulder.

He stared at her, still looking steamrolled. He shrugged helplessly. "It's never happened to the soulless before. I'm as confused by it as you are."

She shook her head and laughed mirthlessly.

"*I'm* not confused by it, Saint. It all seems pretty cut and dry to me. I'm going to find Aidan," she said before she turned and walked out of the room.

Chapter Nineteen

Christina sat beneath a maple tree next to Kavya, both of them watching as Fardusk solemnly instructed Aidan in the yard. The first time she'd seen Aidan shift into his wolf form, a scream had tickled her throat. She started to rise off the ground when Aidan gave a yelp of pain...a yelp that more resembled her human son than the young wolf he'd nearly morphed into. Kavya put his hand on her, stilling her.

"It pains him because he fights the transformation. He will learn not to. Pain is a good teacher," Kavya murmured.

"Mothers cannot idly sit by and watch their children while they hurt," Christina snarled.

"Indeed. But pain is a good teacher for a mother as well as her child." He nodded toward Aidan. Christina watched, mouth hanging open in amazement, as the young wolf frolicked, nipped, and played with the larger, more sedate wolf by his side.

It hadn't necessarily been pleasant sitting there while Aidan familiarized himself with his wolf-nature, but Christina had to admit that doing so alleviated many of the fears she'd acquired during the night. And when the young, sleek brown wolf with the tawny chest and bluish-green eyes trotted toward her later that morning and rested its head on her shoulder, Christina had wrapped her arms around him.

Her heart slowed and she sighed as a profound sense of acceptance went through her. She'd known Aidan was different from the day he was born—no, even while she carried him in her body. Her acceptance at that moment wasn't as surprising as it might seem.

It'd been a long time in coming.

She lifted her face from the soft, sun-warmed fur, and the young wolf raced back into the yard to join Fardusk, who was still in his wolf form. Across the stretch of the wide yard, Christina saw Saint standing in the shadow of an oak. A stream of sunlight filtered down through the branches, turning strands of his tousled brownish-blond hair into pure gold. She felt his eyes on her, even from the distance.

"Why does he deny himself?" Christina asked Kavya quietly, referring to Saint.

"Why does he deny his soul, do you mean?"

Christina nodded.

"He cannot feel it, Christina. And so, in a sense, he is right to say he does not have one."

Christina knew that the wise, otherworldly male who sat beside her sensed her puzzlement and frustration, so she didn't bother to put it into words. He gave her a sad smile.

"Yes, you are right. Saint *does* possess a soul...one that he created for himself through centuries of self-discipline, pain and suffering. In many ways, his soul is more refined than most, because he created it from the terrible friction that comes from the honing fires of restraint, pain, self-doubt, and prayer. Yes, prayer," Kavya repeated when he saw her upraised brows. "He prayed even when he thought it the equivalent of a cockroach asking for a golden god on high to grant him deliverance."

Kavya paused, the expression on his face as he stared across the wide lawn toward his charge both sad and amazed.

"He is a true miracle, and not of my doing. What you must understand, Christina, is that the Magians robbed their planet of its soul over a period of hundreds of thousands of years, mindlessly and foolishly raping fair Magia until the once glorious and powerful song that emanated from her mighty planet-soul throughout the universe became a barely audible whimper. Like your fellow humans, the Magians didn't understand the connection between their own souls and that of the soil from which they sprang. We had become known throughout the galaxy as a planet of cloners, but once the soul of Magia was silenced for an eternity, we were horrified to realize that our clones were missing something crucial as well."

"They were soulless," Christina whispered, fully entranced by his story and the magnetic Magian's deep voice.

"Yes," Kavya replied with a sad smile. "It is difficult for human beings to conceptualize a soul, but they recognize the absence of it quickly enough. It is what forms flesh, graces it…what makes it conscious. The Magians had long ago become sterile as our planet's song waned, which only increased our production rate of clones. For thousands of years, the practice continued, until slowly and subtly our culture began to notice something was missing in the clone class. They began to call them the Sevliss, the soulless.

"Our leaders became consumed with the idea of infusing the soul into Magian-formed flesh. They instigated great contests where the Magian alchemists—you humans might consider us scientists and magicians melded—were challenged to do what only gods had done before us—create a soul."

"Saint told me there are six other Sevliss here on Earth. You and your peers came here for some kind of a *contest*?" Christina couldn't decide if her main emotion was fascination, disbelief, or repulsion. How could something as miraculous as Saint be the result of a contest? It was difficult to imagine beings possessing so much power, and yet being so weakened by their own greed that they were on the brink of destroying their own race.

But perhaps the Magian weren't so different than how humans might be, sometime in the far, distant future?

Kavya shrugged. "It doesn't sound very noble when you say it, but what you must realize, Christina, is that we are here fighting for our very existence. Magians live exponentially longer than humans, but until our progeny are soul-infused, my race's demise looms on the horizon."

Christina just stared at Kavya's handsome, regal profile for several seconds before she glanced over at Saint's preternaturally still figure.

"Have you told Saint these things?"

Kavya glanced at her with polite interest. "Do you think he'd be interested?"

Christina gave a sharp bark of disbelieving laughter. "Uh...*yeah*, I think he'd be interested. He and the other Sevliss princes wonder and speculate about the Magians. It's only natural."

Kavya nodded distractedly. "I am not trying to deprive him of anything, Christina. The formation of a soul is grueling work, and a solitary venture by necessity. It is not information about his origins that will help Saint in the process."

Her spine stiffened in anger. "How can you stand by and watch him suffer? He's your *son*."

"It's his suffering that brought him to this point. It hasn't been easy, but I have done what I must. You call him my son, and I suppose he is. Would you have had me deprive him of the chance for a soul?"

Christina bit her lower lip, scowling as she watched Aidan

run in the grass. Something elemental in her protested Kavya's harsh treatment of Saint, but given the same circumstances, would she do the same for Aidan? Would she have the strength to let him suffer so that he could gain the ultimate prize that a living being could possess?

She exhaled heavily.

"Thank you for not judging me too harshly, Christina."

She gave the Magian a hard glance. "I won't argue with you over what's done. But if forcing Saint to suffer more is in your future plans, forget it. I'm going to make sure he doesn't."

Kavya's sensual lips twitched. "Far be it from me to argue with you."

"So it's done then? The experiment is through?" Christina asked hopefully.

Disappointment flooded through her when Kavya shook his head. "Saint doesn't feel his soul, so what good is it? He denies a part of himself, fights with his dark nature...struggles to vanquish it instead of giving in, and allowing his soul to transform the shadow within. He still has one trial he must face, one more test before he can claim his full identity."

"Teslar," Christina whispered through a throat that had suddenly gone dry. Perhaps Kavya sensed her fear and uncertainty, because he turned and met her eyes.

"Teslar and all the princes' clones were a necessary evil, Christina. Until Saint accepts the dark aspects of his nature that Teslar represents, he will not be able to conquer his clone. He will not win his soul. This is a great secret. One that I'm asking you not to reveal until you judge the moment has come."

Her brow crinkled in confusion. "I can't reveal anything when I don't know what the hell you mean."

He gave her a kind smile. "I have faith in you. I have no

doubt that both you and Saint will do what needs to be done when the time arrives."

She shook her head, suddenly feeling overwhelmed. "I'm just a human, Kavya, a single mom who can't even afford to buy a car, let alone the home my son deserves. You put too much faith in me."

"No," he said simply. Christina started in amazement when Kavya held up his forefinger, his brilliant blue eyes—so like Saint's—seeming to send a shock of awareness through her. "You carry magic, Christina. You are the sacred crucible in which the transformation can occur. Remember this."

Christina just stared, her mouth hanging open in astonishment.

Chapter Twenty

Saint crept silently through the grass. A dove trilled softly in the darkness, sending a shiver of anticipation down his spine. Isi never turned toward him as he approached, but Saint knew that the Iniskium warrior sensed him.

Saint had spent the afternoon tracking in the tunnels with Strix, Bena, and Avadar. There had been no sign of the Scourge, however, and Saint knew that Teslar had dragged his army deep, forbidding them to emerge while Teslar still felt Saint's breath warming his back. Saint had assigned a majority of the Iniskium to guard the crystal chamber, knowing they could defend it with relative ease, given the fact there were only two narrow openings.

He would return again tonight, knowing that Teslar's control of the Scourge would run thin when it came time to feed. Teslar's own control would begin to crack, much as his clone would hate to admit it. Perhaps they would catch a whiff of Scourge stench and follow one of them to their new hideout.

He'd paused in the crystal chamber before leaving the tunnels, absorbing the earth's powerful energies. He knew he needed nourishment before he next saw Christina.

"How long has she been out here?" he asked Isi quietly.

"Twenty minutes or so. She is restless."

Isi's eyes gleamed in the darkness, and Saint understood

that Christina's restlessness had affected the Iniskium warrior. Saint growled softly in warning. It was a purely instinctual reaction, and Isi didn't seem offended as he averted his gaze. How could a virile young wolf not be affected by Christina's powerful vitessence and the pheromones thickening the night air?

Saint felt that same energy; he pulsed with it as he tracked Christina with his gaze. She stood from the steps of the gazebo and began to walk, occasionally reaching out and touching her fingers to the lilac blooms that surrounded the structure.

"Aidan?" Saint asked, his acute night vision focused on Christina's fingertips on the lush petals...wishing it were his skin she touched. A ripple of sensation went through him as if she'd just whisked a caress down his spine.

"He fell asleep right after he ate his supper. Fardusk worked him hard today, but he says the young one did well." Saint felt the Iniskium's eyes on him in the darkness. "Fardusk says the boy has great strength. He says he is something new...different than the Iniskium. Different from you as well...but also alike."

"He is my son."

Saint didn't need to be staring at Isi's face in order to sense his shock. "But I thought—"

"I thought it was impossible as well. Nevertheless, Aidan *is* my son."

Saint hadn't been able to control the fierce emotion that surged through him as he said the words. His voice shook with it. Isi's head swung around and they both stared at Christina as she disappeared behind the gazebo.

"Thank you for watching her, Isi."

He glanced over at the Iniskium when he remained in place, despite Saint's telepathic hint to depart.

196

"I should keep guard," Isi said.

Saint knitted his brows together. "Why? What have you discovered?"

Isi scowled. "Nothing of significance. But something doesn't feel right."

"Does this have to do with Alison?" Saint asked.

"I don't trust her."

"Are you sure it isn't yourself you don't trust?"

The moonlight revealed the flush on Isi's high cheekbones. For a few seconds, Saint thought he wasn't going to respond.

"I don't trust either one of us, to be honest," Isi finally admitted huskily.

Saint gave him a sidelong look. "I'm not sure if I trust Alison either. But she possesses a certain strength we can't deny. I like her, despite myself. And I *do* trust you, Isi. Why don't you keep an eye on Alison?"

Isi took a deep breath, seemingly braced by Saint's words. He melted into the darkness.

The white of Christina's T-shirt caught his eye as she came around the opposite end of the gazebo. Saint stood there, flames of sensation licking softly at his sensitive skin. He inhaled the scent of Christina on the night air. Her fragrance mingled with the odors of fresh earth, lilacs, and the lake in the distance.

His hunger mounted with each passing second until it tightened every muscle in his body. Blood surged into his cock, thickening it...making him ache.

She was his mate. And he hadn't even known it because he hadn't believed he was capable of making such a bond. The wolves formed such ties, but Saint had never fully claimed that part of his genetic heritage, believing himself to be an unnatural creature.

An abomination.

His whole universe had been turned upside down last night when Kavya telepathically told him Aidan was his son. That truth dismantled his old world, but it also made him feel a new rightness, despite his disorientation.

He wasn't an abomination. How could something so godless have helped create something as wonderful as Aidan?

Saint was still struggling to navigate around this entirely new, incomprehensible world, still spinning. Everything had changed, but he suddenly knew one thing for fact. It became the pillar that stabilized his new existence.

Christina was his.

A primal surge of possession went through him. He'd felt it many times before, but quickly learned to dampen the dangerous emotion, shamed by it, not feeling he had a right to it.

Because of his acute night vision, he could see her as clearly at night as he could during the day. She wore her thick, silky hair loose, spilling around her shoulders. Her cheeks were flushed with heat. Her flesh smelled of sweet perspiration and arousal, the scent so thick, he could practically taste her essence on his tongue, even from this distance.

The sure knowledge that she wanted him in that moment as much as he did her made his cock jerk in his jeans.

Her T-shirt was tight. She wore a modest bra, but Christina possessed the kind of nipples that refused to be shielded by cloth. The stiffened crowns pressed against the bra and the shirt, beckoning him as surely as the earth's sublime song. He wondered if they were unintentionally sharing thoughts and sensations, because suddenly she reached up and ran her fingertips over one nipple, lightly pinching it.

A snarl shaped his lips.

He moved silently in the darkness, a hunter closing in on its prey. She started to cry out when he reached for her, but he had already covered her mouth with his hand, trapping her scream. He pressed her to him, her back to his front, making no secret of his flagrant arousal.

He felt a shiver ripple through her. She leaned her head back on his chest and tilted her chin to look up at him, her green eyes wide in her delicate face. He slowly lowered his hand, caressing her neck. Her vitessence popped and sparked, a rich rainbow of color surrounding her. He opened his lips and tasted her richness on the air he breathed. He bathed in it when he gently lifted her jaw, stretching her exquisite neck, and kissed her throbbing pulse.

"I may not be solely a wolf, but I have studied their ways. If we bred together, then you are my mate," he breathed out next to her ear, animal lust making his voice harsh.

"Prove it," she whispered.

His nostrils flared when he sensed the sharp spike of arousal in her vitessence. His fangs distended, the sensation as agonizingly pleasurable as the tightening of an erection so thick it felt ponderous. He spun her in his arms and pressed her to him tightly, snarling at the sensation of her nipples pressing against his ribs.

"You want proof?"

"Yes," she replied between uneven pants.

"Then you'll have it," he growled ominously.

Her lush, parted lips sent him into a frenzy of lust, as if her mouth were an exposed sex organ. He palmed her ass and bent his knees before he fell on her, savaging the honeyed cavern behind her lips. She participated eagerly, tangling with his striking tongue, but it was a consumption as much as a kiss, and it was Saint who consumed, suckling her essence, swallowing Christina down his throat until he felt her essence zipping through his veins, bringing his flesh to vibrant life.

She flicked her tongue over the front of an incisor, a quick, precise tease, and he thought he'd explode then and there.

He moved, only vaguely aware that he wanted something solid behind them, so enraptured was he with burying himself in Christina's taste. She gave a soft *umph* of surprise when he backed her into a thick tree trunk. He softened his kiss by way of apology, but within seconds the madness struck his brain again. He slid his hands behind her thighs and lifted her off the ground, pressing her pussy against his straining cock.

He raised his head and hissed.

Her eyes went wide as she looked up at him, and for a brief second, what she saw flashed into his brain. The moonlight cast his rigid features in bluish light and black shadow. His fangs flashed white and lethal in the darkness.

She gasped and laid her head back on the bark of the tree, exposing her throat. He understood her reaction had come from arousal at the breaking point.

Not fear.

He leaned down and scraped his fangs gently over her madly throbbing pulse, the moment sublime.

When he sunk his teeth into Christina, it was like a velvet cataclysm—an explosion of sensation contained within the softest embrace. The sure knowledge that he would never harm her because he knew love—because he *could* love—flowed through him, an elixir as sweet as Christina's vitessence-rich blood. He heard her sharp inhale, felt her body stiffen against him as pleasure infused them both.

For once, he embraced his pounding lust instead of fighting it.

She made a sound of protest when he withdrew his fangs, the sensation even more exquisite than when he'd sunk into her. His eyes rolled back into his head. He muttered an ancient curse and set her feet back on the ground.

"Take off your pants," he ordered tersely. Stepping away from her at that moment was a pain that made him grit his teeth.

The rapidity of her compliance told him she was just as eager as he was. He tore at his button flies and shoved his jeans down his thighs. His gaze remained fixed on Christina as she worked her jeans down her long, pale legs, jerking her white canvas tennis shoes through the leg holes. When she slid her fingers between her skin and the white panties she wore, he spoke harshly.

"No. Take them off slowly."

She glanced up at him in the moonlight, but he kept his gaze glued to the apex of her thighs. He moved his hand along the underside of the shaft of his cock, shivering at even that light touch. His cock felt huge, heavier than he'd ever known, super-sensitive and teeming with hot blood. His balls were already tight and filled with a seed that felt like it would be released at jet-fueled force.

He lifted his testicles, grimacing as he rearranged them over the leather thong, his eyes glued to Christina's progress all the while. He paused in soothing his aching balls when her sex-lips peeked at him from above white cotton.

"Gods," he groaned. His hand tightened on the swollen base of his pulsing shaft. "You shaved."

"I thought you'd like it," she said softly. She pushed her panties down her thighs and they slipped down her legs to her ankles. She stepped out of them and for a moment just stood still in the moonlight, wearing only her white T-shirt and tennis shoes.

Saint realized that he was staring fixedly at the flushed, glistening folds of her labia while he ran his hand up and down the thick shaft of his cock. She was so aroused that he glimpsed her pink clit swelling between her sex lips. Her pussy-scent pervaded him, fogging the edges of his vision with a red haze of lust. He wanted to eat that flagrantly displayed treat, but he knew his arousal was such that if he didn't bury himself in her soon, he'd be howling at the moon in sheer madness.

He dragged his gaze from that awesome sight and met her stare. "I like it so much that you're going to have to pay. I've never dared to allow myself to feel so much need. I'm going to have to fuck your little pussy hard."

He sensed more than saw how her cheeks flushed with blood, just as the sleek, velvety flower of her sex heated and wetted for him.

He came toward her, both of them gasping when the sensitive crown of his jutting cock brushed against the silk of her thigh. He shrugged out of his shirt and placed it behind her, covering her back and shoulders, protecting her soft skin.

She moaned in excitement when he lifted her and pressed her against the tree, spreading her thighs. He shut his eyes and groaned deep enough to score his throat when he pushed the flared head of his cock into her tight, sultry heat.

He lifted his head and met her gaze.

"Let me in, lovely."

He felt her vaginal muscles convulse around him, sucking at him like a hot little mouth.

"Fuck," he muttered before he drove higher into her, both of them gasping as he sunk several inches.

"I feel huge," he mumbled under his breath.

"You *are* huge."

He glanced at her and saw her small smile. He caught her trembling lower lip between his teeth and bit. Softly. Her blood whispered across his tongue, maddening him. He growled and spread her thighs wider, opening her to him. She wrapped her legs around his waist and her flesh gave.

She cried out, the poignant sound prey makes at the death strike, the soulful sound of a lover claimed. He paused with his balls pressed tight against her, his heart threatening to burst out of his chest he felt so much. He sunk his tongue between her lips and the ravenous urge softened. A little. The protesting ache of his cock made his eyes burn unbearably.

His flimsy restraint evaporated when she nipped roughly at his lips.

"Take me hard or kill me now, Saint."

He blinked open his eyes, surprised. She stared back at him, her blood-red lips parted, her gaze fierce and hot. He snarled and drew his length out of her until only the rim beneath his cockhead was buried in her heat.

Then he drove back into her so hard his balls flung forward against her damp tissues. He held her ass in his hands and jerked her slightly forward as he thrust, flexing his biceps hard, crashing them together, letting his arms take the brunt of his hammering cock and not her back against the tree.

His thighs and ass strained tight as he repeated that long, consuming stroke again and again, rocketing into Christina while she clung onto him as if for dear life. A low, continuous keen of pleasure began to vibrate in her throat, the sound skipping abruptly every time he smacked their flesh together. He gritted his teeth in agony when she gripped him tighter around the waist and firmed her hold on his shoulders, adding her own strength to their frenzied mating.

Strange little detonations of sensation that he'd never experienced before began to leap up the nerves of his back every time he slammed into her consuming heat, traveling from the root of his cock and shooting up his spine in sexually charged electrical bursts. He growled, fangs bared at the untenably exciting sensation.

"I'm gonna explode inside you. I can't stop myself. It's gonna hurt like hell, it'll feel so good," he rasped.

"*Yes*," she replied in a pressurized hiss. He drove into her, hard and deep, the sensitive spot of skin just beneath the rim of his cock stroking her tight walls in such an eye-crossing way that he groaned and pushed higher. When he felt her clasping pussy start to spasm around him, he sank his teeth into the succulent flesh where her shoulder and neck joined. He sucked and plunged deep with his cock...

...and completely lost himself in a torrential rush of pleasure.

Chapter Twenty-one

She cried out, her head thumping against the tree as waves of pleasure shuddered through her. Saint sunk his teeth into her shoulder and she opened her eyes wide on a different universe.

His groan, guttural and harsh, brought her back to herself with a slam. His cock jerked in her pussy. He throbbed inside her as he continued to fuck her with short, demanding strokes, and pleasure continued to wrack her flesh.

His body convulsed in agonized bliss. She cried out in awe at the sensation of his warm seed filling her.

*Over*filling her.

He thrust again and again, continuing to climax. She felt like the A-bomb had just gone off in her.

And she'd been able to contain it.

Her own delicious orgasm waned, but Saint continued to fuck her hard, grunting gutturally, his cock still full and huge. Much to her amazement, she still felt the spasms of his penis, his facial muscles still convulsed in ecstasy.

He was still ejaculating inside her.

The realization of the profundity of his need did something strange to her. She tightened her vaginal muscles around him and ground down with her hips, getting pressure from his thick shaft on her clit. A cry broke out of her throat when she came again. His harsh hiss told her that he felt her climaxing around him. He gave an agonized growl as her pussy finally squeezed out his last drops.

For a stretched, full moment they ran their lips over each other's skin, panting harshly. A cool breeze made the oak leaves shiver around them, but Christina still felt the fever beneath Saint's skin.

She felt his warm tongue on her skin and realized he was licking the small puncture wounds his teeth had made. Some instinct told her his saliva had a healing quality. Maybe she knew that because she innately recognized the cleanness of his taste...the *rightness* of it.

"I'm going to have to have you again in a moment," he rasped with his lips next to her pulse.

She shuddered slightly at his words and the memory of the pleasure that had swamped her when he'd sunk his teeth into her flesh, merging with her in a way that was just as intimate as their joined sexes. He must have felt her internal clutch on his cock, because he raised his head. His eyes were shadowed, but she sensed his stare.

"My cock is so sensitive. It felt like I'd never had a woman before."

She gave him a smile. "It kinda felt that way to me too. And I loved it."

"Stina," he groaned. He seized her lips, kissing her swift and rough. Her pussy throbbed with renewed desire. It felt incredibly exciting to cradle his full, firm cock, knowing how sensitive he was...anticipating the moment he was ready to take her again. She caught the glitter in his eyes when he lifted his head and knew that moment was very near.

"Do you forgive me?" he whispered.

"For making love to me that day so many years ago? In the park?"

He nodded.

"There's nothing to forgive. This..." she flexed her vaginal muscles around him, "...is as natural and right as the dawn."

His lips formed a small snarl at her caress. He exhaled slowly. Christina felt the tension growing in his muscles and the throb of his cock deep inside her and knew another moment of blinding bliss was even nearer. She shivered in anticipation.

"And what of the other?" he asked harshly.

"The fact that you left me on that same day? Denied this?" She squeezed him tightly yet again. His fangs gleamed in the moonlight.

"Yes."

"That might take a little longer to forgive."

She leaned up and lightly licked a sharp incisor. He trembled and his cock leapt inside her. He nipped at her lower lip when she tried to lick him again. She laughed huskily. "I'll let you know when you've made up for all those years I might have had the pleasure of your company, Saint. You have some serious work to do before then. Better get to it."

The low growl that hummed in his throat and his consuming kiss made tingling heat surge through her sex. He whispered next to her lips, "I'm so primed, I think I'll go a long way in making a good dent in all those years in one night."

She yelped when he slid out of her and pushed her legs down until her feet hit the ground. The feeling of his warm, big hands on her skin as he slid her T-shirt up her torso made her nipples prickle in awareness. He removed her bra in the time it took her to blink and gasp. The next thing she knew, he had turned her toward the tree.

"Bend over," he ordered gruffly.

Christina was highly aware of his big hands possessively cradling her hips as she bent at the waist and pressed her palms on the tree. What he did next took her by surprise.

Blissful surprise.

He leaned down and began to scrape his teeth over the skin on her back. He progressed with agonizing slowness. She cried out at the intensity of pleasure that shivered through her flesh, as though his teeth were capable of awakening nerves in her body she hadn't known she possessed. She gasped and moaned, but he just continued to awaken her body with a precise deliberation.

He dragged his teeth across her, sensitizing every patch of skin, pausing occasionally to gently bite at the tender flesh of her hip or to taste her with his warm tongue. If his scraping teeth were gentle, his hands were bold and greedy. He molded the flesh of her hips and buttocks into his palms, shaping it beneath his hungry mouth. He bracketed her waist, holding her in place as he knelt behind her and ran his fangs over the tender flesh of her bare ass.

Her nipples tightened almost painfully at the intimate caress. Her clit pinched in pleasure, causing her to cry out.

"*Saint.*" Christina didn't know how it could be, but if he continued to run his teeth over her tingling skin, she would be cresting in climax. He responded to her shaky plea by pressing a kiss between the cheeks of her ass and rising behind her. She moaned when she felt the heat emanating from his groin onto her bare bottom.

He moved his large, warm hands upwards, the slide of his slightly rough palms against the hypersensitive skin at the side of her body making her tremble. She felt vulnerable bent over like this, naked and raw with need.

But Saint's caressing hands and sinful mouth also made her feel exquisitely prized.

And totally possessed.

She'd been panting, but her breath burned, stuck in her lungs when his hands crept toward her suspended breasts. The thought of him touching her nipples—of him running his fangs over that most tender of flesh—caused a flash of liquid heat to surge through her sex.

"I know what you're thinking."

His roughly uttered words caused the air to explode out of her lungs. He placed his hands on her hips and lifted, spinning her in a fluid movement. One large hand palmed a breast as he pushed her over a supporting forearm, forcing her back into an arch. She sensed his palpable stare on her.

"You have the most beautiful breasts I've ever seen...and I've lived a long, long life," he muttered.

He lowered his head. She felt his warm breath ghosting her skin. Her eyes went wide in shock when he scraped his fangs over the curving underside of a breast.

He put his hand over her mouth a split second before a scream erupted from her throat. He kept her mouth covered as he continued to pleasure her and she keened into his muffling palm.

Obviously, Saint had learned long ago what to expect in these circumstances.

Dear God, she'd had no idea he could evoke such a cataclysm of sensation inside a woman's body. By the time he slipped an aching nipple inside his warm, suctioning mouth and lashed at the captive flesh with his tongue, Christina's entire body shook.

He ran his fangs ever so gently over a beaded nipple. She

clutched at his soft, tousled hair and climaxed.

"That's right. Come for me. Feed me, lovely," she heard him rasp as if from a distance, his lips moving next to the skin of her neck. She felt his teeth sink into her, the sensation causing her orgasm to ratchet up to a level that she checked out for a few seconds, consumed by bliss.

"Stina."

She blinked her eyes open sluggishly when his rough voice penetrated her sensual haze.

"Brace yourself against the tree. You've had your pleasure. Now I will take mine."

Christina realized he'd turned her. He bent at the knees and pressed the front of his naked body to the back of hers. The raw need roughening his voice and the sensation of his hot, teeming cock pressing into the crevice of her ass cheeks made her comply without thought.

He must have sensed her disorientation following her orgasm, because he helped her to position herself, assuring himself that her palms held her secure against the trunk, encouraging her to spread her thighs to accommodate him. Christina stared blindly at the tree bark, every last ounce of her focus on the feeling of Saint behind her...on the sensation of his cock pressed into the flesh of her ass.

He moved and she knew he'd taken his cock into his hand, preparing to enter her. Christina shivered like the canopy of the leaves of the oak tree above her when another breeze swept over her heated skin. But she wasn't cold. She steamed when she felt Saint press the succulent, fat head of his penis into the mouth of her pussy.

He placed his hand at the small of her back and pushed down softly.

"Bend over more," he rasped, his lust-thick voice increasing her trembling.

She complied, sending her tailbone higher. He softly caressed her ass, the gesture striking her as delicious.

"And Stina?"

"Yes?"

"I'm going to ride you hard. Brace yourself."

He separated her ass cheeks and held her in a strong grip. Her mouth dropped open as he slowly sank into her pussy, forcing her soft flesh to give way to his steely length. He pumped, firm but gentle, working his thick shaft into her tight sheath farther and farther with each pass. His low growl as he carved his way into her flesh was like the rumble of the earth before a volcanic explosion.

He paused when he was submerged mid-staff and firmed his hold on her buttocks, squeezing them in a manner that sent a jolt of excitement through her pussy.

"You'd never believe me if I told you how many times I fantasized about taking you just like this." His voice ran through her like a current of energy; it vibrated, not just with emotion, but with the effort of restraint, she realized. "Fucking you here, your scent mixing with the trees and the grass, the moonlight on your naked skin."

"I'm yours to take, Saint. I always have been."

He made a choking sound. A thrill went through her when he tightened his hold on her ass. He sank his cock into her, making her gasp.

He'd been right to warn her to brace herself. He fucked her deep and thoroughly, grunting in primal satisfaction every time he smacked their flesh together. For several sensation-infused moments, her voice box seemed to lock up. Her mouth hung open as he crashed into her, causing a nearly unbearable friction deep inside her body.

Her consciousness narrowed until she swam in a haze of throbbing sensation and jaw-tightening pressure. It was too much, so she couldn't understand why she hissed for him to fuck her harder...daring him to take what was his...taunting him, even. He drove into her, a primed, well-lubricated piston, his actions so relentless and precise that Christina knew he'd accepted her challenge.

Reveled in it.

He gave himself in the way she'd always dreamed he would—no holds barred and without a shred of doubt or constraint. She groaned when she felt his cock jerk inside her and heard his guttural groan. She hovered on the crest of her own climax. He suddenly smacked her ass twice with his palm, brisk and demanding. The unexpected bursts of sensation sent her right over the edge.

He lifted her upper body, dipping his knees and pressing her back into his chest. He buried his face in the juncture of her neck and shoulder and held her tight. His cock throbbed as he continued to shoot his seed deep inside her.

Christina knew she'd never forget the sound Saint made against her skin at that moment. His cry was anguished and blissful at once, the sound of a lost, suffering soul finally coming home.

Chapter Twenty-two

Dawn peeked around the corners of the drapery, casting the bedroom in gray shadows. The silence hung thick and heavy, interrupted only by Saint's low growls of pleasure and the wet sounds Christina made as she took him in her mouth, her movements growing faster and more forceful with each passing second.

Christina had refused to sleep far away from Aidan that night. Not that Saint and she had ever slept...but still. Saint was so energized, not only by the crystal chamber, but also by Christina's powerful vitessence, that he didn't need to sleep in the depths of the earth to revitalize himself. They'd chosen a guest bedroom down the hall from Aidan and proceeded to ravish each other all night long.

His fingers laced through Christina's hair, holding it off her face. He leaned against the pillows, his breath hissing past his lips, his gaze glued to the erotic sight of his cock sliding between Christina's lips. Their minds were exquisitely joined at that moment. He cupped her head gently, knowing she was aroused by the gesture...the subtle hint that he could command her motions if he chose.

His sexual stamina was much greater than the typical human male's, but he'd never guessed at the furthest limits of it until he'd spent a night of unrestrained passion with Christina.

He'd lost track of the number of times they'd made love. He wouldn't have guessed he could become so aroused after drowning in her time and time again, but here he was...

Stiff enough to hammer nails with his cock.

Ripples of pure pleasure went through him at every slide of her firm lips and flick of her quick tongue. She'd quickly learned his sweet spot—a quarter-sized patch of skin on the underside of his cock just beneath the rim. She liked to torture him by giving it a good, hard tongue polishing, making him growl in mixed gratification and warning. Her strong, steady suction told him loud and clear how hungry she was. He massaged her skull in tiny circular motions and spoke to her while she sucked him.

"Such a hot, little mouth. If you had any idea what I want to do to it, you might not be so eager."

Her low, sexy moan vibrated into his cock.

He smiled as she took him deeper, her lips stretching wide around the thick shaft.

"You'd like it, wouldn't you, lovely?"

His cock twitched as she nodded.

A jolt of awareness went through him and he groaned. She glanced up, her shiny green eyes asking a question.

"Aidan just woke up," he muttered. She lifted her head and his cock slid out of her mouth. It fell to his belly with a wet whapping sound. He grimaced at the pain of deprivation. He stopped himself from ordering her to put his cock back in her warm, wet heat immediately.

"Tell him to go back to sleep." He ground his back teeth together at the sound of her voice. It was rough and indescribably sexy from taking his cock so deep.

"What's that supposed to mean?" he rasped, his gaze fixed

on her puffy, reddened lips. He'd ravaged them again and again throughout the night. He couldn't concentrate for thinking about doing it again right that second.

"Use that mind thing you do." She frowned at him when he just stared at her, his brow furrowed. "You're a parent, Saint. Now isn't the time to get all ethical over mind control."

He gave her a wry look. "Fardusk and Kavya say Aidan's strength may one day surpass mine."

"That day isn't today though, Saint." He tensed when she blew softly on his damp erection. The base of his spine tingled with pleasure. "Now, tell your son to go back to sleep. He needs the rest," she proclaimed before she grabbed the base of his cock, lifting it like a tent-pole off his body.

Something feral and hot flared in his chest when he saw her open her lips. He did what she'd suggested in a flash of potent ascendancy, sending Aidan contentedly back to his dreams.

Christina cried out when he grabbed her shoulders and flipped her onto her back, her head bouncing off the stacked pillows. She paused in surprised laughter when she glanced at his face.

She watched him, her green eyes wide as he straddled her and inched his knees forward until they pressed into the juncture of her arms and torso. He held her stare as he placed his hands on the headboard and leaned over her, the head of his cock brushing against her moist lips. They parted hungrily. He transferred his hand to her nape, restraining her from leaning forward and sucking him by gently fisting her hair.

"You're done with teasing. I'll fuck your lovely mouth now. Part your lips. Just a little," he informed her gruffly when she started to open wide to accommodate him. "My cock will stretch them." He couldn't help but smile when he drove between her red lips, demonstrating his point, and her eyes went even wider.

He paused with several inches of throbbing penis penetrating her sultry mouth. He firmed his hold on her hair and adjusted his body, getting just the right angle.

She began to make a low, humming sound when he began to fuck her mouth shallowly, refusing to let her move. It drove him crazy that sound, the tiny vibrations emanating into his plunging cock. He studied her face intently for signs of discomfort, but he needn't have. They were so connected that he easily sensed her profound arousal.

"You like this, don't you?" he rasped as he plunged his cock deeper, and then withdrew along her wet tongue until only the head was in her mouth. She rubbed her tongue over his sweet spot briskly, but he drove into her again, stretching her lips. It felt delicious, and since he wasn't touching the back of her throat, he made free with her, thrusting fast and furious, pumping into her wet heat.

"Answer me, Christina," he demanded thickly. "You like being used for my pleasure. You enjoy letting me fuck your sweet mouth."

She nodded as she stared up at him. Her cheeks hollowed out as she sucked him hard.

"Ahhh," he grimaced in pleasure and pushed farther into her mouth. When he felt the narrow opening of her throat grip at the tip of his cock, he withdrew. She was ready for him when he thrust again, breathing through her nose.

He held onto his restraint carefully while he took her deep. When he couldn't stand it anymore, he held onto the headboard with both hands and fucked her mouth, shallow and fast, plunging into her again and again. He opened his eyes just before orgasm slammed into him, the sight of her wide-eyed stare and spread lips triggering his release.

He continued to fuck her face as he exploded in her mouth. When his intense shudders of pleasure waned, he wrapped his hand around his hypersensitive cock and withdrew it until only the tip rested between her lips. He trembled as he pumped himself and poured his last drops of semen on her beautiful, parted lips. When her tongue came out, quick and furtive, cleaning his come, he groaned and came down over her, belly to belly.

"Stina. What you do to me." He apologized to her telepathically when he sunk his head and ravaged her mouth yet again.

"I'll never get enough of you."

"I go a long way, Saint," he heard her say in his mind.

A smile shaped his ravishing mouth. *"I noticed."*

A minute later, he rested his head on the pillow next to Christina while both of their hearts slowed. A wave of sleepiness struck him, but he resisted its pull. He turned a topic over in his mind, examining it from all angles.

"Do you really think I can be a father to Aidan?"

"Yes," Christina whispered, her breath tickling his cheek.

He turned his head. She watched him in the dim light.

"How can you be so sure?"

"He already loves you. Just spend time with him, like you always have. The rest will come of its own accord. It can't be forced," she replied in a hushed tone.

"So...we'll tell him then?"

Christina sighed and caressed his perspiration-slick shoulder with gentle fingertips. "Let Aidan accustom to this new change in his life first. Then we'll tell him." She met his gaze. "We'll tell him soon, Saint. I promise."

He nodded, accepting. When she noticed how he continued

to study her face, she gave a small grin.

"Why are you looking at me like that?"

"I took from you often this night. Are you well?"

Her smile was radiant. "I have never felt better in my life."

He shook his head in wonderment. "I would never have dreamed it was possible. It must be the crystal chamber that made it so. Or perhaps it's you—the miracle of your strength."

She laced her fingers through the perspiration-damp hair at his nape and rubbed his scalp. Her tender gesture nearly undid him at that moment, for some strange reason.

"I am not the miracle, Saint," Christina whispered before she took his head in both of her hands and drew him down to her breast.

He slept more soundly for the next few hours than he ever had in his life.

Chapter Twenty-three

Fardusk stood beneath the shade of a maple tree and watched the impromptu baseball game, his stony features never shifting except for once, when he'd bellowed for Aidan to "move, young-un," after Aidan had stood staring at the high fly-ball he'd just hit off Alison's pitch.

The ball hit the roof of the gazebo and rolled down toward a quickly approaching Isi. Aidan traveled around the bases as fast as a long-legged gazelle with a leopard on its heels, but Isi"s rapid, supernaturally precise throw to Alison, who now stood at home plate, beat Aidan by a whisper"s breath.

"You're out!" Fardusk shouted.

After Kavya had departed earlier, the Iniskium chief had suddenly proclaimed that they would have a game of baseball. Christina suspected he thought Aidan had trained long enough learning about his wolf-self today, and thought the boy deserved a break.

But there was more to Fardusk's seemingly casual decision, Christina realized as she blinked the dipping sun out of her eyes. Playing on the same team as Saint and Aidan was a fun, relaxing way for them to bond under the unusual circumstances of them learning about Aidan's parentage. It was as if Fardusk somehow knew that, although Aidan, Christina and Saint often fooled around playing baseball in Whitby's yard, they were always divided into separate teams.

But not this evening.

Fardusk moved way up in Christina's estimation. There must have been good reason for him to have been named chief of the Iniskium so many centuries before.

Aidan groaned and kicked at the rubber home plate in frustration at being called out. He gave Saint a sheepish grin when Saint cuffed his head gently, urging him to let go of his anger.

Alison removed Aidan's mitt and shook her right hand, her mouth hanging open in a wince. Her scowl at Isi when he approached thinly disguised a grin. "You frickin' made my hand go numb, you spaz."

Isi's smile flashed white in his dark face. He flexed his biceps beneath the arms of his short-sleeved T-shirt, pointing at the bulging muscle. "That ripped piece of flesh is why your hand went numb. I'm actually impressed you didn't drop it, tasty morsel."

Alison rolled her eyes. "Yeah, not to mention the fact that you're some kind of paranormal freak. And quit calling me that stupid name."

Christina glanced at Saint before she walked out into the yard to pitch.

"Isi hasn't bitten Alison, Stina. Even if he had, the Iniskium are very cautious in the way they take blood. They respect life. Isi's calling Alison tasty *for a much more mundane reason."* Christina blinked when she heard Saint's dry sarcasm resounding in her brain. Saint had obviously also noticed Isi had switched *tiny* for *tasty* in his pet name for Alison.

She threw him a dark glance. When she saw the slight quirk of his handsome mouth, she hid her own smile. She left Saint to do the catching—Alison had complained that Saint's pitches were too fast to even see, let alone hit—and joined Aidan in the yard.

She wasn't sure how she felt about the news that the young couple had a thing for each other. Alison was here because of Christina after all. She was responsible for the young woman's safety until something was done to ensure her security from Teslar. Surely keeping Alison out of trouble didn't involve her getting mixed up with a wolf-shifter who possessed various supernatural powers?

You're not only in love with a similar creature, but your son is one as well, she reminded herself as she took her position on their ad-hoc pitcher's mound. The thought landed like a small blow on her chest. She had to force herself to inhale, slightly unsettled by the new reality of her life.

Besides, Isi was actually ancient, not young, she tried to reassure herself as she studied him while she prepared to pitch to Alison. Although he seemed precisely like a typical, good-looking young man at that moment, strutting around for an attractive female with backyard bravado.

At least, Isi seemed like that when he wasn't glancing at Alison with a narrow-eyed gaze. It occurred rarely enough, but Christina had observed those dark glances and sensed the accompanying brooding emotions emanating from Isi enough times to know his feelings toward Alison were far from simple.

Come to think of it, she saw Saint occasionally watching Alison with that precise same expression on his face.

She became distracted by the sight of Alison picking up the bat.

"You got any heat, tasty?" Isi needled the young woman.

Alison returned Isi's cocky grin in like measure.

"I played on a championship girl's softball team in high school." Alison pointed the tip of the bat toward the tall hedge of bushes that lined the east boundary of Whitby. "Right into the lake, wolf-boy."

Isi raised his dark eyebrows, his smirk letting Alison know he'd believe it when he saw it.

"Hey, Alison!" Aidan yelled from the outfield, running toward the position where he'd just seen her point the bat. "Not in the water, okay? I just got that ball!"

Alison laughed. "No worries, kid. I've got a very precise swing."

Christina threw her pitch. Her mouth fell open in disbelief when the girl smacked the ball in the exact direction where she'd predicted. Alison was halfway to first while the ball still arced high in the air. Christina laughed as she hurried to the outfield.

"To second, Aidan!" she called out to her son, who was running toward the far reaches of the yard, long, thin legs pumping, his eye never leaving the flying ball.

A sliver of anxiety cut through her sense of fun when Saint called out sharply as Aidan neared the tall hedges.

She realized too late what the boy planned. Aidan crashed through the hedge after the ball, his thin body squeezing through what looked like an impenetrable space. She knew there was nothing on the other side of the bushes but a small spit of sand and Lake Michigan. Those tall hedges represented the eastern-most boundary of Whitby, at least in Christina's mind.

And maybe, when it came to magic, a consensual belief that a certain thing consisted of a boundary was all that was required...

She ran past second base and kept going even as she heard Saint call out in his deep, ascendant-rich tone behind her, ordering Aidan to come back. With his supernatural speed, he was just ten feet behind her when she crashed through the tiny opening between the hedges. She was so concerned for Aidan's safety that she ignored the scraping branches on her face and bare limbs in addition to Saint's barking command for her to return.

What she saw on the other side of the hedge struck her like a physical blow. What happened next occurred so quickly, it later became a blur in her memory.

"*Aidan*," she screamed, but the thin body of her son remained unmoving in the arms of the tall, muscular, chestnut-haired male Christina had seen on the subway. He wore a long, thick, black leather coat and gloves, despite the summer sun.

Javier Ash.

Ash snarled at her like a rabid animal, exposing his fangs.

In the distant part of her brain, Christina saw that the Scourge revenant's pale, usually flawless cheek was mottled by a web-work of dark purple blood vessels. Aidan had left his mark on the monster before he'd been knocked unconscious. She remembered what Saint had said about her touch, how she'd felled the Scourge revenant without having any notion of her power.

She flew at Ash.

"Let go of my son," she seethed, fist cocked to strike.

Ash obviously recognized the threat of her. He leaned back, hissing as he avoided her fist. The abrupt movement caused him to slip in the sand. Christina took advantage of Ash's instability and snatched her son. She yanked until Aidan's body fell against her and spun, sensing that Saint was directly behind her.

Saint grabbed instinctively for Aidan's limp body when she shoved him in his arms. A large shadow fell over them. At the exact moment Christina released Aidan to his father, Ash hooked his leather-covered forearms beneath her armpits.

And she was being lifted, the ground soaring away from her at an alarming rate.

"*Saint*," she screamed, experiencing a moment of total disorientation as she rose through the air, flying when her feet had just been on the ground. She glanced back and up, shocked to see that she and Ash were clutched in the bony claws of a huge nightmare bird, the same bird Christina had seen take flight in the subway tunnel. The animal shape taken by—

"Teslar," Saint bellowed, his eyes blazing as he looked into the air above her. He handed Aidan to Fardusk, who had just raced onto the beach. Saint took a running start and leapt, his facial muscles rigid with fury and the great exertion of his impossibly high, flying jump. Christina reached for him—a beautiful, avenging angel—but Ash jerked her back against his body.

And her angel had no wings.

Saint's grasping fingertips brushed fleetingly against hers.

"Better luck next time, Saint," Ash taunted in a rough, snide voice.

Saint let out throat-ripping roar as he fell away from her. His wild, desperate gaze never left her face as he plummeted to the earth. Christina never looked away either. Not even when her struggles caused her to slip in Javier Ash's hold. The revenant cursed viciously and readjusted her, trapping her arms next to her body with his squeezing, steely embrace, forcing her into immobility.

Only when she could no longer see any of the small figures gathering on the beach, only the gray, choppy waters of Lake Michigan, did she look up again.

She saw the underbelly of the blood-red bird and a pair of

beating, leathery wings that encompassed a twenty-five-foot span when spread. The deadly bird—Teslar—dipped its head and pinned her for a moment with its blue-eyed stare.

Christina felt heat rise beneath her skin.

Chapter Twenty-four

Aidan lay in his bed in the coach house, his hand clutching Saint's tightly. A purple bruise had formed just beneath the skin on his right temple where Ash had struck him.

"Javier bashed him a good one, but he'll suffer no long-term damage," Fardusk proclaimed after he'd finished examining the boy.

"But what about Mom?" Aidan muttered, the wild concern in his aquamarine eyes cutting at Saint.

"I'm going to get your mother back. Don't worry about that," Saint stated grimly. He let go of Aidan's hand. "I have to go. You'll stay here with Fardusk."

The boy sat up abruptly, wincing when he jolted his injured head. Their eyes met in the dim room and Saint heard the boy's plea in his mind.

"No. You stay here, son," Saint said softly. Firmly.

He hadn't planned to say it. It'd just fallen out of his mouth in that tension-laden moment. He watched as Aidan's confused expression slowly morphed to one of radiant wonder.

Saint cleared his throat gruffly, more affected by the boy's open-mouthed, amazed stare than he ever would have dreamed. He stood next to the bed. "Your mother and I will explain when I bring her back."

"Do you *promise* you'll bring her back, Saint?" Aidan asked.

"Yes."

"Because it's my fault that Teslar took her," Aidan said, his voice cracking with misery.

"It's no one's fault but my own. And Teslar's," Saint declared. He glanced from Fardusk to the boy. Fardusk nodded almost imperceptibly, agreeing to guard Aidan with his life.

Saint exited the room.

There *was* one other person at fault, but Saint thought it was best not to bring that up to Aidan at the moment.

He stepped onto the front porch, already knowing who approached.

Isi stalked around the corner of the coach house, a fixed, furious expression on his face. He didn't bat an eyelash, despite the armful of kicking, screaming female he carried.

He tossed Alison down on one of the padded recliners so hard air whooshed out of her lungs.

Alison scurried into a sitting position. When she tried to stand from the recliner, Isi bared his fangs and hissed. She jerked back like she'd been burned.

"I found her sneaking through the woods toward the city. I saw Marcellus and Anthony Teethum waiting for her in a car on Sheridan Road," Isi reported furiously. His voice dropped. "You're the biggest little idiot I've ever laid eyes on. Don't you know they would have ripped you to shreds the moment they got you in that car?"

"Shows what you know!" Alison shouted. Tears wetted her pale cheeks as she gazed up at Isi with defiant, anxious, midnight blue eyes. Saint was reminded of a tiny, spitting kitten backed into a corner by a fierce wolf. At any other time, he might have felt a thread of compassion for the vulnerable young woman.

But her betrayal had put Christina in grave danger, and for that, he would not forgive easily.

"Move aside, Isi," he ordered quietly.

It must have been something in his tone that made Alison go entirely still. Her eyes grew enormous in her face when he stepped toward her.

"He...Teslar made me do it, Saint," she entreated in a whisper. "He talked to me...in my head. I *had* to do it."

Saint studied her for a moment, sifting through the young woman's chaotic emotions with his mind. His lip curled in disdain. Alison's tears flowed heavier down her face.

"You thought because you could communicate telepathically with Teslar, you were special. Special to Teslar. Special like Christina."

Alison's gaze skittered over to Isi. Her entire body sagged.

"You have a right to be ashamed," Saint accused. "Sacrificing a life just so you could feel like the special girl, the unique one." He was immune to her bitter tears. He turned up his ascendancy to full throttle, caring little about the discomfort it might cause the young woman. Her spine straightened and she winced. Tears flooded down her cheeks.

"Where did Teslar take her?"

"He...he never told me," she sobbed.

"Why would he?" Isi asked harshly. "Teslar had no use for you other than as a tool to flush Aidan and Christina out of Whitby's boundaries. As soon as your purpose had been served, you would have been dinner."

Alison's face crumpled in misery. "I'm sorry, Isi. I didn't want them to be hurt. Especially Aidan. But Teslar *made* me—"

"You *are* a rare-enough human, Alison," Saint interrupted.

"You actually do have the ability to fight off Teslar's ascendancy. You let Teslar into your mind consciously, because he made you feel special. You will let me in now because it's the right thing to do. Do you understand?"

Alison's wrenching sobs ceased when she gaped at Saint. She nodded once.

Saint plunged into Alison's memories with his mind, making sense of threads and sensations that were just meaningless fragments for her. It was something he rarely did, as it was an aggressive assault on the senses. But he had no choice.

He *had* to find Christina. It cut at him like a twisting blade in his belly to consider what Teslar had planned for her.

He heard Teslar's voice in Alison's memories, heard his clone speaking to her, and so much more. In the distance, he made out the sound of a boat's horn and a male voice speaking on a microphone. Saint strained and sensed Alison's discomfort as he made sense of what was mere sensory debris to the girl.

A moment later, he pulled himself out of Alison's mind, the sensation like peeling off his own skin. Both Alison and he panted in the aftermath of the mind-blend. It had been just as painful for Saint as it had been for her.

But worth it.

"I think I know where they are," Saint rasped.

"Where?" Isi asked tensely. Saint glanced at him, considering. He knew how much the Iniskium warrior wanted to slay Javier Ash, but Saint couldn't afford any mistakes on this mission.

Intense feelings of revenge were likely to cause mistakes.

Saint sighed heavily. He trusted Isi. "They're in the freight tunnels beneath lower Wacker Drive and the river. I didn't think

Teslar knew of that branch of tunnels, but apparently he's discovered them recently. I could hear one of the river tour boats in the far distance. You go to the crystal chamber and bring back the Iniskium. Leave all but a dozen behind in the chamber. That will be sufficient to guard it. I'll meet you in the freight tunnels. Gain access at the storage dock under the Fairview Hotel on lower Wacker Drive."

"Wait," Isi protested when Saint turned to depart. "You can't go into Teslar's den alone."

"You'll be there with the others shortly." He read Isi's unease at the plan.

"You know Teslar. I can't leave Christina there with him a minute longer than necessary."

"But...can Teslar even *touch* Christina?" Isi asked, and Saint recalled that Isi, Fardusk, and he had discussed the surprising development of the revenant not surviving Christina's touch.

"I'm not sure. Either way, he could drain her until she's a husk without touching her. Teslar is not a revenant. *I* can touch Christina, after all. And are Teslar and I not one and the same?"

Saint saw but chose to ignore the shiver of unease that went through Isi's muscular chest.

He turned, willfully entering Teslar's world, and embraced the night.

3.

Chapter Twenty-five

Christina lay on her side and watched as Teslar paced back and forth in front of her. The room where she found herself was surprisingly luxurious. Apparently, Teslar and the Scourge revenants lived like gypsies. They moved around frequently to avoid Saint and the Iniskium, but they carried Teslar's treasures around the tunnels of the underground. The dark, subterranean space had been decorated like a sheik's chamber for Teslar, with rare carpets covering the floors and walls. As well, a velvet couch, rich pillows, flame-lit brass and glass lanterns, several ornate mirrors, and gold-leafed ornaments were spread about the room.

If she weren't scared shitless, Christina would have laughed at the ludicrousness of Teslar's vanity.

She shifted on the carpet, testing her strength. Earlier, Ash had tried to force her down a metal ladder into the tunnels. He'd been clearly frustrated as to how to get her down the shaft without dropping her and so anxious about not touching her that he'd let down his guard. Christina had landed a thwacking punch to his temple.

Ash had howled in pain and knocked her reflexively with the back of his hand. She'd fallen down the thirty-foot shaft, hearing Teslar shout in anguish and fury. Just before she hit the hard earth, she felt hands enclose her shoulders. She'd been falling face-first into the hole. Whoever grabbed her had prevented her body from striking the base of the tunnel, but hadn't fully cushioned the blow to her head.

She must have blacked out for a period of time, because she'd awoken in the luxurious chamber to the sounds of Teslar cursing and the dull thuds of bone against flesh. The scene that greeted her had been an ugly one—Teslar punishing Ash for causing Christina harm, beating him about the face and head with vicious blows. It horrified her to see the way the powerful revenant kept standing and righting himself after each of Teslar's punches, patiently waiting for each blow, despite the snarl of pain and fury that shaped his bloody mouth.

Teslar must be using his ascendancy to turn his first lieutenant into a flesh and blood punching bag.

Her breath had frozen in her lungs when Teslar paused in his beating, his stare meeting hers across the room.

"Get out," Teslar bellowed at the bloody Ash. "You and all the others stay away from this chamber."

Ash stood from his kneeling position, swaying on his feet. When he'd steadied himself, he rushed out of the chamber, obviously concerned Teslar would change his mind. He lifted a hanging crimson, black and beige carpet to find the exit.

Christina had surveyed the chamber with her eyes, trying not to move and draw attention to herself as Teslar washed his hands in a golden bowl. Perhaps there was only the one entrance to the room, but there could conceivably be a tunnel or doorway behind any one of the hanging carpets.

She watched Teslar warily as he tossed down a towel and turned toward her. His blue eyes blazed as he pinned her with his stare. She didn't know what to make of the way he began to pace in front of her like an anxious, caged animal.

Christina couldn't help it. She was fascinated by his

singular male beauty. He wore only a pair of black leather pants that looked like they'd been tailor-made for his long legs and narrow hips. His bare feet padded across the carpet. His lean, muscular torso was a work of art, just like Saint's was. Smooth, golden skin covered rippling, sleek muscle. She couldn't keep her eyes off the narrow path of light brown hair that ran down his flat abdomen into low-riding, supple leather.

She forced her eyes away from the compelling sight and looked into his face.

"Saint will find me."

Teslar paused in his pacing and for a tense moment, just stared at her. If she had to describe the expression on his face, she would have called it *slain*. She pushed up slowly with her arms, cautious of her aching head, but also wary of Teslar's strange manner.

"You don't need Saint. I can make you love me, Christina," he said hoarsely.

She paused in pushing herself into a sitting position, not liking the feeling of lying on the floor while this dark angel towered over her.

"With your ascendancy, you mean?" Her voice sounded level, but her anxiety ratcheted up several levels at his threat. Saint had implied that she could throw off his ascendancy if she chose, but what if her ability to do so related to her and Saint's deep connection? What if what Teslar said was true?

She shivered.

"Is that what you want, Teslar? Another slave for your army? Another sex-doll for your couch?" she taunted, her mouth twisting into distaste.

"*No.*"

She paused, surprised by the passion in his deep voice. It

was impossible not to be affected by the pain and anguish she sensed exuding from him.

"Then why did you bring me here? To draw Saint into your trap so that you can kill him?"

Maybe she was an idiot, but Teslar looked genuinely confused by her questions. She felt pretty damned perplexed herself when he ran his hand through his lustrous, burnished hair, pulling at it as he grimaced in frustration.

"How can you ask why I brought you here? Don't you have any idea what you look like in my eyes?" he asked incredulously. He began to pace again, like a graceful, trapped beast. "You might as well ask why someone wants love."

"Please," Christina muttered sarcastically, forcing herself with difficulty not to be moved by Teslar's supposed anguish. The man could act, she'd give him that. "There are some words you should try to avoid altogether when you're on the stage, Teslar, and love is one of them. Really brings the audience out of the experience with a crash, if you know what I mean."

He stopped abruptly. She stilled an effort to cover her breasts when he glanced down with those hot, soulful eyes. Heat rose to the surface of her skin, but her nipples pulled tight beneath her T-shirt as though she were cold.

Her body's betraying reaction to a sociopathic killer infuriated her.

"I know what you're thinking," Teslar said quietly. His weighty stare returned to her face. "It's true that I hunt humans, Christina, but it's in my genetic make-up to do so. Not just mine, Saint's as well. We feed off humans, true. But in doing so, we're only acting out our nature. I don't suppose you blame a lion for its hunger for flesh?"

"No," Christina replied coldly. "But a lion is an animal, incapable of higher thought. You, on the other hand, know precisely what you're doing when you cultivate fear in your victims. You don't need to kill as you do. Saint has found a way to survive without resorting to murder."

His facial muscles clenched in pain and he resumed pacing again. A groan vibrated in his throat.

"It hurts when you say his name, Christina."

"Do you think I care if it hurts?" she demanded. She glanced around the chamber, her irritation rising as her fear diminished. She knew it was foolish not to be scared of Teslar, but his behavior reminded her more of an angst-ridden teenager than a crazed killer at that moment. "Why don't you let me go?"

His glance was beseeching. Christina swallowed, unable to break his stare. She suddenly became hyperaware of her body— of her throbbing heart, of the blood that rushed through her flesh. A hot, achy sensation pulsed between her thighs.

She blinked and looked away from Teslar's beautiful eyes.

"Stop it, you bastard."

She wished he'd move, wished he'd resume his agitated pacing. Instead, she saw from the corner of her eyes that he remained as still as a statue. She felt his gaze like a touch on her averted cheek.

"I'm not what you think," Teslar spoke quietly. "If you love Saint, then you must love me. Saint and I are part of the same whole, Stina."

She leapt up from the carpet. "Don't you *dare* call me that name. Do you hear me?"

His nostrils flared, but he said nothing. Slowly, he raised his hands. For the first time, Christina noticed that the palms were reddened. A few blisters had risen to the surface.

"I touched you. It didn't affect me like it does the Scourge revenants. It burned, but it was bliss unlike anything I'd ever known. I would sacrifice anything...my very life...to touch you again."

She swallowed thickly when she heard how his voice vibrated with emotion. It wasn't only Saint's voice that came to mind, it was Kavya's. Damn. It would be so much easier if Teslar were a simple, animalistic killer instead of the complex, dangerous creature he was.

She nodded at his reddened palms.

"I still harmed you. If you can't touch me, what do you want from me?" she demanded through clenched teeth.

"To look upon you would be sufficient, I think."

Christina rolled her eyes, breaking their stare.

"If you start quoting poetry, I'm going to be sick."

He smiled, slow and brilliant. The sight snagged her gaze, reeling her in. A dull, unbearable ache swelled in her breast, a painful longing for Saint. She dragged her eyes from Teslar and started walking toward the passageway. To call Teslar dangerous was like calling him cute. Words just weren't sufficient to describe the impact of him.

She needed to get the hell out of that chamber.

"You will be my end, Christina."

She turned, her mouth gaping open. Emotion so deep she couldn't fully wrap understanding around it swamped her awareness when she saw that Teslar's face was wet with tears, despite his radiant smile. Something passed between them, potent and unnamable.

"I told you I wasn't what you thought," he said. "I wasn't what *I* thought. Touching you taught me that. I want to thank you for making me see the truth, Christina."

"You can fake tears," she said accusingly, her voice shaking. She didn't know how she knew that fact, but she did.

Just as she also knew, on some bone-deep level, that what Teslar said next was true, as well.

"I can. But I'm not doing it now."

The energy level in the chamber seemed to grow and thicken by the second. She'd never before been in the presence of magic, but she knew it firsthand in that charged moment.

"*Christina.*"

She spun around, her entire body trembling.

"Saint," she cried out, her voice cracking in both relief and anxiety at seeing him.

He stood just inside the entrance, his heartluster drawn, a still, eerie expression on his face as he pinned Teslar with his stare. He made a beckoning gesture with his hand and Christina moved. Saint pulled her behind him when she approached. She glanced around the arm that held his heartluster, wondering what Teslar would do.

She didn't know if she was surprised or not when Teslar didn't draw his weapon.

"So. You have finally won, Saint," Teslar said.

"What's that supposed to mean?" Saint rasped.

Christina sensed the brittle tension in Saint's coiled muscles. She reached out and touched his waist, soothing him instinctively.

Teslar nodded toward Christina. His cheeks were damp with tears, but he wore a strangely calm, sublime expression, given the circumstances.

"You possess what I would die for." Teslar's words resonated in the subterranean chamber.

"*Speak plainly or shut up,*" Saint snapped telepathically. "*You sound like Kavya, speaking in riddles.*"

Saint was wary of his clone's intentions, but he'd also never seen Teslar look this way, precisely. He seemed dazed...transported.

Teslar shrugged, his eyes still glued to Christina. *"Kavya told me that one day, if I was fortunate, I would encounter something that would forever change my destiny, and in order to have that thing, I would have to sacrifice. I didn't believe him. I didn't understand. When I first saw Christina, I only thought of possessing her for my own."* He held up his palms, and Saint saw they were blistered and red. *"Then I touched her, and found I wasn't worthy enough to do so.*

"It's not what I had thought...my own end," Teslar whispered in Saint's mind, his gaze latched on Christina. *"It beckons to me."*

Christina stirred behind him. He sensed her confusion...shared in it. Teslar's behavior was strange, but also...*familiar* to Saint somehow, as though he'd read a passage in a play long ago, and a scene from that play was suddenly being enacted in real life, and he—Saint—was the main character, a crisis of doubt upon him.

Teslar had long been the nightmare that Saint fought tooth and nail. It suddenly struck him that he hadn't stood so close to his nemesis in centuries, never had the chance to truly examine his clone. It was like staring into a dark mirror, with one difference. Teslar possessed a jagged scar just above his heart. Saint realized with a shock that he had given his clone that scar a century before with his heartluster during one of their many violent clashes.

Teslar met Saint's stare, his blue eyes moist. Saint had the uncomfortable impression that Teslar's calm certitude was entirely genuine. Teslar understood something that was occurring in this moment that Saint didn't—

"You will conquer me," Teslar said in his mind. *"I would do anything to touch her. She is life. I will gladly die in her fires. I will submit to you if you allow me to love her."*

His clone's words reverberated around in his brain. Something coalesced, and Saint understood in a blinding flash what Kavya had always meant when he said Teslar and he were one.

Christina became distantly aware that the two males communicated, but their telepathic exchange was so rapid, so precise, that she couldn't quite capture the content. She only experienced emotion so charged, so subtle, that it raised the fine hairs on the back of her neck and forearms. Saint surprised her by suddenly turning and looking at her.

"I cannot do it," Saint said out loud through a tight jaw.

"The mandate to contain me has been encoded in your blood. You know that, Saint. I permit you the opportunity to control me," Teslar replied. "You must allow it."

A taut silence ensued. A fine tremble began to vibrate Saint's body, as though he held his muscles so rigidly, he would explode from the strain he placed on them.

Christina read his mind with difficulty—he experienced so much chaotic emotion—but understanding dawned slowly.

"Saint?" she asked warily.

The soul that was about to dawn like a fiery new star shone in his blue eyes. Christina knew the moment that Kavya had alluded to had arrived.

"It is your choice to make, Christina," Saint said softly.

"But...Teslar was burned when he touched me."

Saint's angular jaw moved in a tiny, taut, circular motion as he studied her. The amount of tension she felt rising in him both alarmed and thrilled her.

He spoke to her telepathically.

"Teslar and I are one. If I accept that within myself, I will overcome what he represents. I wouldn't ask you to do this if I didn't know it would work, Christina. That it was right." He paused, inhaling slowly. *"You are my soul. If I acknowledge Teslar, he will be able to touch you. Just as I do. He will place himself under my control. I won't allow him to harm you. You will feel only pleasure."*

Christina licked her upper lip anxiously and tasted salt.

"I'm sorry," Saint said out loud. "I didn't understand fully until just now."

"Does he *understand?"* she asked him telepathically, referring to Teslar.

"Yes. He chooses to be controlled by me if I allow him to touch you." He paused and Christina sensed his hesitation. "I tried to explain to you what you represent to beings like Teslar and me. Maybe now...you'll finally know."

Christina swallowed. "All...all right."

Teslar stepped toward them as though her words had released a restraint holding him. Christina wished she could read Saint at that moment, but he just watched her with an impassive expression and fiery eyes.

She came out from behind him and took one step...then two toward Teslar. Her heart felt like it would burst. But suddenly she sensed Saint behind her, his long body ghosting her own, giving her strength. Teslar closed the distance until he stood less than a foot away. Her breath caught when she saw the stark longing in his eyes.

"Don't be afraid."

She blinked. Saint had uttered the words in her ear at the

same moment that Teslar said them gruffly. Teslar raised his hands. Christina saw how they shook. He placed them on her shoulders, and Saint bracketed her waist with his hands. Saint's mouth felt hot and urgent on her neck.

"He is me, Stina. If you accept him, then I can," Saint muttered next to her skin. She stared, transfixed, by the image of Teslar's lowering his head to her own. Saint whispered next to her ear, sharing the arcane secret. "If you accept him, then I can conquer him once and for all."

A convulsion of desire went through her when Teslar covered her mouth with his own. She leaned her head back on Saint's chest while Teslar bent...and devoured her. He tasted much like Saint, with an added hint of bitterness. It inflamed her, that added complexity of flavor to a sensation she loved.

The kiss continued, hot, drugging...delicious. Saint's mouth became more avid, moving next to the skin of her neck, jaw and cheek. The slide of his hands across the bare skin of her ribs made her moan into Teslar's consuming mouth.

They moved in perfect synchrony. Teslar broke their kiss and Saint lifted her shirt over her breasts. Teslar's hands moved to her back. They both stepped back and her bra fell to the floor. She cried out when Saint's hands slid beneath her breasts, caressing and cradling them, forcing the centers to thrust forward into prominence.

"Her breasts are very sensitive," he murmured, and Christina realized he spoke to Teslar. "Run your teeth over them...but gently. Very gently. Yes," he added gruffly as Teslar ran his extended fangs over the upper swell of her left breast and she whimpered in pleasure. "Do you like that?"

"God, yes," she moaned, thrashing her head against his chest as Teslar awakened her nerve endings and a path of molten heat zipped directly to her womb.

Both males' throats vibrated in a soft, yet feral growl when Teslar enclosed a tip in his hot mouth and suckled.

"Let her lie on her back on the floor," Saint said.

Christina knelt at his urging. Her cheeks were flushed and she already panted from arousal. It felt surreal, what was occurring. And yet...on some deep level of her consciousness, it all made perfect sense as well.

She wondered if she could survive the cataclysm of bliss that was sure to follow. Would her body be able to survive the wild fires of transformation, contain the birth of a soul?

The desire that pulsed in her was only amplified when she lay on her back on the soft carpet, watching as both males began to shed their clothing, their eyes glued to her all the while.

Chapter Twenty-six

Both of them paused when they wore nothing but the straps that sheathed their heartlusters. She stared, made mute by the sight of their identical, erect phalluses and firm testicles surrounded by leather.

Their bodies were identical—a long length of sinew and defined muscle gloved in golden-hued skin. The only difference Christina could see was that Teslar had an old scar on his left pectoral muscle, likely the remnant of a long-ago failed attempt by Saint to kill his clone by stabbing his heart.

They removed their weapons as one.

They knelt next to her, two golden gods with fire-lit blue eyes. They bent. She cried out and stared up at the wood-reinforced ceiling of the tunnel, seeing nothing...blinded by ecstasy as each of them worshiped a breast with teeth, tongue, and hot, suctioning mouths. Her pleasure built until it frothed and bubbled just beneath the boiling point.

"Run your hands through Teslar's hair," Saint commanded in her mind.

She complied without thought, glorying in the texture of Teslar's thick, soft mane sliding through her fingers. Teslar lifted his head and winced in pleasure, as though she stroked a sex organ and not his hair.

"You have conquered me, Christina," Teslar growled.

Saint released her nipple from his mouth with a soft popping sound. He sunk his teeth between her neck and shoulder. She shuddered in an agony of bliss, her fists clenched tight in Teslar's glorious mane.

After a pleasure-infused minute, she blinked open her eyes when she felt strong hands shifting her. She was positioned on her hands and knees, although it was Saint's and Teslar's hold that kept her in place, not her will. Her muscles were still slack from her thunderous orgasm.

"Hold yourself up, Stina," Saint ordered, his voice thick with arousal. She focused her eyes and saw that he lay beneath her, his hands supporting her shoulders. She realized that Teslar knelt behind, holding her waist.

Once she'd steadied herself, Teslar deftly removed her shorts and underwear.

Saint leaned up and Teslar lowered. They began a sensual exploration of her body, charting every inch of her skin with their hands and mouth—Saint pleasuring the front of her, Teslar the back. After a few minutes of this sensual torture, she could no longer hold herself in place. Her body began to sag as blissful sensations pounded into her flesh and mind. She swam in a delicious haze of sharp teeth, soothing, warm tongues, strong, shaping lips, and skilled fingertips.

"Oh, please. Please," she begged mindlessly.

Saint lay on his back and grabbed her, one hand on her head holding back her hair and the other on her shoulder. He pulled her down to him.

"*Teslar,*" he said gruffly before he closed his mouth over her parted lips.

The single word must have been a permission of sorts, because Teslar moved abruptly from where he'd been tonguing and gently biting a buttock. He licked along the sensitive inner skin of her right thigh, making her tremble in Saint's hold. She knew her thighs were damp with her arousal. She'd felt her juices wetting her skin while the two males made her body a conduit for pure pleasure.

Her eyes sprang wide when she felt Teslar's tongue swipe across her labia.

He spread her buttocks with his hands, pausing to lift her hips slightly, fully exposing her sex to the cool air of the chamber. She cried into Saint's hot mouth when Teslar slid his stiffened tongue between her labia, laving her clit in a hard, precise caress.

He ate her so lustily, so thoroughly, that Christina was left in little doubt of how much he relished the experience. Sensation overwhelmed her. She struggled in Saint's hold, but he held her fast, forcing her to accept their kisses as they branded her both at mouth and sex.

She climaxed not once, but twice, in shockingly rapid succession. When the shivers of ecstasy eased in her flesh, they broke their kisses at once.

"She is worth it," Teslar muttered from behind her. "She runs like nectar down my throat."

"Lower her down on me," Saint rasped.

Christina blinked several times, trying to focus. Saint's facial muscles pulled tight and his muscles gleamed with a fine coat of perspiration. They locked gazes when Teslar lifted her in his strong arms, holding her back against his chest. Saint held up his cock. Christina noticed the fleshy, arrow-shaped crown glistened with his seed.

Teslar held her with an encircling arm around her waist. His fingers gently parted her sex.

He lowered her toward Saint's awaiting penis.

She shook in Teslar's hold as he slowly impaled her on Saint's cock. Once he was fully sheathed in her pussy and she rested in his lap, she placed her hands on Saint's chest and tried desperately to catch her breath.

She felt so full...so incendiary. Saint placed his hands on her face, cradling her jaw, pulling her down until her hard nipples brushed his chest. His cock lurched and swelled inside her clenching hold.

"I love you," he whispered roughly.

Her face convulsed with emotion and mounting sensation when she felt Teslar part her buttocks.

"I love you too. But I can't. I can't hold you both."

A single tear fell from Saint glistening eyes. "If you cannot, then I cannot contain him. Please, Stina."

She gasped at the feeling of Teslar's hot, heavy, lubricated cock sliding between her buttocks. Her pussy tightened around Saint and his lips twisted into a snarl.

"Yes. All right," she granted.

His lips silently mouthed his gratitude, and Christina was filled with a sense of determination and love.

The crown of Teslar's cock slipped into her. She gritted her teeth as he paused behind her.

"She's too tight," Teslar said in a choked voice.

"No!" Christina managed between pants. "I can do it."

She held Saint's stare as she pressed back slightly and the shaft of Teslar's cock pushed farther into the nerve-packed channel of her ass. The pressure and the ensuing friction of holding both males nearly overwhelmed her. They filled her to capacity. Her entire body quaked when Teslar managed to stuff another few inches into her.

All of them groaned at once.

Christina felt like they'd carefully built a fire in her flesh and a flame was ready to be tossed, creating a conflagration. In the far distance of her consciousness, she felt the earth shudder beneath her. The ancient timbers that reinforced the chamber creaked and moaned. One of them snapped loudly as it splintered.

Saint put his hands on her hips and lifted her several inches off his cock. It gave Teslar the give he needed. Teslar growled as he flexed his hips, pressing his testicles against her ass.

Saint reached with his thumb, rubbing her clit briskly.

"Come for us, Stina," he demanded in a rough whisper. "Come for me."

He settled her back on his cock and she followed his order, exploding in climax.

A moment later she stared down at Saint's enraptured face as her entire world quaked and rattled. Clumps of dirt and splinters of wood fell to the floor of the chamber while Saint held her ass steady and Teslar fucked her from behind, his grunts and growls blending with the creaks of the wood reinforcement and the crumbling earth.

But none of them seemed capable of reacting to anything but the hot inferno of their need.

"Your ass is on fire," Saint growled.

She grimaced as Teslar thrust into her, and his pelvis made a smacking sound against her buttocks. She stared at Saint in dawning wonder.

"I can feel it," he mumbled. Sweat drenched his face now. "We're dying in your fires, lovely."

The chamber shook around them. Teslar plunged into her and an otherworldly howl tore from his throat. Christina felt both males swell inside of her, the sensation causing an orgasm to zip up her spine like lightning. Her scream of shocked pleasure twined with Saint's shout.

A dark veil fell over her consciousness as ecstasy engulfed her.

When she came back to herself she was in Saint's arms, his face pressed against her neck. She felt the wetness of tears against her skin. She glided her hands across his hard chest and shoulders, soothing him without thinking to do so.

Something struck the earth in the distance and lumps of dirt fell to the carpet. Christina lifted her head, blinking to clear the haze of lingering magic and sexual bliss.

Earlier, she'd assumed that the entire earth was shaking around them in a quake, but now she realized the chamber shook because something heavy was being hurtled against the tunnel walls repeatedly.

"Saint," she breathed out warily.

"I know." He gently lifted her off his cock, both of them wincing at the sensation.

"Get dressed. Quickly," Saint ordered.

Christina began to do as he said, despite her rising disorientation. Distant thunder occasionally shook the underground chamber.

She pulled her T-shirt down and stood, fully dressed. She glanced around the now-dusty chamber.

"Where's Teslar?"

Saint glanced up from fastening his button-fly.

"He's gone, Christina. I thought you understood. I used to control Teslar from without. But, because of you, I can now contain him from within."

His magnificent muscles flexed as he drew his shirt over his head. Christina gaped when she saw the scar on his left pectoral muscle. It wasn't the same scar that had been on Teslar...this one was newer, pink, and less jagged looking.

Still, it was in the same position and was precisely the same shape as Teslar's had been.

"Teslar's inside you?" she whispered in awe when Saint stood before her, fully dressed.

"In a manner of speaking," Saint said quietly. "Better to say that because of you, I was able to absorb him. I always told you we were one. Teslar was my shadow...my dark half. We sprang from the same mother cell. But now I hold ascendancy over him. Don't be afraid, Stina."

She wondered what expression had showed on her face to make him say it with so much emotion.

She'd known there was magic at work in their lovemaking, but she hadn't expected *this*.

"I'm not afraid of you," she admitted shakily. "I'm just...stunned. Even though I thought I understood before...it's still quite a shock."

He nodded once.

"We have to get out of here. The Iniskium's attack on the Scourge revenants is going to collapse this ancient tunnel."

"That's what's causing the shaking?" Christina asked as Saint took her hand. They dodged falling earth and timber as he led her out of the carpeted chamber.

He nodded grimly. "And from the sounds of it, it's the worst battle the Iniskium have launched in several centuries."

Saint moved aside the thick carpet and Christina followed him.

They stepped straight into chaos.

Chapter Twenty-seven

The ancient freight tunnel that stretched ahead of them was thick with dust and both inert and writhing bodies. Christina's eyes went wide when a huge, dark shadow came springing in the air toward them. Saint grabbed her arm, holding her in place behind him. He slashed with his right arm and then kicked.

She stared in horrified disgust at the muscular, panther-like prowler that fell to the floor with a dull thud. The severed head Saint had kicked with his booted foot bounced next to its chest, the cruel jaw frozen in a snarl around jagged teeth.

Saint didn't spare the beheaded revenant a glance. He grabbed her wrist with one hand, holding his heartluster in the other, and led her down the chamber. They had to pick their way across dozens of bleeding bodies, some of them still, some in the final throes of battle.

Saint slashed with his heartluster several times as they moved, abruptly ending the struggle of what might have been mortal combats. Once, he knelt and touched a fallen woman's cheek.

"Help is coming, Shrinar. Can you hold out?"

The dusky-skinned female smiled weakly. Blood and dust covered her face. "I saw to it that Marcellus lost his head. I wouldn't dream of leaving the immortal life until I've gloated over that fact for at least a century."

"You did well," Saint said, respect in his tone.

Shrinar shifted her head carefully to glance up at him. "It was like the revenants just gave up there...at the end. You know as well as I do that I'm no match for Marcellus."

Saint's eyebrows went up in interest at Shrinar's words, but he said nothing else and continued leading Christina down the tunnel.

The metallic scent of blood and sulfur burned in her nostrils. She made out a flicker of gold in the distance, the light intermittently occluded by two figures fighting. The battle they waged was vicious, nothing like the waning struggles of exhaustion they'd passed so far in the tunnel.

"Isi," Christina whispered miserably, looking around Saint's body when he paused, still fifty feet away from the dangerous battle.

Javier Ash had just sent a rocketing fist into Isi's jaw, causing the Iniskium warrior to fly against the wall like a projectile from a missile. The earth trembled around them. Much to her shock, Isi sprang forward immediately, a look of determined hatred on his face.

His retaliatory punch and rapid kick to Ash's chin and gut caused the revenant to howl in pain. Saint raised his heartluster in preparation to cross the distance and enter the battle.

"Leave him to me!"

Isi's bellow echoed in the subterranean shaft. Ash struck the wall of the chamber forcefully and fell, motionless.

Saint stilled. Christina sensed his hesitancy as he lowered his sword.

She saw that several figures stood as though waiting in the

far distance—on the opposite side of Isi and Ash. She realized that Isi spoke not only to Saint, but to the other Iniskium who had gathered, watching the fight. Apparently Javier Ash was the last revenant standing guard between the Iniskium and Teslar, Saint, and her.

And Isi had made it his mission to finish his foe one on one.

She let out a tiny scream of shock when Javier Ash suddenly leapt up from his faint. He flew through the air, taking Isi by surprise. The revenant bared a mouthful of sharp teeth, tearing at Isi's shoulder. Blood droplets arced through the air. Both males fell to the floor heavily, shaking the chamber.

Ash's jaw closed and Isi howled in pain.

Ash unfastened his jaw and raised his head, just inches away from biting through Isi's neck. An anguished shout echoed in the chamber and a slight figure raced toward the battling men. Quicker than Christina could think, Saint called sharply and tossed his blade through the distance.

"Alison!"

Saint's heartluster sliced through the air, the metal flashing in the dim light. Alison grabbed the handle and plunged at the same moment that Ash glanced around in surprise.

She drove the sword into Ash's opened mouth.

The blade stifled the revenant's scream; his filmy eyes went wide in shock. Ash didn't even whimper when Isi threw him off his body and withdrew his long knife from the sheath at his waist.

Christina winced in disgust. She wanted to plunge her face into Saint's back and avoid the sight at all costs.

Instead, she watched as Isi sliced through the Scourge

revenant's neck methodically, pausing only to whisk Saint's heartluster out of Ash's throat when metal blade struck sword.

A moment later, Ash's severed head rolled to the floor of the shaking tunnel.

"Ugh. You owe me for this, Saint," she threatened, her face pressed against Saint's back.

He grunted.

"For that, and so much more," he murmured.

"Let's get the injured and get out of here before this tunnel collapses," Saint shouted to the Iniskium.

Christina tripped after him, coughing as earth, wooden planks, and old mortar rained down on them.

Epilogue

There were only thirty-six surviving Iniskium following the tunnel battle, less than half of their original number. Christina sensed Saint's profound sadness for the great loss to an already near extinct tribe of unique beings. They had successfully rescued the injured survivors and the dead for burial before the tunnel began to collapse.

"It's the end of the Scourge revenants, at least in this city," Fardusk said stonily as they all stood on a delivery platform on lower Wacker Drive. They'd been a bloody, bedraggled group and the solemnity of the moment showed on every surviving Iniskium's face. Alison seemed equally as sober as she stood with her arms wrapped around Isi's waist, looking for all the world like she believed she was solely responsible for holding up the brawny warrior.

"Apparently Teslar imparted them with a certain level of strength," Saint had muttered. "When he was conquered, the Scourge revenants were diminished. Only Javier Ash remained strong, but I've thought for a long time that he was no typical revenant. Chances are, he was something unique even before Teslar turned him."

Christina noticed that Saint never stated the manner in which Teslar had been vanquished, and the Iniskium never pressed as to how he had accomplished what was thought to be an impossibility.

They had all gone to Whitby, where Saint designated a plot of land beneath a small grove of redbud trees as a graveyard. This was where Christina found him standing alone in front of the freshly dug graves two nights after the freight tunnel battle.

They had been together frequently over the past forty-eight hours, checking on the injured and spending time with Aidan. Not just Aidan, but Christina and Saint were learning about Aidan's new powers. All three of them were slowly assimilating to the idea that Saint was Aidan's father. Christina knew the process would take time, and Saint seemed to sense this as well.

They'd been together often during the past two days, but rarely had they been alone unless they were making love in the darkness of night, their hunger for one another seemingly only growing stronger, or sleeping in each other's arms.

Until now.

"It's a lovely resting place," Christina murmured from behind Saint, referring to the graves. He didn't turn at the sound of her voice, but she knew he'd sensed her approach. The wind rustled in the trees and she heard the sound of the waves hitting the shore in the distance. She thought of how she'd always sensed the mystery that cloaked Whitby at night, intuited the enigma of Saint himself.

Now that the mystery had been revealed to her, it seemed no less awesome.

Saint turned toward her and held out his arms.

She pressed her cheek to his chest and he combed his fingers through her hair. For several full moments, neither spoke as they held one another, and the night embraced them both.

"Fardusk is taking the Iniskium away from Whitby later

tonight," Saint said after a while.

She leaned back and gazed at his face in the dim moonlight. His chest felt solid and warm beneath her palms. She could feel his heart beating, steady and strong.

"So soon?" she asked in a hushed tone.

Saint nodded.

"Where will they go?"

"To the crystal chamber. Fardusk has a plan for renovating the tunnels around it, making it a more comfortable place for them to live."

"What will they do, now that Teslar and the revenants are gone?"

Saint shrugged. "They will continue to protect those in need. They've fought against evil for too long now to stop. And the gods know there is enough violence and injustice to combat in this city."

Christina had to agree with that.

"Alison has decided to go with them."

Christina started at his words. "Really? With Isi?"

"Yes." Saint must have noticed her doubtful expression. She hadn't been pleased when she'd heard about Alison's betrayal, but she hadn't been surprised either. The girl had a long history of emotional problems, and no matter what Saint said about her supposed strength, Teslar was nearly impossible to resist.

How well Christina knew.

"She's a grown woman. You can't be responsible for every decision one of your charges makes. Don't you think Isi can keep her safe?"

"I suppose. But Alison is so fragile—"

"She's about as fragile as I am," Saint interrupted. Her eyes fixed on his small smile. Saint had to have the sexiest mouth in existence. His lips twitched and she wondered if he'd read her mind.

"Alison insisted on going with Isi to the tunnels the other night. He couldn't talk her out of it. I don't know how hard he tried to stop her, considering how angry he was with her for having betrayed you and Aidan. Maybe he figured she had whatever was coming to her if she came up against a revenant."

"Well he doesn't feel that way anymore. Not after Alison stepped into the middle of that fight and saved his life. I wonder if they can actually be happy together," Christina mused.

"They've got their own battle ahead of them, that's for sure. Ought to be interesting," Saint said wryly.

"I suppose it makes sense that Fardusk would take them to the crystal chamber," Christina murmured. "Since they can take nourishment from it."

Saint's eyes gleamed in the moonlight.

"What?" she asked, intuiting that he wanted to tell her something.

"I have not been to the crystal chamber for days now, Christina," he said gruffly.

Her eyebrows knit together in confusion. "I...I had noticed that. But I thought it was because of our lovemaking. I thought I was sustaining you," she whispered.

He slowly shook his head. His eyes seemed to glow in the moonlight. "I am able to eat more...to take nourishment from food. Only the food you prepare, food infused with vitessence...with your soul. But I've been eating it regularly. I've been able to eat your food occasionally since I've known you, but only in small amounts. Only your meals appealed to me."

"Really?" she asked in amazement, thinking of how he'd told her at the party—had it really only been several weeks ago—how he could only eat her food, and she'd assumed he was joking.

He nodded before he leaned down and nuzzled her nose with his own. His lips brushed against hers in a warm, firm caress. She shivered, but the topic at hand was too important to let Saint's delicious kisses sidetrack her.

"But what does it mean?" she asked.

He kissed her slowly and thoroughly. She tasted the new, subtle hint of bitterness in his rich, delicious flavor and embraced the complexity and sheer power of his soul. His kiss enveloped her, and she promptly forgot what it was they were discussing as her body began to hum with increasingly familiar potent sexual arousal.

"I spoke with Kavya about it," Saint said huskily next to her seeking lips a moment later.

She blinked, recalling their conversation. "And?"

"He says that when I absorbed Teslar, when I accepted my dark self and took domain over it, that my soul was fully crystallized. I can feel it now, Stina. I am no longer one of the soulless ones. I can give as well as take."

She looked up at him through tear-filled eyes, moved by the depth of feeling in his voice. She figured now wasn't a great time to tell him that he'd always given to her, always shared himself in a way that made her feel vibrant and alive.

"I'm so grateful you realize it now, Saint."

He swallowed thickly and bent his knees. He pressed his forehead to hers.

"That isn't all. Kavya says that through the transformation that occurred in the chamber...I became mortal. In gaining a soul, I set the term of my life."

She leaned back in alarm. "*What?*"

He gently placed his hand at the back of her skull and pressed their foreheads together. His breath was warm and fragrant as it brushed against her nose and lips.

"I'm not dying now. Kavya wasn't sure how long I will live, but he guessed I will begin to age now in a way that's similar to other humans. Is that so bad? For us to grow old together, Christina?"

A tear skipped down her cheek when she shook her head. "No, *no*. I would love nothing more than to grow old with you."

"Stina," he growled softly. He enclosed her in his arms and kissed each of the tears that fell from her eyes.

Then he settled on her mouth hungrily.

A moment later, he pulled her down to the soft, cool grass and lay on top of her, belly to belly. She sighed blissfully, loving the feel of his weight and hardness pressing against her. He nuzzled her breast with his nose and mouth and then, ever so gently, bit the tip, scraping his teeth over a beaded nipple until she shivered.

"You gave me my soul," he whispered gruffly into the darkness.

"No, Saint." She threaded her fingers through his soft, tousled hair and pulled him down to her. "You earned it."

About the Author

Beth Kery loves a sexy romance and a good story, whether it be of the contemporary, paranormal or historical variety. She grew up in a huge house built in the nineteenth century where she cultivated her love of mystery and the paranormal. When she wasn't hunting for secret passageways and ghosts with her friends, she was gobbling up fantasy and romance novels along with any other books she could get her hands on. Currently she juggles the demands of her careers, her love of the city and the arts and a busy family life. Her writing today reflects her passion for all of the above. To learn more about Beth Kery, please visit www.bethkery.com, send an email to bethkery@aol.com or join her Yahoo group to join in the fun with other readers as well as Beth, http://groups.yahoo.com/group/totalexposure

They've been hiding from the past.
Now it's time to fight for their future.

Sanctuary Unbound
© 2010 Moira Rogers
Red Rock Pass, Book 4

New England is ideal for vampire Adam Dubois. His cozy home in the Great North Woods reminds him of a happier time when werewolves and witches were stuff of legends, and he was a simple lumberjack.

Hiding from past failures has worked for over eighty years, but a life debt owed to the Red Rock alpha has forced him to leave his retreat—and come face to face with a woman who challenges and tempts him on every level.

Hiding secrets is a lonely business, and Cindy Shepherd is lonely with a capital L. Red Rock isn't exactly crawling with available men, but her interest in the mystery-shrouded new vampire in town seems mutual. After all, it's only sex—there's no danger he'll dig deep enough to unleash the demons of her past.

Casual flirtation turns deadly serious when Adam discovers that the vampire plaguing Red Rock is using his mistakes as a road map. When it comes to his life, he knows Cindy has his back. But in order to secure the future, they both must trust each other with more—even if it means sacrificing themselves to save everything they hold dear.

Warning: This book contains epic werewolf battles, mystical vampire blood bonds, unexpected sex on the kitchen floor and a dangerous attraction between a secret-burdened werewolf and a vampire lumberjack.

Available now in ebook from Samhain Publishing.

When it comes down to love or duty,
pick a side—and pray your heart survives.

Death, the Vamp and his Brother
© 2009 Lexxie Couper

Death exists for one purpose and one purpose only: to sever the life-threads of the living. She does her job with pride and an unwavering commitment. Nothing ruffles her. Until she encounters Patrick Watkins. The Australian lifeguard pushes all her buttons—and makes her tailbone itch like crazy. And when her tailbone itches, it means trouble is brewing. Big trouble.

Ven's gut tells him that Death is taking aim at his kid brother. He should know—he died and was turned vampire while trying to prevent another failed murder-attempt eighteen years ago. Patrick is meant to do something important in the world, and Ven will do anything to keep him safe. Even take on Death herself. In more ways than one.

As far as Patrick's concerned, the whole thing is a load of bull. But what if everything Death tells him turns out to be true? How is he expected to save mankind from the worst fate of all—the Apocalypse? Especially when all he can think about is how quickly he's falling in love with the most feared Horseman of them all...

Warning: This book contains enough heresy to shame the Devil, more scorching sex than one person can handle, Oh, and lots of Australian colloquialism. A bloody lot of Australian colloquialism.

Available now in ebook and print from Samhain Publishing.

HOT STUFF

Discover Samhain!

THE HOTTEST NEW PUBLISHER ON THE PLANET

Romance, fantasy, mystery, thriller, mainstream and more—Samhain has more selection, hotter authors, and everything's available in ebook.

Pick your favorite, sit back, and enjoy the ride! Hot stuff indeed.

WWW.SAMHAINPUBLISHING.COM